Acclaim for the authors of
PRIVATE SCANDALS

JOANNA WAYNE

"Wayne creates compelling relationships
and intricately plotted suspense...."
—*Romantic Times*

"Joanna Wayne...delivers romance and excitement."
—*Romantic Times*

"With great storytelling excitement and energy,
Joanna Wayne shines...."
—*Romantic Times*

JUDY CHRISTENBERRY

"Judy Christenberry's stories touch the heart."
—*New York Times* bestselling author Debbie Macomber

"Judy Christenberry stirs romance and humor
into the perfect blend."
—*Romantic Times*

TORI CARRINGTON

"Tori Carrington...scorches the pages...."
—*Romantic Times*

"Characters of emotional and sensual depth always
come to life at the skilled hands of Tori Carrington...."
—*Writers Unlimited*

"Tori Carrington is a writer of exceptional merit
whose books continually awe and impress."
—*Rendezvous*

"Known for writing passionate and emotionally
moving scenes, Tori Carrington is one of category
romance's most talented authors."
—*Escape to Romance*

JOANNA WAYNE

lives with her husband just a few miles from steamy, exciting New Orleans, but her home is the perfect writer's hideaway. A lazy bayou, complete with graceful herons, colorful wood ducks and an occasional alligator, winds just below her back garden. When not creating tales of spine-tingling suspense and heartwarming romance, she enjoys reading, traveling, playing golf and spending time with family and friends.

Joanna believes that one of the special joys of writing is knowing that her stories have brought enjoyment to or somehow touched the lives of her readers. You can write Joanna at P.O. Box 2851, Harvey, LA 70059-2851.

JUDY CHRISTENBERRY

has been writing romances for over fifteen years because she loves happy endings as much as her readers. A former French teacher, Judy now devotes herself to writing full-time. She hopes readers have as much fun reading her stories as she does writing them. She spends her spare time reading, watching her favorite sports teams and keeping track of her two daughters. Judy's a native Texan.

TORI CARRINGTON

The power behind the pen name Tori Carrington is husband-and-wife duo Lori and Tony Karayianni, who have twenty-one steamy books to their credit. When they're not creating romance novels they're enjoying their own twenty-year-old romance, and exploring ways to expand and spice up both. Along with their sons, Tony Junior and Tim, and their ever-growing family of felines, they call Toledo, Ohio, home base, but travel to Tony's hometown of Athens, Greece, whenever possible. For more information on the authors and their books, visit their Web site at www.toricarrington.com.

PRIVATE SCANDALS

JOANNA WAYNE
JUDY CHRISTENBERRY
TORI CARRINGTON

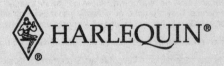

HARLEQUIN®

TORONTO • NEW YORK • LONDON
AMSTERDAM • PARIS • SYDNEY • HAMBURG
STOCKHOLM • ATHENS • TOKYO • MILAN • MADRID
PRAGUE • WARSAW • BUDAPEST • AUCKLAND

ISBN 0-373-83582-5

PRIVATE SCANDALS

Copyright © 2004 by Harlequin Books S.A.

The publisher acknowledges the copyright holders of the individual works as follows:

SHADOWS OF HER PAST
Copyright © 2004 by Jo Ann Vest

FAMILY UNVEILED
Copyright © 2004 by Judy Christenberry

SLEEPING WITH SECRETS
Copyright © 2004 by Lori and Tony Karayianni

This edition published by arrangement with Harlequin Books S.A.

® and TM are trademarks of the publisher. Trademarks indicated with ® are registered in the United States Patent and Trademark Office, the Canadian Trade Marks Office and in other countries.

Visit us at www.eHarlequin.com

Printed in U.S.A.

CONTENTS

Dear Reader,

Welcome to HIDDEN PASSIONS, my new series from Harlequin Intrigue. Come and travel with me throughout the sultry Southern states. These are stories about real people thrust into situations that force them to call on all their strength and courage to survive. But they are also sensual romances where the passions of the hero and heroine lie as deep as the secrets that haunt their souls. The settings may be the mysterious bayou country of southern Louisiana, a rambling house on a deserted beach, a haunted orphanage or anywhere in between. But wherever the stories take you, you can always be assured that the ending will find the hero and heroine safe and in love.

When the heroine in "Shadows of Her Past" wakes up in the room with a dead man, she's certainly not expecting to find understanding from the victim's rude and arrogant brother. But when he's the only person in town who believes her innocence, she is forced to accept his help. Their story is proof that princes don't always ride in on white horses. Sometimes they drive a pickup truck.

I love to hear from readers. Please visit my Web site at www.eclectics.com/authorsgalore/joannawayne and enter the Authors Galore contest. You can also write me at P.O. Box 2851, Harvey, LA 70059. If you'd like, you may send an SASE for a free bookmark and newsletter.

Happy reading,

Joanna Wayne

SHADOWS OF HER PAST

Joanna Wayne

To women everywhere who are searching for their rock of a prince, with wishes that one day their prince will come.

CHAPTER ONE

JESSICA LEWIS awoke to the piercing buzz of an alarm clock. She hammered one hand into the pillow and reached to shut off the irksome noise with the other. She groaned at the dull thud of pain as her knuckles banged against the edge of the table.

Finally her hand found the clock. She shut off the alarm, rubbed her eyes and tried to bring her mind into focus. She pushed to her elbows, but the muscles in her back and neck protested movement and her head throbbed as if she'd beat it against the wall for last night's entertainment.

Wetting her dry lips with the tip of her tongue, she scanned the small hotel room. She was in Bankstown, Georgia, to see the headmaster of Carruthers Boarding School. The appointment was for nine o'clock—an important meeting so she'd better get her butt in gear.

Stretching, she kicked from beneath the covers, then realized she was fully dressed, except for her shoes. Not a good sign, especially when she didn't even remember crawling into bed last night. She'd been dead tired and she'd had a drink. She did remember that much. Maybe the combination of fatigue and alcohol had been a little too potent.

But at least she was in her own room. That was her worn blue luggage on the rack and her black leather jacket tossed over the chair. She yanked her sweater down over her stomach and threw her legs over the side of the bed, determined to get up and get going. The room started spinning, and whatever she'd eaten last night came alive in her stomach. Groaning, she fell back against the pillow. She must have caught some awful virus on the plane yesterday.

Or maybe it was just being back in Georgia that was doing her in. Her past was the type much better left behind, and she'd spent years working to accomplish that. A counselor called it denial. She called it survival—which is what she'd best concentrate on right now.

She forced herself out of the bed, then started to the bathroom. Halfway there she tripped over a shoe and went sprawling across the floor.

And that's when she saw the body.

A man, on his back, a black handle of what

appeared to be a knife poking out of his chest. His eyes were rolled back in his head, but every strand of his thick dark hair was in place. His gray suit was barely mussed, except for the section with the crimson stain.

Still on her knees, she closed her eyes tightly and prayed she was lost in a nightmare. When she opened them again, the body was still there. A clammy feeling crawled across her skin as she inched to the man's side and fit her fingers around his wrist. Cold and lifeless, as she'd expected. She dropped it and shrank away.

Nauseous and weak-kneed, she stood, walked to the phone and punched in a nine and a one before caution stopped her. She broke the connection but still cradled the phone in her trembling hand. Once she made the call, the police would show up in minutes. But what would she tell them? That a deranged stranger had broken into her hotel room during the night and stuck a knife in his own chest?

She hung up the phone and dropped to a chair as troubling images staggered through clouds of confusion. She'd gone to the hotel bar last night for a glass of wine, thinking it would help her relax and fall asleep more quickly. The dead man had been there, only he'd been alive then.

They'd talked for a minute, and she'd had the distinct impression that she'd known him from somewhere, though his name didn't register. Damn. She couldn't even remember his name now—or coming back to her room. Temporary and selective amnesia. The cops would love that.

Maybe she should call a lawyer first. No. That would only make her look more guilty. She'd done nothing wrong and she had no reason to worry. All she had to do was to make a call to the authorities. The cops would believe her and understand.

It was a reassuring scenario. Too bad she didn't buy it.

JESSICA JUMPED at the hammering on her door, then rushed to unlatch the safety lock and swing it open. The man who greeted her wasn't in uniform, but he flashed an ID that looked official. "Sheriff Boyd Latimer," he announced in a lazy drawl. "Are you the woman who reported an alleged murder?"

"I'm the woman who reported finding a body."

He pushed past her, stared at the body for a second, then looked back to her. "You better have one hell of a story, lady."

"I woke up and found the body in my room just as I told the woman when I called 9-1-1."

"Uh-huh. Sure you did." He slid one hand to the butt of his revolver. "Spread your legs and put your hands against the wall."

"What?"

"You heard me."

She did as he said, the way she'd seen it done in movies and on TV. It was pretty disgusting to have his hands on her body, but at least he did it quickly.

"Okay, you can drop the position."

"Thanks. I know how this must look, but the truth is I have no idea—"

"This will go a lot better for you if you admit everything."

She threw her hands up in exasperation. "There's nothing to admit. The body was here when I woke up this morning—on the floor, the same as it is now."

"What's your relationship to the senator?"

"Senator?" Crapola! This was growing worse by the second.

"Surely you're not claiming you didn't know this here's Senator Marcus Hayden?"

"No. I mean yes."

"So which is it?"

"I didn't know."

His face screwed up as if he'd caught a whiff of rotten fish. "Do I look like I just fell off a turnip truck to you?"

"Excuse me?"

"I may be a country boy, lady, but I'm not an idiot. Ain't a soul in Georgia old enough to speak wouldn't recognize Marcus Hayden. Hell, he's better known than the president around these parts."

"I don't live in Georgia."

"Then how did you meet up with the senator?"

"I didn't *meet up* with him. I only exchanged a few words with him last night in the hotel lounge. He didn't even mention politics—at least not that I remember."

"I see. You two met in the bar. You came onto him. One thing led to another. So you invited him up to your room."

"Absolutely not. We exchanged a few words and then..." She massaged a spot above her right temple as the headache intensified. "I don't really remember what happened."

"You don't remember? Now ain't that convenient?"

"I know how this must sound, but I can't remember leaving the lounge or coming to my room. I drank the wine and then…'' Of course, why hadn't she thought of this sooner. "Someone must have put something in my drink.''

"Now you're claiming you were drugged?''

His drawl made the word into two long syllables and she cringed at the incrimination that crackled in his voice.

"Are you alert now?'' he asked, his eyes squinted under his bushy brows.

"I don't feel too well, but I'm alert.''

"Then you have the right to—''

"Whoa! Am I a suspect?''

"The body's in your room. You're the only one here. You figure it out.''

"Then I want to talk to a lawyer.''

"I kind of thought you might. But I will need to get your fingerprints while I'm here.'' He pulled a pen and a small black notebook from his shirt pocket. "And, for the record, will you state your full name, permanent address and your reason for being in Bankstown?''

He had her spell every word as he wrote, then stuck the notebook back in his pocket. "Okay, Miss Lewis, you're free to call your lawyer now. Then stay out of the way. I'm going to have to get a little backup in on this.''

"You surely don't think I'm dangerous."

"Not that kind of backup. This ain't no everyday murder here, you know. I'll have to have the crime scene fully investigated before the body is moved and hopefully before the media finds out about this and comes shoving in here like a bunch of wild hogs."

"The media?"

"You better know it. This is the biggest thing to ever hit Bankstown. Way bigger than that little bank robbery we had a couple of years ago. This here'll bring out CNN."

She dropped into the room's one chair, her head feeling as if her brains had been scrambled and fried, and her stomach so queasy, she thought she might have to run for the bathroom at any second.

"I need to call my boss and let him know what's happened," she said, trying to get a grip on the trouble she was in. "And I need to call Carruthers school to let them know I can't make this morning's appointment."

"Go right ahead. Make all the calls you'd like, as long as you have a cell phone."

"What's wrong with using the phone in the room?"

"You'll mess up the prints."

"I doubt the dead man used the phone."

"Don't get cute, and don't touch anything."

"My prints are already on the phone and almost everything else in here. And I need to get in the bathroom to wash my face and brush my teeth."

"You're not brushing your teeth in my crime scene."

"It's also my hotel room."

"Not anymore."

She glared at him, wishing she'd had the foresight to shower and dress in something a little less rumpled and more professional than the stretch slacks and cotton sweater she'd slept in last night. But the sheriff was here and there was nothing she could do but follow orders.

And try to find a really good lawyer to keep her out of jail. A good, *cheap* lawyer. Talk about an oxymoron.

ONCE HER FINGERPRINTS had been taken, Jessica skimmed the Yellow Pages under Attorneys. There weren't that many with addresses in Bankstown, but Jessica still found the task of randomly picking a defense attorney daunting. Closing the phone book, she watched Latimer's hodgepodge of a crime-scene team stumble over each other in their efforts to locate evidence. She'd watched plenty of cop shows on TV before. The scene in front of her bore little if any resemblance.

She'd managed to reach the school and cancel her appointment, though she hadn't given them any of the pertinent details. She hadn't reached her boss. It was an hour earlier in Houston and the office phones were still being manned by computer. The fact that she was a suspect in the murder of a famed Georgia senator didn't seem the kind of message to leave at the tone.

After what seemed like an eternity, four of the officers left, leaving only Latimer and a tall, thin blond guy the others had called Slim. The sheriff walked over to Jessica. "You are not to leave town under any circumstances and—"

He stopped midsentence as a new visitor arrived on the scene. The man marched right past the both of them and planted himself over the body. He was a good six inches taller than Latimer, broad-shouldered, hard and muscled. His manner shouted authority, though he was dressed in faded jeans and a denim work jacket, and unruly dark hair poked from under a Braves' baseball cap.

"Sonofabitch!" He turned back to Latimer.

"You'd think someone would call and notify the family and not leave us to hear this kind of news on the radio."

"Damn, Conner. I haven't given anyone authority to release this to the media."

"Then I guess someone didn't think he needed your okay."

"I'm gonna have to ask you to leave. This is a crime scene."

"Okay. You asked." The man motioned toward Jessica. "Who is she?"

"Jessica Lewis. This is her hotel room."

"Did you kill my brother?" he demanded, moving into her space and locking his gaze with hers.

"N-no," she stammered, then grew aggravated with herself for letting this obnoxious bully get to her. She might be scared to death, but she didn't have to give him the satisfaction of showing it. "I don't appreciate your tone," she said, standing and propping her hands on her hips defiantly.

"How did you know my brother?"

"I didn't."

"Do you make a habit of having men you don't know spend the night in your hotel room?"

"I didn't *have* him up here. I just woke up and found the body on my floor. Now if you'll all excuse me, I'm taking my things and getting out of here." She opened the drawer and grabbed her panty hose and bras, ready to stuff them back into her carry-on bag.

"And just where is it you think you're going?" Latimer demanded.

"To find another hotel, hopefully one with no bodies."

"I doubt any hotel in this town's gonna want you 'round," Slim said. "You better stay put or you might be sleeping on the ground."

"What happened to innocent until proven guilty?"

"You ain't in jail yet, are you?" Latimer reminded her.

"Pack your things," Conner ordered. "I'll at least get you a new room."

First, he accused her of killing his brother. Now he was going to get her a room, and he said it all in the same brash, condemning tone. She doubted they were actually blood brothers. The senator had been sophisticated and handsome. This guy was arrogant and ill-mannered, with a jaw that was too squared and a slightly crooked nose.

"Are you going to pack or stand there? I haven't got all day."

"I don't need your help," she quipped, though she wasn't at all certain that was true.

He glared at her. "Suit yourself." He asked Latimer a few more questions, frowning as he listened to the part about her passing out. Then he put up a hand as if he'd heard enough—or wasted too much of his time. He turned back to her, gave her one last once-over from top to bottom, then left the same way he'd entered, as if he were the general and the rest of them were lowly privates.

The sheriff muttered a string of curses under his breath. "Not so fast with the packing. I'll take a look through that suitcase first."

"That there was Conner Hayden," Slim said, directing his comment to her. "He's the senator's brother."

"He has an odd way of showing grief," Jessica said, watching while the sheriff rummaged through her clothes. When he didn't find a weapon, he shoved the carry-on out of his way.

Latimer strung another length of crime-scene tape. "I wouldn't be so quick to make an enemy of Conner Hayden if I was in the trouble you are, Miss Lewis."

"Why? Is he a politician, too?"

"With that disposition?"

"What does he do?"

"Owns a construction company. Lives right here in Bankstown."

"Yeah," Slim said. "He's a little rough around the edges and don't cotton to a lot of nonsense, but he knows this town better than anyone. So if he gives you advice or any other kind of help, you oughten to take it."

"Why would he?"

"Him and Marcus didn't gee-haw together too well, if you know what I mean?"

"I suppose you mean they didn't see eye-to-eye on everything."

"It was a tad more serious than that," Slim said, hitching up his khaki trousers. "They don't even speak to each other."

"Stifle it, Slim," Latimer ordered. "You don't have to explain Conner to the suspect."

A second later a tall, sandy-haired man stuck his head through the door and flashbulbs started popping. Jessica groaned. Sick as a dog, her thick red hair tangled, and wearing clothes she'd slept in—the worst possible presentation for her fifteen minutes of fame.

Welcome back to Georgia.

CHAPTER TWO

CONNER HAYDEN stormed down the four flights of stairs, stopping at the front desk only long enough to insist they give Jessica Lewis a new room. Until he figured out what was going on, it was far better she stayed where he could find her.

With that out of the way, he marched to his truck, made painful phone calls to his sister and Marcus's wife Sheila, then let his thoughts travel back to the last time he and Marcus had been in the same room together.

It had been four years ago, a week after his mother's funeral. They'd argued. Marcus, in one of his few physical outbursts, had slugged Conner. The punch had caught him off guard and Conner had fallen backward into his mother's china cabinet, sending a stack of antique plates to the floor in a shower of broken china.

Conner hadn't hit him back. At that point he'd been too angry to do it with any kind of finesse and would probably have loosened a few of his brother's perfect teeth. Besides, besting Marcus at a physical fight would have been like beating a six-year-old at a game of pool. A waste of energy and a total absence of satisfaction.

They'd talked on the phone a few times since then, mostly dealing with things having to do with settling the estate. But the issues between them had never been resolved. Now Marcus was dead.

And the number-one suspect was a young woman with a bizarre story and a disposition to match her fiery red hair. Pretty, of course. Marcus wouldn't have been with a woman who wasn't. A little thin for Conner's taste, but Marcus liked them petite. Only how could a woman that size have managed to sink a knife so deeply into Marcus's chest without his putting up some kind of fight? More to the point, what was the motive?

He might get a better handle on what had actually happened in that room last night if he could talk to her alone—and before some slick-talking lawyer convinced her that silence was not only golden but probably her best defense.

He hesitated just long enough to wonder why he was getting involved in the investigation at all when Marcus had made it plain that he didn't want Conner's involvement in any part of his life.

But Marcus didn't have a life now, so all bets were off.

JESSICA LET HERSELF INTO her new room, this one on the second floor. It was smaller than the last and looked out over the parking lot, which was considerably more crowded now than it had been when she'd arrived last night. Another news van pulled in while she watched.

Turning away, she plopped her one piece of luggage on the side of the bed and took out her toiletry kit. Her teeth felt as if they'd grown moss overnight and yesterday's mascara was caked in her lashes. Those were not the least of her problems by any means, but those were things she could do something about.

She'd just squeezed a stream of toothpaste onto her brush when someone rapped on her door. No doubt the return of Latimer who'd escorted her to her new room only minutes ago. But when she opened the door, Connor Hayden stood in front of her, the baseball cap he'd had on earlier clutched in his hands.

"I did not kill your brother," she said, starting to feel like a maniacal parrot.

"I'm not accusing you of anything. I just want to talk."

"I'm sure. You certainly don't want to listen to what I have to say. You or the sheriff."

"Actually, I *would* like to hear what you have to say."

His tone was far more civil than it had been earlier, almost sympathetic. Oddly enough, that made things worse. As long as she was enraged, she could hold her own. But it wouldn't take more than a touch of kindness to have her jangled nerves give way altogether and set her sobbing.

"You weren't interested when you were here before," she said, holding on to a thin edge of anger.

"I was in shock. I'm calmer now."

She opened the door a bit wider and he stepped inside. His gaze bore into hers and, for the first time, she noticed signs of what might be actual grief.

"We got off to a bad start earlier," he said. "Let's try it again. Why don't we both sit down and you tell me everything you know?"

"I'm not saying anything else until I talk to a lawyer."

"I'm not a cop, Jessica. I'm trying to help you, not nail you."

"You're Marcus's brother. Why should I trust you?"

"Because you're in serious trouble and I might be able to help you."

"There's no reason to sit," she said. "I woke up this morning and practically fell over your brother's body. I called 9-1-1. Latimer came barreling in. End of story."

"Then let's go back to last night."

She sighed, hating the prospect of going through this with Conner, yet almost needing to talk about it if only to help get the events straight in her own mind. "I think I was drugged."

"By whom?"

"I don't know, but that's the only thing I can think of to explain my passing out after a glass of wine." She paced the room a few seconds, then dropped to the edge of the sagging mattress.

Conner leaned against the small bureau. "Start from the beginning," he said. "When did you arrive in Bankstown?"

"I flew into Atlanta yesterday and rented a car. I arrived at the hotel about seven-thirty. I was starved, so I ordered the grilled-steak sandwich from room service.''

''And when did you run into Marcus?''

''After I finished eating and unpacked, I went down to the hotel lounge for a glass of wine to help me relax. Your brother was sitting at the bar. I'm not certain of the exact time, but it must have been about nine.''

''Was Marcus by himself?''

''He was at first.''

''So you joined him?''

''No. I took a seat at a nearby table. He walked over and started a conversation. He recommended the Merlot he was drinking, then went back to the bar and got it for me.''

''What did you talk about?''

''Things strangers usually talk about. The icy conditions of the road. Places to eat in the area. He asked what had brought me to Bankstown.''

''Why are you here?''

Conner listened without interrupting while she described the purpose of her visit, but he seemed distracted and she felt as if she could all but see the wheels of doubt and speculation turning in his mind.

''So you and Marcus were talking and having a glass of wine. Then what happened?''

"I excused myself to go to the ladies' room. When I returned, your brother had taken a seat at the end of the bar and was talking to a dark-haired woman. Their heads were close and they were speaking in low voices."

"Can you describe the woman?"

"She had long, straight hair. Very dark and shiny. And she was petite. That's really all I could see since her back was to me."

"Did you finish your drink?"

"I'm not sure. I think I took a few sips. My memory gets really fuzzy at that point."

"Was there anyone else in the bar besides you, Marcus and the woman?"

"Just the bartender."

"How long did you stay?"

She shook her head. "I have no idea. I don't even know how I got to my room. I woke up just like this." She ran her hands down her wrinkled sweater, suddenly feeling so grungy she wasn't sure she could stand it another minute. "Fully clothed except for my shoes."

"And when you woke up this morning, Marcus was in your room with a knife in his chest."

"Yes, but there is one other thing. When Marcus joined me, I remember thinking that he seemed familiar, though I couldn't place him."

''That's no surprise. He's been in politics all his adult life.'' Conner exhaled a long stream of air. ''His *short* life. He was only forty-eight, ten years older than me.''

''I'm sorry. I know it must be difficult losing your brother. Believe me, I'd help identify his killer if I could.''

''I appreciate that.'' He pulled a pen from his pocket and scribbled a name and a phone number on the pad of paper next to the telephone. ''Call this number and ask for Beth Delaney.''

''Why?''

''She's local, but the best lawyer in the whole state. Her office is out by Selby Lake. Have her give you directions.''

Jessica picked up the paper and stared blankly at the number, completely aware that Conner's sudden desire to help her made absolutely no sense.

He walked toward the door. ''If you're wondering why I'm doing this, it's pretty simple.''

''So you read minds, too. I should have known.''

''Yours was pretty easy to read in this case.''

''So why are you going out of your way to help me?''

''If I don't, Latimer is going to railroad you

right into jail—and let my brother's real killer go free.''

''What makes you so sure I'm not the real killer?''

''No one guilty of murder would come up with a story that lame, so I figure it must be the truth. Now lock the door behind me and don't open it for strangers unless you want your picture on the front page of every newspaper in the country. And don't talk to anyone else before you talk to Beth.''

She watched him leave, not sure if she was thankful for his help or pissed that he thought he could just tell her what to do. But any way you looked at this, she was stuck in a bed of quicksand and the only rescue line was dangling from the rugged hands of the victim's brother.

Things couldn't get much worse. So why was she certain that they would?

CONNER BEGAN PUNCHING numbers into his cell phone even before he reached his truck. The first two calls were to verify Jessica's story. All the details of employment and reason for being in Bankstown checked out. He wasn't surprised. He was usually a good judge of character; he'd liked the way she'd come at him so straight, just threw everything out there and almost dared him to doubt her.

Conner punched in one last phone number, then went through Beth Delaney's secretary before he got her on the phone.

"I heard the news, Conner. I'm sorry."

"Yeah. Thanks."

"I know you and Marcus had your problems, but still, this must be a shock. Are you doing all right with it?"

"Do I have a choice?"

"No, but you don't have to sound so tough."

"It's a front."

"I know."

"That's the problem with us, Beth. You know me too well. But I didn't call for sympathy."

"I'm sure you didn't. What's up?"

"I don't know how much you heard, but Marcus's body was found in a woman's room at the Mountain View Hotel."

"Has the woman in question been arrested?"

"Not yet." He took a deep breath and wondered once again if he'd lost his mind. "Her name is Jessica Lewis. I'd like you to see her, Beth."

"You're surely not asking me to take her on as a client?"

"I'd like you to consider it."

"Why?"

"I think she's innocent." He explained his meeting with Jessica and recounted the story exactly as she had told it to him, knowing that it had all the earmarks of poor fiction.

"This woman must have really gotten to you."

"It's hard to explain."

"Taking in a woman suspected of murdering you brother is not like picking up some stray dog from the side of the road, Conner. If you get involved with her in any way, it's going to have repercussions."

"Have you ever known me to get as involved with any woman as I do a stray dog? I just want you to talk to her. After that, you're free to decide whether or not to represent her."

"That's big of you. I won't be affected by some blonde batting her big blues at me."

"She's a redhead. And her eyes are green."

"Is she pretty?"

"I didn't notice."

"You're a man. You noticed. So I'll take that for a yes."

"It's not why I believe her story."

"I hope not. But if I'm going to consider taking her on as a client, I want to see her as soon as possible—before she says any more to the police.''

''I already gave her your phone number. She should be calling anytime.''

They finished the conversation and Conner guided his truck down the narrow main street of town, past the hardware store and Jackson's Pharmacy. The town was still fairly quiet, but the circus would start soon. Reporters from across the country would descend like buzzards to fresh roadkill. All digging for dirt while the cops dug for clues.

Talk to me, Marcus. Who killed you? Give me a sign and I'll try to see that you rest in peace even if you weren't interested in living that way.

But Marcus wasn't talking.

BETH DELANEY'S OFFICE was in the west wing of a three-story house that sat atop a hill overlooking a small lake north of Bankstown. Beth herself was stunning. Somewhere around forty, Jessica guessed, with short, smoothly coifed blond hair that stopped an inch above the jawline and piercing eyes just a little deeper shade of blue than the lake.

She sat across from Jessica, not behind the

barrier of an impressive desk, but in an uphol-
stered chair that gave the impression they were
two old friends chatting. Jessica didn't buy it for
a second. She was all too aware that she was
being measured and found wanting as she went
through the story she'd shared earlier with Conner.

"My five-year-old niece could come up with
a more believable tale," Beth said.

"You asked for the truth," Jessica said.
"That's what I gave you."

"I hope so."

Jessica fingered the strap of her handbag.
"But you don't really believe me?"

"My believing you won't keep you out of
prison. My ability to convince the jury that
you're telling the truth will. I won't have much
chance of doing it with that scenario, though you
seem to have convinced Conner that you're innocent."

Jessica felt the scrutiny intensify and she had
the unsettling feeling that there was a new un-
dercurrent charging the air. If there was some
kind of romantic entanglement between Beth
and Conner, she certainly didn't want to be
thrown into the middle of it. "Perhaps it's best
if I look somewhere else for an attorney."

"Perhaps—but I doubt it."

"Are you that good?"

"I'm good enough, but even more important, I know things about Marcus Hayden that most of his constituents don't. Conner knows a lot more and, for some reason, he wants to help you. Your best bet to beat the charges is to stick with me, but I'll want a few commitments from you before I agree to take your case."

No doubt money. And Jessica was fairly certain she couldn't afford Beth Delaney.

"I'll have to know everything about you and your past—and I do mean everything. I can handle your worst secrets up front, but I don't want any surprises when I step into that courtroom."

Jessica looked away as the realization of what she might be about to face pressed into her mind. "I need time to think."

"You don't have a lot of options," Beth informed her.

"It's a long shot, I know, but surely there's a chance that the cops might find the real killer in the next few days and I won't need an attorney at all."

"I doubt they'll wait a few days before they arrest you."

Arrest her and lock her up in jail, as if she

were a common criminal—or not so common. Jessica took a deep breath and stood, pulling on her coat and hugging it around her chest. "I'll get back to you later today," she promised, already walking toward the door.

A few seconds later she was in her car, huddled behind the wheel and shaking like a cat just dropped into pen of wild dogs. Finally, when she became steady enough to drive, she started the engine and began to back down the steep, sharply curved driveway. The view from the rearview mirror was one of towering pine trees, and the sparkling surface of the lake beyond.

The peaceful setting did nothing to ease the fears that pummeled Jessica's mind or to stop the cold sweat that made her hands stick to the steering wheel of the small rented car. The past and the present, about to collide, and there might be no way for her to protect herself from the impact.

She hit the gas, then let off quickly as the car skidded on a patch of ice and careened sideways, sliding off the pavement and into the mud for a harrowing second before she managed to straighten it.

Back on the driveway, she pressed the brake to slow the descent. Her foot sank to the floorboard as the car picked up speed. She was flying toward the trees; even if she managed to maneuver between them, she'd plunge into the lake.

Impulsively she fought the wheel, then grabbed the key, turned it and killed the ignition. But the car was skidding across the icy ground, completely out of control as it slipped between two towering pine trees and plunged into the icy water of the waiting lake.

Shock and panic hit with paralyzing force, and all she could do was stare at the water that bubbled and churned around the car. The second the cold water seeped through the floorboard and began creeping up her legs, she bolted into action.

She turned the handle and shoved against the door, throwing her shoulder against it so hard that pain ripped along her muscles. The door didn't budge. Frantic, Jessica beat her right fist against the thick pane of glass as she loosened her seat belt with the other. The glass stayed intact.

She closed her eyes and tried to think. Instead of a way to escape, the face of Marcus Hayden flooded her mind, his eyes no longer glassy and vacant but condemning.

And in that second she knew where she'd seen Marcus before. But it was too late to matter. The water was rising, up to the seat now, and swirling along the bottom edges of the side window. She screamed and hammered against the window. She wasn't ready to die. Not yet. Not like this.

But the water just kept rising.

CHAPTER THREE

CONNER DROVE UP just in time to glimpse a red compact car as it skidded out of control on the icy decline and plunged into the lake. He didn't recognize the car, but instinctively swung into action, fueled by a burst of adrenaline and gut instinct. Sliding from behind the wheel, he grabbed a small hammer from the tool chest in the truck bed and took off running.

His feet slid on the iced pine straw as he raced through the trees, but somehow he kept his balance until he reached the bank. The car was sinking slowly, it wouldn't be long before it was totally submerged. He kicked off his shoes and wiggled out of his jacket, then jumped into the icy water.

The shock of the frigid temperature was painful, but he swam with steady strokes toward the car. The tumble of red hair was the first thing he saw. When he glimpsed Jessica's eyes, wide and frightened, a new urgency surged inside him.

He struggled with the door, but apparently the lock was stuck. Damned electrical systems. He let his feet touch the bottom and discovered that if he stood on his toes, he could keep his mouth above the surface.

He held up the hammer. "I have to break the window," he yelled. "Get back."

She nodded and scooted away, covering her face with her arms. Conner slammed the hammer against the window, then broke out the pieces of busted glass. "Shimmy through here. Quickly, before the car sinks completely."

She followed his orders, taking his hands and kicking through the opening. When she was clear, he took her in his arms and waded toward the shore.

"Thanks," she whispered through chattering teeth. "I'll owe you for this."

"Big time." But relief and the icy shock of the water had affected his mind. Strangely, he felt as though he and Jessica were bound by something far stronger than the situation…as if she belonged in his arms.

"How did you know I'd need help?" The words bounced along her shivers.

"I didn't. I'd come out to talk to Beth. I didn't even know it was you until I reached the car."

"Oh."

She tightened for a second, then relaxed in his arms. He felt her breath on his neck, a stark contrast to the bone-chilling cold. He set her down in the truck, then tore the soaked flannel shirt from his body, threw it into the bed of the truck and crawled in behind the wheel.

"You should get out of those wet clothes," he suggested as he started the engine and turned the heater on high. "You'll get warm a lot faster."

She shook her head. "I'll be okay."

He jerked the truck into gear and gave it gas, shooting out a stream of gravel and mud behind them. "I only live a mile down the road. Less than five minutes to a roaring fire and thick blankets."

"I'm starting to like you, Conner Hayden."

"Just because I save you from a plunge into an icy lake and offer you a blazing fire? Who said you weren't easy?"

For the first time in a morning that would live in infamy for both of them, Jessica Lewis smiled. And Conner felt a strange twisting inside his chest. He chose not to think about what it might mean.

SPRING STREET CAFÉ, Bankstown's only open-for-breakfast eatery, was filled with locals and newsmen by midmorning, all clamoring for coffee and Myrtle's famous homemade biscuits. Sheriff Latimer and his deputy sat in a back booth, talking with each other in between countless interruptions by reporters or friends and neighbors wanting the real scoop on what he'd discovered that morning in Room 404 of the Mountain View Hotel.

But Latimer wasn't talking—at least, not much. The state attorney general had ordered him to keep his trap shut. This was bigger than Bankstown, he'd said, and he wanted the Atlanta police department to conduct the investigation, along with the sheriff's help, of course.

"We'll do the dirty work. The big-city boys will get all the glory," Slim said.

"Yep. It would be different if we needed them, but we don't. I told Bennigan this is an open-and-shut case."

"Who's Bennigan?"

"The detective they assigned to the case. Some smart-assed, college-educated cop who thinks he knows it all. I have no intention of just sitting back and taking orders from some whippersnapper probably don't even know how to spit a proper stream of tobacco.''

Slim sopped up red-eye gravy with a hunk of biscuit. ''You think Jessica Lewis is definitely guilty?''

''Guilty as a man caught with his pants down in bed with his neighbor's wife.''

Slim poked the biscuit in his mouth. ''She's awful pretty,'' he said, talking with his mouth full and spraying crumbs down the front of his khaki uniform. ''Don't look like no killer to me.''

''Probably wasn't before last night. Nothing more dangerous than a woman scorned. Never forget that, Slim.''

''How could she be scorned if she didn't even know the senator?''

''She was lying through those pretty white teeth or my name's not Boyd Jacob Latimer.''

''Yeah, but, still it don't add up. If she was guilty, why did she hang around and call us?''

''She didn't until she had time to sober up and come up with that stupid story about being drugged. Besides, she couldn't go hauling the body out of the hotel without someone seeing her. And the room was registered to her, so even if she'd left, we could've tracked her down.''

''Sounds mighty circumstantial to me.''

''Circumstantial or not, she's guilty. The knife's being checked for fingerprints right now, and I'd bet my next paycheck that Jessica Lewis's are there. If they are, she'll be in jail by this time tomorrow.''

''I reckon you're right, but she just don't look like a killer to me.''

''That's why I'm the sheriff and you're the deputy, Slim. I can see through women like her as if they were made of glass. Trust me on this one. Jessica Lewis is probably hiding out in her motel room right now ruing the day she landed in my county. Now let's get out of here. We got work to do.''

JESSICA HUDDLED beneath the woolly blanket Conner had provided when he'd put her soaked clothes in the dryer. Conner handed her a mug of steaming hot chocolate, then poked the burning logs in his mammoth stone fireplace with an ash-crusted poker. He'd changed into dry jeans, a gray sweatshirt and black work boots.

She appreciated being saved, but her feelings toward him were confusing. He was tough when he talked, yet tender when he'd held her in his arms and carried her from the freezing water to the warmth of his truck. He'd ordered her around as if she were a slave, yet he had brought her home with him, built her a roaring fire and made hot chocolate for her. All of that after his brother had been found dead in her hotel room.

If her own life were not such a chaotic mess, she might be able to figure him out. As it was, she had no choice but to deal with issues in the order they flew at her and that included taking him as he was or walking out. The first seemed the only logical response, at least until her clothes came out of the dryer.

Conner turned to face her. "Are you warm yet?"

"On the outside. I'm still shaking on the inside, but I don't know if it's from the cold or the ordeal."

"Probably a little of both." He reached down and covered the tips of her bare toes with the trailing blanket. "What made you lose control of the car?"

"I hit a patch of ice and started to skid. I managed to get the car back on the drive, but when I tried to slow it down, the brakes didn't hold."

His eyebrows shot up. "It was a late-model car. Seems unlikely the brakes would have worn out."

"My luck. First I wake up with a dead senator. Now I've sunk a rental car. I don't even want to venture a guess at what's waiting for me back at my hotel room."

"You're not going back there."

There he went giving orders again, but this time Latimer had beat him to it. "The sheriff said I was not to leave town."

"That doesn't mean you have to stay in the hotel. I have plenty of room here."

The statement stunned her. "Give me one good reason why I should. Better yet, give me a reason why you'd want me here."

"I didn't say I *wanted* you here. I said you could stay."

"Why?"

He added another log to the fire. Flames licked their way around it, then shot up the chimney as if he'd angered them. He planted a booted foot on the hearth and stared at her. "I told you earlier. I want to find out who killed my brother."

"Isn't that for the cops to do?"

"They want an arrest. I want the truth."

Which was exactly what she wanted, so maybe they weren't so far apart, after all. "I've told you all I know."

"There is one other reason I want you here."

He stared at her with his piercing brown eyes and she felt something strange and compelling slither up her spine. She was alone in a house with a rugged man who'd just saved her life. Some kind of awareness would be only natural, but this was different—a touch of fear, a tremble of anticipation, as if they were partners on some strange adventure.

"I think you may be in danger, Jessica."

"But if the man who killed your brother had wanted me dead, he had the perfect opportunity last night."

"Men have been known to change their minds."

"I get the feeling you know more than you're saying, Conner."

"After I left you, I paid a visit to the bartender who was working in the bar at Mountain View last night. His mother said he wasn't there. I had her check his room. His duffel bag and his hunting rifle are gone. My guess is he was in on the murder."

"That would explain how the drugs that put

me under got in my drink. But why would a bartender in Bankstown want to kill a senator?''

"That's the question I keep asking myself.''

"And even if he wanted to kill him, why did he drag me into the situation?''

"That could have been a spur-of-the-moment decision. You walked in on the scene, Marcus brought you into a conversation, and the bartender—or someone working with him—decided you'd make the perfect scapegoat.''

"It seems to have worked. The sheriff's convinced I'm guilty.''

"Latimer's looking for glory, and he loves the media attention.''

"And if I stay here, you'll be drawn into the line of the media's fire, as well.''

"Not if they don't find out you're here.''

"I'd have to tell the sheriff where I'm staying.''

"Hopefully he could be persuaded to keep that information to himself.''

"Why risk it?''

He grimaced, then stepped closer, keeping his gaze locked with hers. "I'd hate to jump in frigid water to save your life only to have you lose it to a killer.''

She shuddered, apprehension suddenly thick

as cold grits. "You really do think I'm in danger, don't you?"

"What's one more body to a person who's already killed?"

She sucked in a deep gulp of air, then tugged the blanket higher under her neck, as if she could somehow shield herself from the possibilities that kept coming at her.

"It makes sense for you to stay here, Jessica. It's the last place anyone will look for you."

"Unless the killer was watching when you pulled me from the water and followed us here."

"We weren't followed. I made sure of that." Conner paced the room, then came back and hunched down beside the hassock she was sitting on. "I hate to leave you here alone, but I have to drive into Atlanta this afternoon to help with funeral arrangements."

Jessica sighed and bit back her own frustration. In the midst of her own problems, she'd all but forgotten that he was dealing with the loss of his brother.

He stirred the fire again, then walked to the kitchen door. "I'm going to make us some lunch now. After we eat, I'll show you around the house. You should be safe here, but I have a pistol. You can keep with you—just in case."

"I wouldn't know how to use it."

"It's simple. I'll show you. I was a small-arms instructor with the National Guard for about five years."

"Even if you show me, I doubt I could pull the trigger and shoot someone."

"You might be surprised what you can do if put to the test."

But she'd been put to the test years ago. And Marcus Hayden had been there. She should tell Conner that now, but she couldn't without bringing up all the horrid details of her past. It had no bearing on the present, though she doubted either the cops or the tabloids would agree with that assessment.

Jessica Lewis. Orphan. Troublemaker. Murderer of babies.

Her breath came hard. It had been years ago. Another lifetime. Yet she felt herself being sucked back into the mire and shame as if it were happening all over again.

Only this time she wasn't alone. It wouldn't last. But for some reason she couldn't begin to fathom, a rugged, take-charge man with piercing eyes and strong arms seemed determined to help. Wariness persisted, but it was either stay here with a man she didn't totally trust or go back to

the hotel room to face a hoard of persistent reporters and possibly a killer.

"Chicken noodle or vegetable beef?" Conner
asked. "Canned, of course."

Her stomach growled in anticipation of food
or in complaint that she hadn't refilled it since
last night's steak sandwich. If there were any
doubt before, the odds tilted in favor of staying.
At least here she'd get fed.

JESSICA HAD CLEANED UP the kitchen after Conner left, then spent a good half hour mentally
going over what she could remember of last
night's events. She'd scribbled a few notes and
tried to come up with some reasonable explanation for how the body had gotten in her room.
Bottom line. There was none.

After an hour of frustration piled on top of
panic, she'd given up, shed her clothes and taken
a long, hot shower in the master bath where
Conner had laid out a supply of caramel-colored
towels and washcloths before he'd left. She'd
hoped the shower would help her relax, but instead she seemed to grow more tense with each
splash of water.

The dead body, the encounter with Latimer,
the plunge into the lake had all taken their toll,

but it was the not-knowing-what-to-expect-next that was really getting to her. If Conner was right, someone wanted her dead. But who? And why? It certainly wasn't as if she knew anything.

Too restless to sit still, she paced, back and forth, down the long hallway to the kitchen, the spacious den and back to the bedroom. If houses had a gender, this one would definitely be male. Rich woods, supple leather, oversize furniture, earth-colored Mexican tile, and so many windows the place seemed part of the woods that surrounded it. Rustic. Masculine. Mysterious. A lot like Conner.

And that was another problem. She was staying in the middle of nowhere with the brother of the man the police suspected her of killing. She and Conner weren't friends. They were barely acquaintances, yet she was wandering through his house all alone, exploring his private space. She'd used his soap when she'd showered, massaged his shampoo into her hair, dried her dripping body on his fluffy man-size towel. Now she was in a blue flannel robe she'd found on a hook behind the bathroom door.

The robe smelled of Conner. Musky with just a hint of wood smoke. She imagined him slipping into it after a shower, the hairs on his chest holding drops of clinging water, his stomach taut, his... Damn. The last thing she needed now was lustful thoughts about Conner. It wasn't as if he were some irresistible hunk. He wasn't even handsome—at least not in the usual sense. He was incredibly virile, though. Mostly he just had a way about him that made her feel safe and protected.

She jumped at the jarring ring of the phone. Conner hadn't said for her not to answer the phone if it rang, but then he hadn't said for her to answer it, either. It could be Latimer—or a reporter. Or the killer.

But then again, it could be Conner. She was still staring at the phone when the answering machine clicked on and Beth Delaney's voice filled the room.

"I know you're there, Jessica, so please pick up. There's been a new development in the murder case."

She grabbed the receiver. "Hello, Beth."

"I was beginning to think you'd taken off on your own."

"No. I'm staying here—for now."

"I'd recommend it. Look, I'm sorry for what happened at my place this morning."

"It wasn't your fault."

"No, but I should have warned you that the drive is sometimes hard to maneuver when it's icy. Not that the information would have helped much without brakes."

Apparently, Conner had told Beth everything. Their relationship was hard to figure. If it was romantic, she seemingly didn't care that he'd brought Jessica home with him. Whatever their relationship was, it was no concern of Jessica's and she'd be smart to remember that.

"I just wanted you to know that if I'd seen your plunge into the water, I'd have come out to help."

"Thank you."

"That's the one thing about this house I don't like. With the drive at that angle, I can't see it from anywhere inside the house, so I never know who's coming or going. I did hear all the commotion earlier, though, when some of Conner's men were trying to get the car out of the lake."

"His men?"

"Guys who work for his construction company. They were ready to have it towed away when Latimer showed up and had it impounded."

"Is that the new development?"

"One of them. The other is that Latimer has the prints back from the murder weapon."

Jessica's grip tightened on the receiver. "And…?"

"Your prints are on the knife. We also have more information on the knife itself. It was one of the oversize steak knives from the hotel kitchen."

"I didn't kill him." It was the same mantra she'd chanted that morning, but even to Jessica's ears, it seemed to have lost its former power. Now it just rolled with the dread that was churning in her stomach.

"I'm not accusing you, Jessica. I'm only telling you what I know."

"How did you find out?"

"I have friends in low places."

"How low?"

"The crime lab."

A deafening silence hung on the line. Jessica knew she should say something, but the images of the morning were playing in her mind again. The knife. The blank eyes. The bloodstains. Was it possible that in a drugged stupor, she really had let Marcus into her room and then killed him?

"I contacted Latimer to let him know I'm

your attorney and that any requests to talk to you should go through me."

"How could you do that when I haven't hired you as my attorney yet?"

"Conner hired me. He said to spare no expense in defending you. He'll take care of everything. I thought you knew."

"When did he do that?"

"A few minutes ago, when I told him your prints were on the knife."

All the evidence pointed to the fact that she'd killed Conner's brother, yet he was paying for her defense. There was no way this made sense.

"How well do you know Conner, Beth?"

"Well enough."

"What were the problems between Conner and Marcus?"

"You need to ask Conner that question."

"He does a lot better at asking questions than he does at answering them."

"He does tend to be a bit controlling."

"A bit?"

"He'll take control if you let him, but he's a good guy, Jessica."

"I guess. It's just hard to fully trust a man I know so little about."

"I'm a defense attorney. I'm served up lies,

cruelty and deceptions every day of my life. I trust very few people, but I'd trust Conner with my life.''

But could Jessica? That was the question that haunted her as they finished the conversation. The spacious house seemed suffocating now, as if the walls were closing in on her. She opened the back door and stepped outside just as a clap of thunder crashed in the distance. Wind pummeled the tall pines and the bare branches of some ancient oaks that stood a few yards from the house.

She closed her eyes and gave in to her own storm, a barrage of painful memories colliding with the present. Running through it all was a hard line of fear, soul deep and bone-cold. And the mind-numbing certainty that the past she'd tried so hard to leave behind was somehow going to rise again. But this time it might destroy her.

JESSICA JERKED AWAKE. The den was eerily dark, lit only by glowing embers from the dying fire. She'd only planned to lie down for a few minutes, but apparently she'd fallen asleep on Conner's sofa, still dressed in the robe she'd slipped into after the shower. She shivered and pulled it tighter.

The storm that had threatened earlier raged outside, sending sheets of rain pelting against the windows. Jessica flicked on the lamp, then shuddered as the room remained dark except for the lighting provided by a zigzagged streak across the night sky. The thunder that followed seemed to shake the whole house.

Evidently the storm had knocked out the electricity, which explained why the house had grown so cold. There was nothing to do but to rebuild the fire, then get dressed again and wait for Conner to return.

She had the first log in hand when she heard the unmistakable sound of breaking glass coming from the back of the house. The wind must have blown something into the window with enough force to knock out one of the panes.

Or else someone had just broken into the house.

CHAPTER FOUR

IT WAS LIKELY the wind, Jessica reminded herself. It was howling around the corners of the house and a pine sapling outside the window swayed almost to the ground.

You could be in danger.

But she couldn't take chances. She needed the gun, the frightful weapon she'd left on the bureau in Conner's room when she'd showered. Down the narrow hallway, toward the sound of the breaking glass.

A cold draft swept through the house, as if a door had swung open. The log slipped from her hands, clattering against the metal fire screen before it landed on the stone hearth.

The years slipped away and she was eight years old again, deep within the musty basement of the orphanage. But even then she hadn't been alone. Her friends had been with her, holding hands in the darkness, listening to the cries of the ghost baby.

Jessica fit her hands around the handle of the poker. It wasn't a gun, but it would have to do. She waited, watching for shadows, listening for footfalls from the back of the house, though she knew there would be no way to hear them above the storm.

But it was the front door that creaked open with a blast of cold air that practically knocked her off her feet.

"Jessica."

Relief swept through her. She lowered the poker and let it slide from her hands and crash to the floor. "I'm here, Conner." She didn't wait for a response, but simply propelled herself into his strong arms.

CONNER'S TRAITOROUS BODY reacted much too swiftly to the pressure of Jessica's body against his. He held her close, shaken by a rush of hot desire.

"I think someone else may be in the house, Conner. I heard glass breaking in the back of the house and felt a draft as if a window or door was opened."

He dropped his hold on her, the desire dissolved by a blast of adrenaline. "Where's the gun?"

"I left it on the bureau in your bedroom."

"Damn." He flicked the light switch, then realized why she was waiting in the dark.

"The storm knocked out the electricity," she whispered. "I was about to light the fire when I heard the window break."

He reached into his pocket for a penlight, shone the tiny beam around the room and noticed the log and the poker sitting cockeyed on the hearth. Evidently that was what he'd heard fall when he'd opened the door. He reached for the poker. "Stay here," he whispered. "I'll check it out."

"No. You can't go back there. Let's just get in your truck and leave."

"It's probably just the storm. I didn't see any sign of a car when I drove up." He fished his keys from his pocket and pressed them into her hand. "If I call your name, run to the truck and take off."

"Go with me, Conner. Please, just go with me. We can call the cops and let them check out the house."

"I'll be okay. You will, too. Just do as I said." He eased past her and crept toward the back of the house, sticking to the wall, the poker ready to strike if need be. He waited at the end of the hall, listening for breathing or movement, for some sign that the man who'd killed Marcus had come here searching for Jessica. There were only the sounds of the howling wind and the driving rain.

When he reached his bedroom, he shot a beam of light at the window. The right bottom pane was broken. The opening was large enough to let in a draft but too small for a person to have crawled through it.

"Thank God."

He turned at the sound of Jessica's voice. "I told you to stay put."

"I couldn't just leave you by yourself."

He held his hand out to her and she slipped hers inside it. It struck him that it had been a very long time since he'd held a woman's hand other than to shake it. He let go and stepped away, afraid he was giving her the wrong impression, though he had no idea what the right impression might be.

"I'll get a towel," she said, "and blot up some of the water."

"Thanks. I have some heavy plastic in the garage. I'll tack some over the opening. That should keep most of the rain out until I can get the window fixed."

"Do you have candles?"

"Yeah. And some gas lanterns, too. Always have to be prepared for losing the electricity when you live in the woods."

Jessica grabbed a towel from the bathroom and started working, and Conner was hit with a another round of the desire that had surfaced when he'd held her in his arms. This wasn't like him. It had to be the circumstance. They were caught up in a situation that reeked of danger and tension and surprises that wouldn't quit. He'd gotten the latest just as he'd turned onto the dirt road that led from the highway to his house.

He'd have to tell Jessica as soon as she settled down. Tonight it had merely been the storm that frightened her. Next time it could well be a killer.

Two large gas lanterns provided illumination and lent a surprisingly cozy feel to Conner's well-equipped kitchen, especially now that the rain had slowed to a pleasing pattering instead of a pelting downpour. Jessica's earlier fears had subsided, leaving her emotionally drained and mentally exhausted. She craved a taste of normalcy and was glad for the opportunity to help with preparing food.

"You have a lot of pots and pans for a man who serves canned soup," she teased as she pulled a skillet from the cupboard.

"Beth's doing. She stocked the cooking supplies and linens."

Jessica tried to ignore the goading wave of jealousy the statement produced. It was unacceptable and unexplainable. "You and Beth must be quite close," she said, striving for a tone of casual interest.

"Yeah." Conner pulled slices of bacon from the slab and arranged them into the skillet she'd set atop the gas range.

"Yeah" wasn't exactly the answer Jessica was looking for, but then maybe it said it all. It certainly wasn't a denial. "Beth is very pretty."

"Yes, she is. Smart and down-to-earth, as well."

"Is she married?"

Conner stepped over, stopping a little too close for comfort. "Are you checking out Beth or me?"

Heat flushed her cheeks. "Neither of you. It was just a question."

"There's no husband, at least not anymore.

Jake died two years ago in a boating accident. He was my business partner at the time—and the best friend I'd ever had. But, for the record, there's nothing between Beth and me except friendship.''

Jessica was glad for the information but hated that she'd asked the question. Now he probably thought she was attracted to him. She wasn't. Well, she was, but it was a natural reaction to a stranger who'd not only saved her life but become her literal port in a storm.

When they sat to eat, he took the chair across the square kitchen table from her. "Hope you don't mind breakfast fare for dinner," he said. "The only alternative was a couple of steaks in the freezer, but it was a little late to wait for them to defrost.''

"Bacon and eggs are fine."

"I stopped by the hotel and picked up your luggage. I'll get it out of the car after we eat."

"How did you get in my room without a key?"

"I know the owner."

"I see. And now he knows where I'm staying, as well.''

"Actually, I led him to believe you'd left town, though I'm not certain he bought it. But even if he didn't, he probably won't mention it to the media. You're making the Mountain View Hotel a hot property.''

''Because your brother was the senator.'' The uneasiness surged again, the feeling that she was being as much managed as saved. ''What happened between you and Marcus, Conner?''

He kept eating, didn't even look up, but his muscles tensed at the question. ''It's a long story.''

''We have plenty of time.''

He ignored the comment.

''I know it's none of my business,'' she continued, ''but sometimes it helps to talk to a stranger.''

''Is that what we are, Jessica? Strangers?''

''We only met a few hours ago,'' she reminded him.

''A few hours in which my brother was found dead. Hours in which someone tried to kill you.''

''You don't know that for a fact. The brakes might have simply failed due to some kind of mechanical problem.''

He put down his fork. This time when he met her gaze, there was no teasing. No reassurance.

Just an intensity that turned his eyes even darker. "It wasn't an accident."

"Are you sure?"

"Positive. Latimer had them checked at my insistence. The brake line was cut, which means someone followed you to Beth's and saw your parking on the incline as a window of opportunity."

"But why, when it would have been so easy to kill me last night?"

"Maybe the killer was interrupted before he could finish the job. Right now the why is not as important as the who, and the question of how we stop him before he succeeds."

She pushed her plate away. "What kind of enemies did Marcus have? Who would hate him enough to plunge a knife in his chest and just walk away?"

"Marcus was great at making enemies—and friends. My guess is the culprit is someone he used and then sold down the river."

This time there was no mistaking the pain that had crept into Conner's voice. It seemed out of character. He was strong, determined, a man who always seemed in control, yet even that didn't assure him a life free from hurt.

"Is that what happened between the two of

you, Conner? Did Marcus sell you down the pro-verbial river?''

He exhaled sharply. ''I don't want to get into this, Jessica. Not tonight.''

Not ever, she suspected, and who better than her to understand that there were some things about a person's life they preferred to leave bur-ied in the furthest recesses of their mind. A shiver crawled along her spine and, as if on cue, the dark memories claimed her mind.

The baby is dead, Jessica. Do you know what happens to little girls who kill babies?

''It's okay, Jessica. You'll be safe with me. I won't let anything happen to you. I promise you that.''

She hadn't even been aware that Conner had reached across the table and taken her hands in his, that their fingers were entangled the way their lives had become.

''Thanks, Conner. I don't understand you or the reason why you brought me home with you, but I'm really glad I'm here.''

''Me, too. And if it's any consolation, I don't understand me, either.''

CONNER STOOD at the back of the group of fam-ily members and friends gathered at the burial site. Reverend Thomas had encouraged him to take a seat in the front row beside his sister Susan and her husband, but Conner was more comfortable standing and maintaining his space.

His emotions were raw, like an open sore, festered and exposed. Their depth surprised him. He hadn't been sure what he'd feel. They had never been close, but a guy couldn't grow up in the same house with an older brother and not feel something for him. So maybe he was grieving for what they'd never had and now never would.

Shifting, he pulled his overcoat around him. It was cold, gray and threatening rain, or possibly sleet—a fitting day for a funeral. The church had been packed with Marcus's family, friends and constituents. But the cemetery service was supposedly private, though Conner saw more than a few faces he didn't recognize. The pastor was talking about peace and closure. Conner felt neither. They were hard to come by when whoever had killed Marcus was still on the loose, still a threat to Jessica Lewis.

Jessica had been at his place for three days now, but he hadn't seen that much of her. He'd had Brad, the largest and toughest of his crew, stay with her while Conner had spent his days taking care of family obligations surrounding Marcus's death and asking endless questions about the murder. He hadn't found any answers, and as far as he could tell, neither Latimer nor Detective Bennigan had made any notable progress toward finding the villain, either.

All they really knew was that the bartender was still missing, there were no fingerprints on the knife except Jessica's, the dark-haired woman who'd been at the hotel with Marcus that night had not been identified and the brakes on the rental car had been deliberately disabled.

Latimer was still making sounds like Jessica Lewis could be guilty, insinuating that the brakes might be a ruse to throw them off balance, claiming that if Conner hadn't happened along, Jessica would have escaped from the sinking car by herself.

But Latimer hadn't seen the look of pure terror in her eyes when Conner had pulled her from the wreckage or held her trembling body when she'd dissolved in fear over a window broken in the storm. Jessica was innocent. And that might be the only thing Conner was certain of at this minute. That and the fact that having her in his house morning and night was really starting to get to him.

None of which should be claiming his mind now. The service was concluding. His sister was weeping softly. Sheila was dry-eyed, but pale and shaken, holding on to her sister who'd come to offer moral support. Apparently Marcus and Sheila had shared some kind of bond that wasn't affected by Marcus's sexual indiscretions or Sheila's self-indulgence and spiteful temper.

Conner turned away and started the long walk back to his car before anyone could corner him to offer more condolences. All he wanted now was to go home. His hand was on the door handle when he felt a touch on his shoulder. When he turned around, Sheila was looking at him through moist, red eyes rimmed in black mascara that hadn't smudged.

"Are you coming by the house, Conner?"

"I haven't been invited there in four years, Sheila. It doesn't seem right that I'd come now."

"More right than running home to spend time with the woman who killed your brother."

"Jessica Lewis did not kill Marcus."

"That's a matter of opinion. And you can't deny that she's staying at your place."

"How did you find out?"

"It doesn't matter how I found out. I did. And

if I know about it then other people do, too. You may as well as spit on your brother's coffin, Conner."

Damn. He should have known word would get out. Beth wouldn't have talked. That left Latimer or Bennigan or maybe the manager of the hotel. His bet would be on Latimer.

"I want that woman out of your house, Conner, and I want her out now."

"I'll decide who's welcome in my home, Sheila. Not you."

"Then you need to read this note." She pulled a folded slip of paper from the side pocket of her purse. "I found this today when I was going through the glove compartment of Marcus's Mercedes. It was stuck in the back. The cops apparently overlooked it when they examined his car."

"I don't need any information you found by snooping."

"I think you do. It regards a rendezvous."

"Marcus is dead, Sheila. Let it go."

"This time I can't. And neither can you. It's proof that your houseguest was involved in Marcus's murder."

Conner felt the foreboding. It took the steam right out of him, like a hard punch to the gut.

He ached to turn his back on Sheila and walk away. Instead he took the incriminating note and read it right down to the signature line.

Love, Jessica.

CHAPTER FIVE

I'LL BE AT THE MOUNTAIN View Hotel in Bankstown. Can't wait to see you, sweetheart, and spend another night in your arms.

Conner read the words again, pictured Jessica in Marcus's arms and experienced an almost overwhelming urge to smash his fist into something.

"So now do you believe me, Conner? Or do you still buy that bizarre story your sweet little redheaded killer concocted?"

"Get out of my face, Sheila."

She grabbed the note from his hand. "Very well, Conner. Play the part of a fool just like your brother did. Maybe the vixen will sleep with you, too…unless you've already been together."

Conner didn't answer. What was there to say?

JESSICA HAD EXPECTED Conner to be down and a little distant when he returned from the funeral, but watching him sit and drink one beer after another was not helping things. Worse, he appeared to be deliberately avoiding conversation with her, seemed barely able to look at her. She walked up behind him and put a hand on his shoulder. The move was impulsive, but the awareness that shot through her was swift and powerful. "Let's go for a walk," she said, suddenly needing to escape the confines of the house.

"It's freezing outside."

"You have a closet full of jackets."

"And I have a warm fire right here and another six-pack in the fridge."

"Then go for me. I need to get out of the house."

He set his beer on the table a lot harder than necessary. "Are you tired of my company, Jessica?"

"No." That was the only thing she wasn't tired of. "I just hate to see you like this. So walk with me, Conner. In the woods where it's quiet and we can see our breaths in the cold air and watch the squirrels scurry from beneath our feet, where life goes on with some kind of normalcy."

"You're right," he agreed. "We should get out of the house. But not walk. The weather's too nasty for that."

"Where will we go?"

"A surprise. You like surprises, don't you?"

She hated his tone and the look in his eyes, but she could understand it. It couldn't be easy going to the funeral of a brother that you'd been at odds with. She'd prefer to walk, but getting out of the house to go anywhere was better than this.

"I'll drive," she said as he picked up a beer for the road.

"Why not? It's your show."

JESSICA KNEW she should have held out for the walk the second they stepped inside the doors of Cleo's. It was empty except for a paunchy, bearded bartender, and the smoke from last night's cigarettes still hung thick in the air. The lights were dim and it took a minute for her pupils to adjust so that she could see the full length of the bar and the pool tables that lined the back of the narrow building. A jukebox in the corner belted out an old Elvis tune.

"Conner Hayden, it's been a while," the bartender said.

"Guess it has."

"Sorry to hear about your brother."

"Yep."

"What will it be? Beers? Whiskey?"

"Jack on the rocks. A double," Conner answered.

"A light beer," Jessica said. "Whatever's cold." She seldom drank more than an occasional glass of wine, and never in the middle of the afternoon, but she needed it now. She'd hoped getting Conner out of the house would shake his depression, but apparently she'd been overly optimistic. Still, he'd been there for her for days. She could put up with Cleo's awhile for him.

Conner waited at the bar for his drink, though he didn't sit. When it arrived, he downed half of it in one gulp, then turned his back to her and strode away. "Grab a cue," he said, his tone biting, his words starting to slur as he walked to the back of the room.

"If you'd like, but I haven't played pool in ages. You'll be certain to win."

"I seriously doubt that."

Jessica hesitated, then followed Conner to the pool table where he'd already started racking the balls. This was a side of him she'd never glimpsed before. It was as if he was deliberately trying to start a fight with her.

"Ladies first," he said, chalking his cue.

"Okay." She tried, but her fingers shook and the ball moved only inches.

"I expected you to be far better at ball crunching, Jessica. Here, let me help you." He pressed against her, his chest to her back. Fitting his hands over hers, he helped her make a shot. The balls scattered in all directions.

Then without warning, Conner jerked her around to face him. His gaze was piercing, cold and hot all at once, and it was as if something both frightening and exciting had erupted between them. And then his lips were on hers. He was too rough, his kiss too hard and demanding, yet she didn't pull away. Instead she exploded with a hunger she'd never known. The emotions of the past few days purged themselves in the kiss. Wet and wanton. Probing and excruciatingly satisfying.

She would have made love with him right there—on the floor…on the pool table. Outside in the cold. She was that hot for him, that lost in the desire that stripped her bare. But he pulled away and wiped his hand across his mouth as if that could remove the passion.

"I'm sorry, Jessica. I didn't mean to do that."

Her heart was pounding in her chest. "No harm done." Except to her heart. And maybe her soul. "Is it the funeral, Conner. Was it horribly painful?"

"No."

"It's…it's the situation." He turned away. "And something I heard today."

"Something about me?"

"Did you know Marcus before this week?"

So her secret was out. She should have known the past would rear its ugly head and spit out its venom. "Yes. I knew him."

His face couldn't have looked more stricken than if she'd slapped him.

THEY RETURNED to the truck where they could talk without the blare of the jukebox for backdrop. The kiss lingered between them, hard evidence of the sizzling tension that punctuated their relationship.

"I was raised in the Meyers Bickham orphanage about thirty miles north of here. Your brother Marcus held some kind of position with the orphanage. I was only ten when I came into contact with him, so I'm not certain what his job was, only that in my mind, he was someone to be feared."

"How long ago was that?"

"Nineteen years." And yet the memories and dread filled her mind now as if it were yesterday. The loneliness. The fear. The guilt. "My mother abandoned me, just dropped me off at the orphanage one day and never returned. Years later I learned that she'd died from a heroin overdose."

"And your father?"

"I never knew him. My mother wasn't married

and there was no name but hers on my birth certificate.''

Conner looked straight ahead, holding on to the steering wheel as if it might fly out of his control if he loosened his grip though they were still sitting in the parking lot at Cleo's. She studied his profile. It was hard, angular, his expression impossible to read.

"Tell me about your relationship with Marcus."

"There was no relationship. He came and went. When I got in trouble they made me go and talk to him while he was there. And I was always in trouble.''

You let the baby die. Mr. Hayden will have to be told. You let the baby die. You let the baby die.

Tears welled in her eyes and the knot in her throat made breathing almost impossible. Nineteen years ago, but the shame and hurt were still potent.

Conner turned to face her, his expression still unreadable. "What about now, Jessica? What was your relationship with Marcus before he died?'' There was no mistaking the accusation in his tone.

Finally she got his message. She didn't know what he'd heard at the funeral, but it had obviously made him change his mind about her innocence. She felt twisted inside, hurt and angry, but at least now she knew what was going on.

"I didn't kill Marcus, Conner. I hadn't seen him in nineteen years, and I wish to God I hadn't seen him that night at the hotel. And I didn't lie about not knowing who he was. I had worked hard on leaving the painful memories of my past behind and it wasn't until I was in the sinking car that I remembered why he looked familiar."

Her voice was as shaky as her insides. She opened the door and jumped from the truck, reeling from Conner's betrayal. She was on the edge of the road miles from town, but she didn't care. She'd find a ride back to Bankstown, go back to the hotel and face the media—and the killer if it came to that. But she had to get away from Conner.

"Get in the truck, Jessica." The voice came from right behind her.

She kept walking at the same fast pace. "Leave me alone, Conner. Go back to your world."

"We live in the same world." He caught up with her and grabbed her arm, pulling her to a stop. "Let's go home. We can talk there."

"Going home is not an option for me. I'm a murder suspect, remember? Apparently you discussed that very fact at the funeral. Troubled girl with a history of causing problems. Why would anyone believe me?"

"I was out of line, and I'm sorry. It's been an emotional day. I just wasn't thinking clearly."

"You're thinking like everyone else in town, the same way the jury will think."

"Beth will handle the jury."

"No. She's not my defense attorney. *You* hired her."

"For you. Jessica. For the same reason I want you with me. To keep you safe."

"No." But she was weakening. Tears burned at the backs of her eyelids, and she ached to press her body against Conner's and hold on tightly. But the hurt was too real. For once she'd let herself trust blindly, and this was what came from it. "Just leave me be, Conner. Just leave me be."

"I can't do that."

"Why?"

"I was wrong, Jessica. I overreacted to something I heard. I know you didn't kill Marcus."

"How do you know, Conner, when every shred of evidence points against me?"

He cuddled her face in his large, rough hands, forcing her to meet his gaze. "Because you're honest and real—and too damn soft."

The tears broke loose then, sliding down Jessica's cheeks in torrents. Conner picked her up and carried her back to the truck. She held on, lost in her need for him though she didn't understand it any more than she understood anything else that had happened since coming to Bankstown.

But even if she didn't understand it, she couldn't deny the truth. She'd never felt as safe as she did in Conner's arms.

CONNER LEANED BACK IN the passenger seat, hating himself for the complete fool he'd been. He didn't know where the note Sheila had shown him had come from, but he wouldn't be surprised if she'd written the damned thing herself or at least signed Jessica's name to it.

She'd found out Jessica was staying with him, hadn't liked it and had decided to do something about it. Manipulate, lie, play her little games of deceit. Any other time, in any other situation, he'd have ignored her pointed barbs and insinuations—tossed the note to the ground and walked away. But she'd caught him off guard, his nerves rattled, his emotions raw.

And the result had been that he'd hurt Jessica. It was unforgivable, considering she was probably the only innocent involved in all of this. Even now he'd be hard-pressed to explain to a unbiased stranger why he was so sure she hadn't killed Marcus. It didn't matter. It was enough that he was certain of it, and that she was here so he could protect her.

"The funeral must have been difficult for you," she said once they'd started back to his house.

"It was." He stretched and massaged his neck and the niche at the base of his skull. "You asked me once about what had happened between Marcus and me."

"I'd still like to know, but we don't have to talk about it now."

"It goes way back. My father and my grandfather were in politics. It was all we knew growing up, and both Marcus and I were expected to follow suit. We should be groomed for the White House. It was Dad's trademark expression. It worked with Marcus, but I was a major disappointment."

"In what way?"

"I was a maverick, drank beer instead of fine wine, preferred jeans to designer suits, and choose my friends because I liked them, not for what they could do for me. I still do. What you see is pretty much what you get with me."

She reached across the seat and lay a hand on his thigh. "I like what I see."

"Thanks, but there's more to this story. About four years ago, I found out that Marcus was taking bribes and payoffs from some major Mafia players.''

''What did you do?''

''Went to him first. He denied it, told me to stay out of his life and punched me in the nose.''

''And that was when you stopped seeing him?''

''Shortly thereafter. Someone else found out and they took it to the attorney general. Marcus was certain I'd turned him in. Beth was working for the D.A.'s office at the time, and she was ready to prosecute.''

''What happened to the case?''

''It was dropped for insignificant evidence. From that point on, the battle lines were drawn. Aunts, uncles, cousins, family friends—they all blamed me for Marcus's problems. Only my sister stayed friends with both sides.''

''What about your parents?''

''They were dead.''

''We're a fine pair, Conner Hayden. Both of us with our troubled and convoluted past.''

He squeezed her hand and tried to think of a worthy response, but his attention was claimed by the ring of his cell phone. He punched the button. ''Conner Hayden.''

''This is Carl Epson. My mother said you were looking for me.''

"Where are you, Carl?"

"I'm staying in a friend's boathouse out at Selby Lake. I know why you're looking for me, but I didn't have nothing to do with the senator's murder."

"So why did you run?"

"I was scared, man. You know, spinning out. Besides, I'd sniffed a little that night, you know what I mean? I didn't need no crap from the cops."

"I'd like to talk to you in person."

"I'll talk to you, but not the cops. I mean it, Mr. Hayden. I can smell cops a mile away, and if I do, I'll disappear in the woods faster than you can blink your headlights."

"Exactly where on Selby Lake is this boathouse?"

He gave his location. It was less than twenty miles from where they were right now, a mere half mile from where Beth lived.

"Don't leave the boathouse. I'll be there in under a half hour."

"That was the bartender, wasn't it?" Jessica asked when he'd broken the connection.

"Yeah. He's ready to talk."

"Finally."

He could tell from her sigh of relief that she thought the news would all be good. He prayed she was right, but he had his doubts. But then he was far too much a realist to take anything good at face value.

THE BOATHOUSE was not much more than some used lumber nailed together haphazardly over a half-rotting dock. There was no boat. There was only blood—and a body.

CHAPTER SIX

JESSICA'S STOMACH TURNED inside out and stayed that way. For the second time this week, she was standing over a dead body. Only this time, it was not neat and orderly. There was no clean, puncture wound, no expensive suit to soak up the blood. And the pistol that had likely delivered the gaping and deadly wound was lying only inches from Carl's outstretched fingers.

Conner murmured a string of curses, his tone even harsher than it had been the morning he'd first walked into her hotel room. Only now she understood him better, knew that his toughness was a false barrier, that he was never truly protected from his feelings.

The wind rustled in the tall grass at the water's edge and Jessica sidled closer to him. ''The killer could still be nearby.''

''From the looks of things, the killer and the victim are one and the same.''

''You think he shot himself?''

"It looks that way."

"But you just talked to him on the phone."

"I know, I just don't get it. I can't believe he didn't at least wait until I got here."

"Do you think he killed Marcus?"

"I don't know, and we may not find out, not unless he left some kind of note."

"We should call Latimer."

"Another minute or two won't hurt Carl, and I'd like to check out the boathouse." He put a hand on her shoulder and pulled her into the curve of his arm. "Are you okay?"

"No, but I'm still breathing. Right now I'll settle for that."

She followed him into the boathouse. The place was littered with beer cans and empty chip packages. There was a half-eaten hamburger on the table, sitting on top of a paper bag from a fast-food chain—and a handwritten note. A huge cockroach scurried away from it when they approached.

She looked over Conner's shoulder as he read it, her mind trying desperately to mesh the pieces of what Carl had written with her memories of the night Marcus had been murdered.

Carl claimed he was high on speed when she'd come in. If so, she hadn't noticed, but then

Marcus had actually gotten her drink for her, so her interaction with Carl had been minimal. According to the note, he'd slipped some roofies into her drink, whatever that was, and she'd passed out.

The senator had helped Carl get her back to her room, and then Carl and the senator had gotten into an argument when Marcus had wanted the bartender to leave him alone with Jessica. He'd pushed Carl. Carl had grabbed the knife from the room service tray and the senator had slipped and fallen into it.

"Lots of detail for a suicide note," Conner said. "Almost reminds me of one of Beth's closing arguments."

"But it makes sense. At least it seems to. What's a roofie?"

"Rohypnol. More commonly known as the 'date rape' drug. I saw a special on TV about it just the other night."

"What do we do now?"

"Call Latimer. It's his show from here on out. His and Bennigan's."

She read the note again while Conner made the call to Latimer. Carl had admitted everything in the note. She'd no longer be a suspect. Her name would be cleared.

She should be overcome with relief, but two men were dead and all she felt at the moment was a kind of blanket sadness, overwhelming fatigue and...gratitude.

"Thanks, Conner."

"For what?"

"For being you and being here."

He took her hand and squeezed it. It was simple a gesture, but it felt good and right. And she knew she was falling much too hard for a man who'd been thrown into her life by circumstance and whom, once this was over, she might never see again.

BUT TWO DAYS LATER, Latimer had still not given Jessica permission to leave town. So on Saturday, Conner suggested a road trip.

The Meyers Bickham Children's Home hadn't existed in that capacity in over ten years, but the old church that had housed the institution still remained. Conner had passed it before, though he'd never given the orphanage much thought. He'd always suffered from too much family rather than too little.

He was no psychologist, but even a novice like himself could tell after just a few days around Jessica that she needed some kind of closure on the time she'd spent there.

Ghosts and bogeymen that could be bigger than life to a frightened kid had a way of dissolving in the glaring light of adulthood. They'd driven in silence most of the two-hour trip, but they were getting close now and she was growing more antsy with every passing mile.

"I'm not convinced this is a good idea, Conner."

He snaked a hand across the back of the seat and rubbed his thumb along the tight tendons of her neck. "Have I steered you wrong, yet?"

"This is different. You may be biting off more of a challenge than you wanted."

"I can handle it." He hoped. Volunteering to jump head-first into emotional issues had never been his style before, but nothing about his reactions to Jessica Lewis matched his usual behavior patterns.

Even when he'd been angry and felt betrayed by her, the sexual urges had been so strong he could have taken her right there on the pool table in the back corner of Cleo's. Fortunately his brain had checked in and conquered his libido—at least temporarily.

Damn. He was getting worked up now just

thinking of making love to her. "Where are your foster parents now?" he asked, knowing he'd best get his mind on something else.

"Papa Leo died from a heart condition five years ago. Mama Clarice died last year of a stroke."

"What were they like?"

"Good people. They'd lost their daughter in a shooting accident—young people fooling with a supposedly unloaded hunting rifle. She was an only child and they were too old to have or adopt another. I was the replacement."

"That couldn't have been easy on you."

"Easier than living at Meyers Bickham. I'm sure they even loved me in their own way. It's just sometimes I think I worked against them."

"Knowing you, that's hard to believe."

"Believe me, I tried to do everything right. It was the closest to thing to a real home and family I'd ever known and I wanted to stay with them. But having me there was a constant reminder of the child they'd lost." She clasped her hands in her lap. "I don't know why I'm you telling you this."

Neither did he. He was glad she felt comfortable enough to do it, but it also made him uneasy. Every bit of personal information they shared, every touch, seemed to bind them closer together. It insinuated a real relationship, and relationships frightened him a lot more than a killer. Probably because he wasn't a big enough fool to believe this one could possibly last.

Jessica would be out of his life in a matter of days.

JESSICA STOOD in front of the church, struck by how much smaller it looked than it had in her mind. The arched double doors were just that and not the entryway to a dungeon of doom as she'd imagined them before. Still, it filled her with a dread so real she could taste it.

Conner put an arm around her waist. "It's just a building, Jessica. There's nothing here that can hurt you."

Having Conner beside her made it easier. So did the sun that beat down on the back of her neck and the light wind that feathered her hair and sent the hem of her skirt dancing against her thighs. Maybe she had moved further past the old hurts than she'd realized.

Conner took her hand and led the way up the broken concrete walk to the weathered doors. He turned the knob and pushed, but the door held tight.

"I guess we could go through a window," she said, "though I never imagined I'd be breaking into this place."

"We will if it comes to that, but I think the door's just stuck."

Jessica caught herself holding her breath, her stomach tightening into knots as Conner heaved with his shoulder. The door gave, the wood scratching along the concrete like an old man's raspy cough.

"Ready or not, here I come," she said, taking a deep breath and stepping over the threshold into the shadowed old church that had once been her home.

It smelled of mildew and standing water, and giant cobwebs hung from the door facing and the few light fixtures that still dangled from the crumbling ceilings. The floor was littered with dirt and trash, and huge clods of dirt stuck to the walls.

"And I thought it was bad when I lived here," she said, brushing webs from her cheeks and eyelashes.

"Home for spiders, dirt dobbers and probably rats now," Conner said.

"It was always home to rats, large brown ones

that scurried around the basement like watchdogs.''

"Don't tell me they made you go down into the basement with rats.''

"Actually that was our escape. My friends Daphne and Sara and I sometimes sneaked down there late at night to talk—and make up stories about our being bewitched princesses held prisoner by a tribe of wicked witches.''

"Waiting for your prince to come?''

"White horse and all.''

And now he had, or at least Conner had been a prince of a man this week. Gruffer than the man of her dreams, not nearly as handsome, but brave and strong and... A blush crept to her cheeks. Sexy. It hadn't been her first impression of him, but there was no doubt about the way he made her feel.

She stepped away from him, moving deeper into the desolate building.

"Where did you sleep?'' Conner asked, skimming the piles of lumber that were scattered around the sanctuary.

"Our rooms were in the back. At least, that's the way I remember it. The offices were out here.''

"Not much left of them now.'' Conner

walked to a stack of cardboard boxes along the wall, stooped and blew layers of dust off the top one. He pulled out some old manilla folders, riffled through a few, then returned them to the box.

Jessica continued on without him, her legs growing shaky as she neared the door that led to what had been the bedrooms and living area for the children. Memories consumed her, but there was little connection between them and the empty space in front of her.

"How are you doing?" Conner asked, stepping beside her.

"I'm glad we came. Seeing it like this makes it lose a lot of its potency." She stopped at an old metal chest, the kind they'd used to hold their meager belongings. Hunching down beside it, she lifted the top. It was filled with framed pictures.

Conner knelt beside her. "That's Marcus," he said, pointing at a man in the center of a group of mostly women. He trailed his finger along the listing of names at the bottom.

"'Marcus Paul Hayden, Chairman of the Board of Directors for Meyers Bickham Children's Home.' And, I'll be damned. That woman standing on his left is Sheila, his wife. I never realized it, but he must have met her here.''

Jessica's gaze moved to the woman. The old shame washed over her like a hurricane-driven wave. And the sound of a baby's cry exploded in her brain.

"It's okay, Jessica," Conner said, picking up on her distress and taking her in his arms. "It's just a photograph. There are no ghosts."

"But there are." She pulled away from him. "There always will be. It's not just memories, Conner. I killed a baby."

"What are you talking about?"

"Sheila was one of the caretakers. She made me take care of the sick babies, and I didn't, at least I didn't do it right. One of the babies died."

Jessica's voice quivered and her arms were heavy with the weight of the dead infant. "I never told anyone. Not my foster parents. Not any of the counselors they took me to see. Not even Sara or Daphne my best friends here at the orphanage, though they heard the ghost of the baby crying the same as I did."

Conner rocked Jessica to him, finally understanding how traumatic her time in this place had been, aching for her but also stunned by Sheila's brand of cruelty. "You were just a kid,

Jessica, not old enough to be responsible for infants, especially sick ones.''

"I know, but the baby cried so hard. I wanted her to stop. I prayed she'd stop—and then she did."

"It was a terrible thing for you to have to deal with, but it was never your fault. You surely can see that now."

"I'd like to go, Conner."

He kept his arm around her shoulder as they walked back to his truck, but his thoughts were on Sheila. Had she recognized Jessica's name after all these years? Was that why she'd written that note and signed Jessica's name? But what would be the point, especially when she was supposedly stricken with grief over the loss of her husband?

It stayed on his mind as he drove home, added a new and prickly layer of doubt to the suspicions that were already brewing there. Had Carl's suicide and note wrapped things up a little too neatly?

JESSICA STOOD UNDER the pulsating spray of the shower for a quarter of an hour, letting the heat and moisture soak into her muscles and ease the tension while her mind dealt with the memories.

Conner was right, of course. She wasn't responsible for the baby's death, no more than she was responsible for her biological mother's abandoning her for a life of drug addiction. It was time to let go of things she had no power to change, to break their hold on her and to go on with her life.

A life selling software and looking for love and happiness. A life without Conner.

A week ago she'd have never imagined that she would share her most terrifying secrets with the arrogant man who'd stormed into her hotel room. A lot of things had changed in a week, but seven days didn't make a relationship. Conner had only kissed her once in that time, and then he'd pulled away almost before it had begun. Still, what a kiss it had been.

She grew hot at the thought. She trailed her fingers down her wet body and let them linger on her breasts, her stomach, the triangle of red curly hairs at the apex of her thighs.

There was no denying that she wanted Conner. In her arms…between her thighs. His mouth on hers. The length of him sliding inside her, hard and demanding and setting her on fire.

She didn't know what would happen after tonight. He'd never talked of anything beyond protecting her from a killer, but whatever else might come of her time with him, she wanted the memory of making love with him to take with her when she walked away. Hot, heated, loving memories to push away the ugly past that had lived inside her much too long.

Racked with a need she didn't fully understand, she stepped out of the shower and dried her body on the fluffy towel. She didn't bother with the robe. Naked would do just fine for what she had in mind.

CONNER FINISHED his conversation with Latimer and hung up the phone. He'd received news that did a lot toward dispelling the theory that the bartender's note might have been planted.

Carl Epson had a lengthy record of drug abuse, and he'd been charged but not convicted of slipping Rohypnol to, and actually raping, some girl he'd picked up in a bar a couple of months ago in Atlanta. She'd dropped charges a few days later, no doubt to avoid having her personal life go on trial with Carl.

As far as Latimer was concerned, this made everything perfect. Carl was the guilty one. Marcus had likely come to Jessica's aid and been killed for the effort. Carl had the motive, the opportunity and he'd already given himself the death sentence. Case closed. Jessica was free to leave town.

Damn! All good news. So why did Conner feel as if he'd been hit in the gut with a two-by-four? He walked back to the hearth, poked the burning logs a few times just to hear them crackle, then tossed another one onto the pile.

When he turned around, he got the surprise of his life.

CHAPTER SEVEN

JESSICA STEPPED TOWARD him, and every part of Conner's body reacted at once, throwing his equilibrium so far off balance he could barely stand.

"Conner."

His name was a mere whisper, but her voice was rich with desire. He swallowed hard and tried to speak, but his mind was too far gone to come up with words. Instead he opened his arms and she stepped into them, her lips raised to his.

The kiss was tentative at first; he had the feeling that this was only a mirage and when he pressed against her she'd simply evaporate.

She didn't. Instead the kiss deepened and she responded with a need that seemed every bit as fierce as the one that raged inside him. If he'd been able to think at all, he might have doubted it could be true. But his brain was mush. The rest of his body rock-hard and fire-hot.

She tore at his clothes, unbuttoning his shirt,

tangling her fingers in the hairs on his chest. Every movement seemed unbelievably erotic as she pressed her lips against his bare flesh, tasting, nibbling, while her hands worked to unbuckle his belt.

He didn't help her. His hands were exploring, as well, tracing the outline of her perfect breasts, kneading the pink tips of her nipples, reaching below her waist to slide between her thighs. She was already moist. Anticipating *him.* The marvel of it hit again and he shuddered as a new wave of desire ripped through him.

They half fell to the carpet in a tangle of arms, legs and lips. He wiggled out of his jeans and stretched beside her, her breasts melded against his chest, her left leg sliding between his thighs. He knew he should take it slowly, taste and touch every inch of her, make sure he was satisfying her. Only his heart was pounding, his blood rushing, his body so ready it ached.

He murmured her name and she moaned softly.

"Take me, Conner. Take me now." She kissed him hard as her hand slid to his erection and guided it to her.

She was torrid and slick as he thrust inside her. Her legs wrapped around him, and his breath came fast as he found his rhythm and they became one in a burst of passion that sent him cresting over the top.

She came with him, moaning and calling his name as they climaxed, both of them lost in an act as primal and natural as life itself.

Even when they were done, they didn't talk. What could he say that didn't sound as corny as some Hollywood script? That he'd never lost himself so completely in a moment of passion. That he'd never felt so uninhibited. That nothing had ever felt this right before.

He couldn't say it, but, scary as it was, that was all true. He was thirty-eight years old. He'd had sex lots of times with several different women. But this was the first time he'd ever made love.

So they lay together, her pressed against him, the afterglow of their lovemaking wrapping them in a silken cocoon. Finally she stirred, and he kissed her again, then got up, dimmed the lights and went to turn on a little mood music and to pour them a couple of flutes of wine. She was getting up when he got back to her.

"Where do you think you're going?" he asked.

"To get dressed."

"Not yet. Unless the floor's uncomfortable?"

"Very comfortable."

He pulled her back into his arms. "I just want to lie here and hold you—at least until my strength returns."

"And then what?"

"Then I'm going to make love to you the right way."

"If that was the wrong way, I'm not sure my heart can survive the right way, Conner Hayden."

But he held her close and his body that was spent only a few minutes ago stirred back to life.

JESSICA WOKE in the wee hours of the morning, the room pitch-dark, but the gentle ache between her thighs reminding her that making love with Conner had been more than a dream. Now she was sharing Conner's bed. The sounds of his steady breathing filled the room and she listened intently, wanting to memorize the sounds so she could play them back in her mind on lonely nights.

Stretching between the cool sheets, she turned toward him, loving the way he looked with locks of his thick hair falling into his face. Awake, he was always alert, authoritative, the lines in his face angled and hard. Asleep, with his muscles relaxed, he looked somewhat boyish, almost gentle.

He was as complex as he seemed. Smart and tough. Protective and thoughtful. A real man who had made her feel more loved last night than she'd ever felt in all her life.

Yet as marvelous as last night had been, he hadn't mentioned having any kind of special feelings for her. He hadn't asked her to stay on in Banksville so that they could get to know each other better. He hadn't even mentioned the possibility of their getting together again.

Easing to the edge of the mattress, quietly so as not to wake him, she swung her legs over the side of the bed, stood and tiptoed to the window. A Georgia sky, studded with sparkling stars and a glorious moon. She'd dreaded coming back here. Now she dreaded leaving.

An unfamiliar ache swelled in her as the truth hit home. In all her life, no one had ever actually loved her, so why would Conner Hayden be any different. Still she'd never be sorry they'd made love. It had been absolutely perfect and the memory of it would linger in her soul for a long, long time.

CONNER STOOD in the office, doing his best to focus on work when his mind was on a red-headed woman who in one short week had turned his world upside down and taken complete control over his mind—not to mention what she was doing to his emotions.

One minute he was riding high, all hot and bothered and full of thoughts of how it had been last night. The next he was lower than the fill beneath a cement slab, imagining what it was going to be like after she'd walked out of his life.

He could be with her now. Instead he'd left her alone to pack while he'd driven into the office, claiming he had things to do that couldn't wait when the truth was he couldn't bear to watch her getting ready to leave.

"Guess it was a rough week with the funeral and all."

Conner looked up as one of his foremen walked into the narrow office carrying a rolled-up blueprint in his hand. "Rough enough," he answered.

"You could take a couple of days off. I know you don't believe it, boss man, but the work goes on even when you're away."

"That's not what Ron Hampton says."

"That pious jerk. What's he complaining about now?"

"He thinks you took too long on his framing job."

"Tell him we could work a lot faster if he'd stay clear of the site and quit harassing my crew with his stupid questions."

"I already told him, just not in those exact words."

The foreman grinned. "Bet you didn't mince words too much. Any chance you can get me a roofing crew on the Perkin's job tomorrow?"

"When are they supposed to show up?"

"Not until Thursday, but we're running ahead of schedule and I'd like to get finished with the exterior before the next stretch of bad weather hits."

"I'll see what I can do."

Ryan flashed a thumbs-up sign and disappeared.

Conner scribbled himself a note to check on the roofing crew, then finished the last of the coffee he'd already let grow cold. If he left now he'd have time to stop by the Hampton site to check on the progress before he picked up Jessica to drive her to the airport.

Or maybe he'd just get her in the truck and

keep driving. Or hop a plane with her, fly to Cancun or Acapulco and check into a fancy resort on the beach and spend the rest of his life making love.

A nice thought. A fantasy. Too bad Conner was so firmly entrenched in reality. He wasn't husband material, and anyone with half a brain would know Jessica would never have given him the time of day if she hadn't been in fear of her life. She was young and beautiful, could have her choice of men.

He was ten years older than her. Nothing special in the looks department. Definitely lacking in the charm category. Not exciting on any level. She was attracted to him now because he'd saved her life, but give her another week and she'd be ready to hit the road again.

Better to have it over and done with now when all the memories of what had happened between them were good ones. He grabbed his Braves' cap, plopped it onto his head and headed for his truck. His cell phone rang before he'd backed from the parking area. "Conner Hayden."

"Are you back at work?" Beth asked.

"Man's gotta make a living. What's up, counselor?"

"A tidbit on Marcus that I thought you might find interesting."

"What's that?"

"He'd talked to a lawyer about filing for divorce the day before he was killed."

"There must be some mistake. Marcus would never divorce Sheila. It wouldn't fit the image of a good Georgia boy on his way to the White House."

"Maybe something more important than the White House had come along."

"Like what?"

"A woman."

"There have always been women in Marcus's life—discreet affairs with lovers who knew to keep their mouths shut. A divorce is ugly and public."

"My source is very reliable, Conner."

"Who?"

"I'm not at liberty to say."

"I'd say the person is wrong, no matter how reliable they usually are."

"I don't thinks so. Speaking of women, how's Jessica?"

"She's fine."

"You're not just letting her walk away, are you?"

"No. She's flying. It's quicker that way. I'm driving her to the airport in about an hour."

"Don't make light of this, Conner. You're crazy about her and you know it."

"Like I always say, you know me too well."

"Did you tell her how you feel?"

"No point. It would never work between us."

"Not with that attitude."

"Gotta go, Beth, but thanks for the info on Marcus."

"But not for the advice concerning Jessica. It doesn't matter, Conner. I'm still going to tell you what I think about that."

"Somehow I knew you would."

"You've been dodging any kind of serious relationship ever since I've known you. You pretend to be tough, but when it comes to women, you're scared to death."

"I just know my limitations."

"No. You know the limitations your parents drilled into you. You may not have been politician material—in my book, that's not a bad thing. But you are a super guy and any woman would be lucky to get you. That includes Jessica Lewis."

"Is that the end of the lecture?"

"Pretty much. Give her a chance, Conner.

Give yourself a chance. If you don't, you may regret it the rest of your life. Love doesn't come along every day. Take my word for it. I know.''

He said goodbye and hung up the phone, knowing Beth was right about at least two things: he was a coward and love didn't come along every day. But love didn't guarantee the absence of regrets.

He forced thoughts of Jessica from his mind and concentrated on the news about Marcus. A divorce. No way. Sheila would never have let him humiliate her like that. She'd have killed him first.

JESSICA'S LUGGAGE was packed and sitting by the front door even though it was an hour before she expected Conner to return to drive her to the airport. Grabbing her black leather jacket, she slipped into it and stepped outside.

The temperature had climbed into the sixties over the past few days, but a cold front had moved in overnight and it had dipped back into the low thirties this morning. The chill factor had to be a lot lower, she decided as a gust of icy wind all but blew her over.

She considered ducking back inside but decided even the cold was better than wandering through Conner's house, thinking about him, re-living every moment they'd spent together. Reaching into her jacket pockets, she pulled out her red fleece hat and gloves and finished dressing for the weather.

She strode the small clearing that surrounded the house and took a well-worn path that led into the woods. The forest was a mix of towering pines interspersed with oaks, red maples and a few dogwoods.

There was little underbrush beneath their thick canopy, but the pine straw rustled from a host of squirrels and a couple of rabbits who didn't appear too thrilled about her company. A crow cawed loudly from a branch over her head. For a second, she felt as if it were warning her not to go on.

A bit of paranoia, she assured herself, spawned by the events of the past week or so. But she was enveloped by nature in an isolated section of forest no more than a few yards behind Conner's house. What could possibly harm her here?

Her confidence returned and she walked on, slower now, so lost in her thoughts that she was barely aware of her surroundings. She already missed Conner, just knowing that after today she might never see him again.

She'd walk away without telling him how she really felt. Just take what life handed her and be grateful for small favors. After all, her own mother hadn't wanted her, why would anyone else?

Her spine stiffened. That was the old Jessica. She wasn't that frightened girl anymore. She was a woman with wants and needs that couldn't be denied. And what she wanted was Conner Hayden. Admitting how she felt to Conner would mean facing the possibility of rejection once again. But not telling him meant she'd be giving up without ever giving them a chance.

"Well, well. What a surprise. Little Jessica Lewis, all grown-up."

Startled, Jessica spun around at the sound of the high-pitched female voice. The woman was standing only a few feet away.

"You don't recognize me, do you?" the woman asked, her tone caustic.

Jessica stared and tried to place her. She was petite and attractive with shoulder-length, ash-blond hair that was partially covered by a hat that matched her full-length dark mink. Both hands were buried deep in the pockets of the luxurious coat.

"I don't recognize you," Jessica admitted. "Should I?"

"I'd think so, since you came after my husband."

Her husband. Jessica's heart plunged to her toes. No wonder Conner hadn't mentioned seeing her again or asked her to stay. He was married. And Jessica was a naive fool.

"I didn't know," she said. "He didn't tell me he had a wife."

"Oh, come now, Jessica. Sheriff Latimer and Conner may have been taken in by your charming guile, but I know you better than that. You were always a troublemaker, you and those other two ungrateful urchins who snooped around the orphanage with you."

"How do you know about the orphanage?"

"Oh, I know all about you, including the fact that you purposefully went after Marcus to get back at me."

"Marcus?"

"Right, Marcus. My husband. Your lover."

Jessica's heart sprung back from the depths. Conner hadn't lied to her. This wasn't his wife. "You must be Sheila."

"How perceptive." Sheila took her right hand from her pocket, revealing a silver pistol—pointed right at Jessica's chest.

Jessica tasted the fear, felt it pit like acid in her stomach, but this was a mistake. She just had to make Sheila understand. "You have me confused with someone else, Sheila. I didn't have an affair with Marcus."

"You were at the hotel the night he was killed."'

"I ran into him in the lounge. It was the first time I'd seen him since leaving the orphanage. We talked, but I swear I didn't know who he was."

"He went there to meet you. I have the note you sent him. Only you didn't count on my showing up. Neither did Marcus."

"I didn't send a note. You have to believe me, Sheila. I didn't kill Marcus."

"Of course you didn't kill him, Jessica. Why would you? You weren't the one he was leaving." Sheila stepped closer, laughing as if they'd just shared some private joke, and Jessica got her first real look at the madness that lurked beneath Sheila's anger.

"You were the one who killed Marcus, weren't you?"

"Marcus was going to divorce me. After all I'd done for him, all the dirty little affairs I'd tolerated, he was leaving me for a worthless slut like you. He deserved to die, just as you do."

The fear intensified, swelling inside Jessica until she could barely breathe. This was all some kind of sick mistake, a giant misunderstanding, but if Sheila pulled that trigger, Jessica would be dead.

The pistol was in Sheila's hand and a trembling finger was on the trigger. Fear and adrenaline merged in a wave of energy as Jessica dove into the woods and took off running, cutting a zigzagging path around the trees.

The sound of gunfire shattered the quiet of the cold morning. Sheila was firing at her, but Jessica kept running, dodging branches and trying not to get caught in the thorny brush that grew low to the ground.

Another shot rang out, this one hitting a tree just inches from Jessica's head, making shrapnel of bark fragments and sending them flying into her face. She ran all the harder, but the underbrush grew thicker, tangling her feet.

One of her shoes got stuck in the mud and stayed. Twigs and pinecones dug into the bottom of her bare foot like sharp glass. Gasping for breath, she fell against the trunk of a tree, holding on to a low-hanging branch so that she didn't collapse.

But a second was all she got before the next shot rang out. She lurched forward, determined to keep going, but her bare foot slipped into a hole. Her ankle twisted and she fell to her knees as an excruciating stab of pain shot up her leg.

She swallowed the cry that flew to her throat, but it wouldn't have mattered if she'd screamed at the top of her lungs. Sheila had already found her. She stood over her, the gun only inches from Jessica's head.

Jessica knew she was going to die, yet she couldn't stop herself from releasing some of the pain that had lived inside her so many years. She pulled herself to a sitting position. "I didn't have an affair with Marcus and I never killed a baby. I was just a kid and you tried to destroy me. You tried to destroy us all."

The sound of the firing bullet was deafening as Jessica fell back to the ground in a volley of pain and blood.

CHAPTER EIGHT

CONNER RUSHED TO JESSICA and took her in his arms, his heart tearing around inside his chest like a warring buck.

She opened her eyes, blinked repeatedly, then simply stared at him. "You're not real, are you?" she whispered. "You're just an angel who looks like Conner."

"Last time I checked I was real, and I'm pretty damn sure I'm no angel."

"But the shot. The blood. The pain."

"The gunfire was mine. The blood is Sheila's. I shot the gun from her hand, probably just as she started to shoot. The pain is from your leg. Your ankle is twisted badly, if not broken."

She raised to her elbows and looked around. "Where is Sheila?"

"Running like a wounded bat out of hell the last I saw of her."

"You can't let her get away. She killed Marcus."

"She won't get far. Latimer's on his way out here. He'll probably have her in custody before she gets to the highway," he said, already lifting her in his arms. He held her close and started the long walk back to the house, his senses reeling from all he'd been through in the last few minutes.

"How did you know I was in trouble?"

"A lucky guess. A very lucky guess." And some timely information. Amazing that with all the underhanded political games Marcus had played, it was his private indiscretions that had cost him his life.

Conner had called Jessica as soon as he'd finished talking to Beth. When she didn't answer, he'd driven home at breakneck speed only to arrive to find Sheila's car parked in his driveway. He'd gone crazy then, calling Latimer, grabbing his own gun and fortunately spying two sets of fresh footprints in the damp earth that led to the path.

When he'd heard gunfire, he'd experienced a kind of panic he'd never known existed before that terrifying second. But the sound had led him to Jessica. He wasn't sure himself how the rest had happened. Instinct had taken over and God must have steadied his hand.

"I must be heavy," Jessica said.

"No way. Anytime you need a pair of strong arms, I'm your man."

"Is that a promise?"

"You bet." At this moment he would have promised her the world with the moon and stars thrown in as lagniappe. And he wouldn't think beyond this moment. Jessica was alive and safe and that was all that really mattered.

JESSICA SAT on Conner's coach, her swollen ankle propped on pillows. Conner was on the phone, looking very serious and talking in low tones. But the fire was blazing and the lights were low. She'd probably never find a better time to tell him what was in her heart.

"That was Latimer," he said once he'd finished talking and returned to the couch. "Not only is Sheila in custody and blabbing a mile a minute, the mystery woman finally appeared."

"The one with long black hair who was in the bar with Marcus that night?"

"That's the one. Natalie Givens. She claims that she and Marcus were in love and that he was going to divorce Sheila and marry her. Her story is that when she left the bar that night, you had gotten drunk and passed out at your table.

Marcus and the bartender were about to carry you to your room. Marcus was going to meet her later in a smaller, lesser-known motel out on the highway. That's pretty much all she knew. Apparently Sheila confessed the rest.''

"Is Sheila the one who drugged my drink?''

"She paid Carl to do it—but the drugged drink was intended for Marcus. Somehow your drinks got confused.''

"Then Sheila and Carl were in this together?''

"Not before that day. She'd driven straight to the hotel when she'd found the unsigned note from Natalie. She was already furious that Marcus had asked for a divorce, so she offered to pay Carl to help her out.''

"Then she did go to the hotel that night to kill Marcus?''

"Not originally. At least, that's what she's saying now. She only planned to confront him and his lover. She just thought it would go better if he was sedated and she had the upper hand. Carl misunderstood what she had in mind and put in a far more potent amount than she'd intended.''

"When I came in and Marcus started talking to me, she must have assumed I was the lover.

But that doesn't explain how Marcus ended up in my room—and dead."

"Sheila followed Carl and Marcus when they carried you up the back stairs to your room. And while you slept, Sheila and Marcus had a shoving and shouting match. Carl picked up the knife you'd left on your room service tray to subdue Marcus. Just as he did, Sheila rammed Marcus from behind, pushing him into the blade of the knife."

"Then it was actually Carl who killed Marcus?"

"More like a joint endeavor. But Sheila murdered Carl."

"Why would she?"

"She'd promised to cover for his killing Marcus if he'd help her kill you. You were part of her betrayal and she wanted you dead. So Carl followed you to Beth's that day and decided cutting the brake line was the best way to bump you off and make it look like an accident."

"I still don't see why she killed him. He was doing what she said."

"To keep him quiet. He started running scared and told her he was going to call me and confess everything."

"Only Sheila got to him first."

"Unfortunately."

"What will happen to her?"

"That will be up to a jury to decide. She's claiming temporary insanity brought on by the stress of Marcus's asking for a divorce."

"Such a twisted situation," she said. "And so sad. For Marcus. For Sheila. For Carl. And for the other woman who fell for the wrong man."

"I'm just glad it's finally over."

"You got a lot more than you bargained for when you took me in that first day."

"Lot's more."

He nuzzled the back of her neck and desire grew hot inside her in spite of the pain still emanating from her ankle.

"I'd do it all again in a New York minute," he said.

"Really?"

"Really."

This was the opening she'd been waiting for. She took a deep breath and gathered all the courage she could muster. "I'm thinking I shouldn't leave here, Conner."

His brows arched. "Is that right? Tell me more."

"I'm thinking we're terrific together, and that…that…"

"And that?"

"That I care for you." She took a deep breath and started over. "It's more than that. I know you like me, and I think I'm falling in love with you. I know this is sudden, but maybe I could get a job and stay in Bankstown awhile. We could date or have dinner or something occasionally and see what happens between us."

"I'm thinking that's not a good idea."

"No?"

"No." He trailed a finger from her forehead to her lips. "I'm not big on trying things out. So maybe you should just plan to move in with me."

"Move in with you?"

"Sure. I could buy you a ring and you could go shopping for one of those white dresses with a long veil."

Her heart did a triple somersault. "Did you just propose?"

"I guess if you have to ask, I must have done it all wrong. I am totally crazy about you, Jessica. I've never been in love before, but I'm pretty damn certain this is it. So, will you marry me?"

"Yes! Yes! Oh, Conner I love you and everything about you. I'll marry you tomorrow. Tonight if you want."

"The sooner the better."

He kissed her then, long and sweet. She kissed him back as tears slid down her cheeks. She didn't try to stop them. She'd waited a lifetime for this moment and she didn't want to miss one tiny iota of the joy.

Little Jessica Lewis was in the arms of her rock of a prince. The past was finally behind her. Love had found her—at last—and it was here to stay.

Dear Reader,

When offered the opportunity to start a new series, I couldn't resist. One of the themes of my stories is the importance of family. I've read other stories with similar plotlines, but I wanted to do my own version of a young woman who didn't know she had siblings somewhere in the world. And I wanted her mother to play an important role. So I came up with the Berry family.

I hope you enjoy the journey these long-lost siblings travel to bring their family together again, each one finding romance along the way. I truly feel that sharing the joys and sorrows of life makes the experience richer and makes the individual stronger.

The CHILDREN OF TEXAS series will be published in Harlequin American Romance over the coming year. A variety of characters will populate these stories. I hope you'll join me in future books as the CHILDREN OF TEXAS come together.

Best wishes,

FAMILY UNVEILED

Judy Christenberry

CHAPTER ONE

WILSON GREENFIELD checked his watch. His latest client was due any minute. He hadn't wanted to take this case, but a private investigator had to keep business coming in to pay the bills.

But this woman rubbed his nerves raw. She reminded him too much of his wife. Ex-wife, he amended. She had lived for money and had left him when he couldn't earn enough to suit her, finding instead a wealthy man to marry and support her.

This lady, his client, was wealthy already. She could buy whatever she wanted. And she'd wanted his help.

When the fortysomething Vivian Shaw had entered his office a couple of weeks ago in her designer suit, a string of real pearls around her neck, he'd suggested she have her lawyer contact him. He'd no doubt she had a lawyer; that kind of woman *always* did. A male lawyer. Will made most of his money working with men at insurance companies and law firms, and preferred to deal with men.

Mrs. Shaw had refused.

Because one of the law firms for whom he did a lot of work had recommended him, he couldn't turn her down. Which led him to this moment. He'd intended to mail her his report—along with his bill—but she'd insisted on coming down. This woman might be petite and genteel, but she was stubborn and bossy.

He hated women who had to have their own way because they had money.

"Will?" His assistant, Carrie, stood in the doorway, staring at him. "Didn't you hear me? Mrs. Shaw is here."

Carrie worked for him part-time while she went to school. For three years she'd read his mind, done the dirty work and smiled. He didn't think he could manage without her, even though she was female.

"Okay. Show her in."

He shrugged into his suit jacket. At forty-eight years old he was beyond the game-playing of power suits and ties, but he was a good enough businessman to maintain decorum in case she reported back to the law office.

Standing behind his desk, he greeted her. "Come in, Mrs. Shaw. Please, sit down."

The attractive strawberry blonde wore another pastel designer suit, this time with a gold necklace and diamond studs. She neatly sat down in the wing chair in front of his desk, looking lost in it. Her expression was eager.

"You said you had news for me."

"It's all here in my report."

"I'll read it, of course, but tell me what it says."

He gave a disgusted sigh. So much for hoping it would be a brief session. "I have the names and ages of the other five children. Your daughter was the youngest. According to the agency in Longview, where the family was from, they were all adopted within a four-state region...except for the two oldest."

The woman gasped. "What happened to them?"

"They weren't adopted. Both boys were considered too old at seven and nine. They were placed in the system."

"What do you mean, 'placed in the system'?"

"They were put in foster homes until they were eighteen."

"Oh, poor dears."

He hardened his heart against the soft sympathy in her voice. Society women always appeared concerned, he knew, but they really didn't do much for anyone but themselves.

"There's enough information for your daughter to find her family if that's what she wants."

"Her?" the woman asked in surprise. "I thought you understood that if she's interested, I want *you* to find the children. She may not— That is, they may not be suitable for Vanessa to— I want her to know what she's getting into if she decides to follow up on your information."

"That's really not necessary. It's easy to—"

"No! I'll double your fee, Mr. Greenfield. I don't mind the money, but I want my daughter protected."

He'd sat back down at his desk after she'd settled in the chair. Now he crossed his fingers under the desk. "She may decide not to look for these siblings. You can call me once she makes up her mind."

"No, you might have taken on other work and not have time for us. I want you to tell her about it tonight and get her decision."

Will stood up. "Whoa, lady. I never agreed to break the news to your daughter. That's your business. You can call me tomorrow. I won't have time to find another job by then." Unless he got up early and called all his contacts, which, of course, was exactly what he'd do.

"Mr. Greenfield," the woman said as she drew a checkbook out of her purse and scribbled across it. "I want you to join us for dinner tonight and talk to my daughter about the gift I want to give her. I want you to explain the disadvantages and the advantages."

Then she ripped out a check and pushed it across the desk. "If, after doing so, my daughter chooses not to pursue the matter, our business with you will be finished, and you may keep the money. If, however, she wants you to find these siblings, I will expect you to continue. I'll be glad to write checks whenever you need more money."

Exactly the kind of woman he hated. They thought they could buy the world. With a sigh, he looked at the check. Five thousand dollars. That was more than he made in a month.

He hated himself even more as he nodded his head. "I'll come tonight, but not for dinner. What time will you be finished eating?"

"Why not dinner?"

"I like to keep my social life separate from business."

She glared at him and stood. "Very well. I'll expect you at eight o'clock."

Then she walked out of his office.

As he sat in his chair, he realized he was sweating. From nerves. For some reason the woman made him nervous. The way she bulldozed him into doing what she wanted. The way she had him selling out for a four-figure check. The way she looked so proper, almost regal in her conservative suit cut to reveal none of her womanly curves. He'd bet underneath that jacket beat the heart of a tigress, a woman long denied and just waiting to pounce—

Whoa! he called out mentally. Where did that come from? He almost laughed as he tried to figure out how he'd put a sexy tigress and Vivian Shaw in the same thought. No, Will told himself, he was better off not trying to figure it out and simply stick to the business at hand. And remember his own motto about keeping separate his social life.

Wiping the beads of perspiration off his forehead, he shook off the errant thoughts.

"Carrie?" he called, as he quickly endorsed the back of the check.

"Yes, Will?"

He waved her toward the desk. "Go deposit this in the bank. Then write yourself a check for this month's salary. Do I owe you more than that?"

"No, Will. You paid me last month, when you did that big case for Global Life."

"Oh, yeah, right. Thanks, honey."

She gave him a cheery grin. "Any time, Will."

Thanks to his failed marriage, Will had never had any kids, but he thought of Carrie Rand as his daughter. The only family this only child had, now that his parents had died. She was a sweetheart. He didn't know what he'd do when she actually finished school and started a career.

Picking up the report he'd prepared, he read through it again. He hadn't done that much work. He'd found out the younger three were adopted, a boy, age five, and twin girls, age two.

He had a photograph taken just a week before the parents were killed in a car wreck. He hadn't met Mrs. Shaw's daughter, Vanessa, but judging by the beautiful twins, he'd bet the baby of the family was a hell of a looker.

Man, he didn't want to do this job. Mrs. Shaw was going to tell her daughter she was not her biological child, and not the only child Vanessa believed herself to be, but one of six children. She wanted to do that because her husband had died last year and neither she nor her husband had any living relatives. When she died, she didn't want her daughter to be alone.

Nice sentiment. Didn't fit the society-lady profile.

Maybe he'd be able to talk the girl out of it.

"DARLING, YOU DON'T have plans for tonight, do you?"

"Some of my friends were going to take me out for my birthday, Mom, but I can put them off if you need me."

Vivian thought again how fortunate she was in her daughter. Since Vivian's husband, Herbert, had died, Vanessa had been even more considerate than normal, not wanting her mother to feel lonely.

"I'm sorry to ask, dear, but I do need you to help me entertain a guest this evening. I didn't know he was coming until this afternoon."

"He? Who is this guest? Have you been seeing someone on the sly, Mom?" Vanessa leaned forward, a teasing smile on her full lips.

Vivian turned a bright red. The thought had

never entered her mind. "Of course not. Your father's only been dead a year, darling. I would never—"

"Mom, I know you loved Dad. But a year is long enough to mourn. And you're only forty-three. You're still a young woman."

Vivian grinned. "The gray strands I've been finding in my hair make me think you're wrong, young lady."

"Your hair is beautiful. All my friends are envious of me for having such a beautiful mother. I wish I'd inherited strawberry blonde hair instead of Dad's. Plain brown is so dull."

Vivian mentally rebuked her daughter's description. Vanessa's dark brown hair had russet highlights that illuminated her face. Thick and well-cut, it fell below her shoulders. But after countless discussions, Vivian knew it was pointless to argue. Instead, she returned to the original subject. "The man— I mean, this is a business meeting, sort of. It's about your birthday."

Vanessa sobered. "A business meeting about my birthday? Mom, really, I don't need anything big. Let's just keep it simple."

"No. I've made up my mind. But the final decision is up to you."

"Did you talk it over with Uncle Harry?" Vanessa leaned forward, concern in her hazel eyes. "Dad said you should always check with Uncle Harry before you invested in anything."

Harry Browne wasn't really Vanessa's uncle, but he was her godfather, as well as her father's real-estate business partner. As such, he stopped by their Highland Park estate frequently to check on them.

"No, I haven't talked to Harry about this. I made this decision by myself."

"You're worrying me, Mom."

The doorbell rang.

Vivian looked at her watch. "Oh, my. He's right on time." She got up to go to the door, but the housekeeper, Betty, called out, "I'll get it."

"Um, dear," Vivian said to her daughter as she paused, "this man is a little, uh, crusty. Just ignore his attitude. He's supposed to be one of the best." She started out of the room. Then she stopped to look at Vanessa again. "Go to the library. I'll bring him there."

Vanessa did as her mother asked, but she wasn't going to let her give her an extravagant gift. She suspected the man she intended to introduce to her was a car dealer, since her mother had been hinting that it was time to get rid of her Honda Accord. It was a good car, only three years old and Vanessa saw no reason to change.

Put out by her mother's behavior, she settled in one of the wing chairs by the fireplace. There was no fire there, because it was May in Dallas, already getting warm.

When the door opened and her mother's light footsteps were followed by heavier ones, she slowly looked up.

Where her mother was petite and slender, looking much less than her forty-three years, the man beside her had gray lightening his black hair at the temples. Quite distinctive, actually. He was tall and well muscled, she noticed, though he wore a suit jacket. His clothes were nice, but not terribly expensive.

In fact, Vanessa was feeling better about whatever was going on, because she kind of liked him. He looked honest.

She stood. "Good evening."

Vivian smiled, approving her manners. "Darling, this is Will Greenfield. Mr. Greenfield, my daughter Vanessa."

The man nodded, saying nothing.

After an awkward silence, Vivian said, "Shall we be seated?"

Mr. Greenfield moved to the other wing chair

opposite Vanessa's. He stood by it until her mother pulled up a chair between them and sat down. Then Mr. Greenfield sat.

Still he didn't speak.

Vanessa sensed a reluctance in him for whatever was going on. Which only made her leery once more.

"Darling," Vivian began, "I've tried to think of a good birthday present for you. Finally, I decided to do what I thought I should have done a long time ago. Your father didn't agree." She paused and licked her lips.

Vanessa seldom saw her mother nervous.

"Mom, what is it? You always agreed with Dad."

"No, just most of the time. But you see, I couldn't have children."

Vanessa sat up straight, surprised. "But what about me?"

Her mother reached out and took her hand. "Your father found a baby we could adopt. You. You're not my birth daughter, but I love you very much. You've made my life so wonderful!"

Vanessa fought back tears. The same tears she saw in her mother's eyes. "Mom, I didn't know! You've never hinted—"

"I had no reason to tell you. But when your father died, leaving just you and me, with no other relatives, I knew I had to do so."

"Why, Mom? It doesn't change anything."

"Yes, it does, darling. You see, you have five siblings."

"What?"

"Your birth parents were killed in a car crash. You were only three months old, so I'm sure you don't remember. But there were five other children." She told her the ages of her siblings. "My gift for you is to help you find your brothers and sisters…if you want to."

Vanessa felt as if she were in a state of shock. "I—I can't—"

"That's why Mr. Greenfield is here. He's a private investigator and has promised to help you if that's what you want to do. Right, Mr. Greenfield?" Vivian turned and smiled at the man.

Vanessa could see the smile was not returned. Instead he sat there and glowered at her mother.

CHAPTER TWO

WILL CLEARED HIS THROAT. "If you are interested in meeting your siblings, Ms. Shaw, I can
probably find them. I can't tell you how long it
will take because adoption records are sealed.
The two older boys won't be as hard to find."

The beautiful young lady nodded, her eyes
wide.

"However, your siblings probably weren't
adopted by wealthy parents. They may want
money from you. Or they may try to cheat you.
There's a price for having relatives. You may
find them to be less than desirable."

She said nothing.

"I do have a picture of your family taken a
week before your parents died."

"May I see it?"

He reached in his pocket and brought forth the
picture. He stood and took it to her. Then he
returned to his chair. He tried to think of some-

thing else he could tell her, anything to discourage her.

"They could even be criminals," he added. "Who knows?"

"How would you find them?"

"I do a lot of work on the computer. I've actually located the two boys who weren't adopted." He hadn't wanted to break this news.

"You have?" Vivian asked, leaning forward.

"It was in my report," he assured her grimly.

"Why weren't they adopted?" Vanessa asked.

"They were seven and nine, considered too old for adoption. They were put in foster homes until they turned eighteen."

"Where are they?" Vanessa asked.

"Your oldest brother, James Barlow, enlisted in the army and fought in the Gulf War. Now he's in Iraq as a Blackhawk helicopter pilot."

Vanessa sat back, considering his news. "I see."

"I'm afraid your other brother, Walter Barlow, also joined the army and was killed in the Iraqi war."

"Killed? How old was he?"

"Twenty-eight."

Vanessa looked at her mother with tears in her eyes and Vivian held out a hand to her daughter.

"You should've told me," Vivian said softly to Will.

He stiffened. "It was in my report."

"But you kept the report," she reminded him.

"I offered it to you. You're the one who chose to leave it behind."

While they'd argued, Vanessa had made up her mind. "Mr. Greenfield, I want you to find my remaining siblings as soon as possible."

"I think you should take some time to make your decision. Once the genie is let out of the bottle, it's almost impossible to get it back in." He watched her carefully.

"These are my brothers and sisters. I've already lost one. I don't want to lose any more of them without getting to know them, offering them help if they need it."

"You should proceed cautiously, Ms. Shaw."

She leaned her head to one side. "You seem reluctant to take on this case. Why?"

Will glared at the young woman and then looked at her mother. "I can do the work. I just want you to be prepared for the results."

Vanessa nodded. "Thanks for your concern, but I've made my decision. Please begin at once."

WILL WAS IN HIS OFFICE working on the Shaw case, when he heard the outer door open. Carrie was on the job, so he knew she'd deal with the visitor.

"Carrie?"

He thought he recognized the voice. Vanessa Shaw. But how did she know Carrie?

"Hello, Vanessa. Are you here to speak to Mr. Greenfield?"

"Well, yes, but how are you? I tried to contact you several times, but I couldn't find you."

"We moved. Just a minute and I'll let him know you're here."

Will waited for Carrie to step into his office. Something was wrong. Usually Carrie was quite relaxed and friendly, but he heard the tension in her voice. And saw it in the tight set of her face.

"Will, Ms. Shaw is here to see you."

"How do you know her?"

Carrie bit her bottom lip and shook her head.

Will knew what she wanted. "Very well. Show her in."

Vanessa entered, but her attention wasn't on Will. She was staring over her shoulder at Carrie. Head down, Carrie merely walked out of his office and closed the door.

"So, Ms. Shaw, how do you know Carrie?" he began.

His client seemed surprised by his question. "We were freshmen together at Southern Methodist University."

"I see." Freshman year. The time when Carrie's life had shattered to pieces. Carrie had had a relatively easy childhood. But she'd told him when her father died her freshman year, she'd discovered they'd lived a life based on credit cards and juggled finances. After his death, she'd assumed control of her mother's life and tried to straighten everything out.

She'd been forced to sell their house, their cars, her mother's jewelry, anything that would bring in money. Now she and her mother shared an apartment near a local junior college where Carrie took one class a semester. Her mother worked as a receptionist at a law firm.

"Did she transfer to another school?" Vanessa asked, her gaze going back to the closed door.

Will knew Carrie was a private person, and he respected that privacy. He quickly changed the subject.

"What is the nature of your call, Ms. Shaw? I've been working on your case this morning, but I don't have much information yet."

"Please, call me Vanessa. No need for us to be formal when we'll be working closely, Will." She took a seat in his guest chair. "I'm here to pick up the report Mom said you had prepared. And I'd like to have a copy of the photo you showed me last night."

"Excuse me," he said. Then he raised his voice. "Carrie?"

The door opened slightly. "Yes, Will?"

"Bring me the Shaw file, please."

"Yes, sir." She closed the door.

Will wondered if he should go get the file. Obviously, Carrie didn't want to face Vanessa. But she had no reason to be ashamed. In fact, he'd been impressed with her strength and courage.

The door opened again and Carrie, looking straight at Will, brought the file to his desk and left the room, not speaking to either of them.

"Why is Carrie acting as if she doesn't know me?" Vanessa was frowning at the closed door.

"That's Carrie's business, not mine." Will opened the file and pulled out one of the copies he'd had made of the Barlow family.

"Here's an extra copy."

"Oh, thank you. I was going to offer to make my own copy. I'm going to have it enlarged and framed. I also would like to have James's address so I can write him and introduce myself."

"Are you sure you want to do that? Soldiers can be pretty rough, Ms. Shaw."

"I'm sure, Mr. Greenfield. He's my brother."

With a sigh, he pulled out the mailing address of Captain James Barlow.

"He's a captain?"

"Yes. Your brother distinguished himself in the Gulf War and was encouraged by his commanding officer to get his degree and become an officer himself."

"I see."

"I have a copy machine in Carrie's office. If you'll make a copy of the paper and return it to Carrie, please, I'd appreciate it."

"Of course. And your report?"

He opened his desk drawer and withdrew the folded report. "Here it is."

"Well, thank you very much, Will. And you'll let us know as soon as you have any more information?"

"Yes."

He stood as she left. Then he sat back down,

listening intently through the open door to make sure she didn't upset Carrie. He heard quiet voices, but soon the outer door closed and he knew Vanessa Shaw had gone.

He got up again and walked to the door. "You okay?" he asked Carrie.

She nodded but didn't speak.

He stepped into the outer office and went to the front of the desk. The paths of tears marked her face as she looked up, startled by his move. Quickly she rubbed her cheeks dry and looked away. "Do you need me to do something?"

"No. I want to know why you're crying."

"I'm being silly, Will. It's nothing."

"I won't have that young woman coming in and upsetting you. If she was rude to you—"

"No! No, she wasn't rude. Vanessa is very sweet. She just reminded me of a more innocent time when I took a lot of things for granted. That's all. See, I told you I was being silly."

Will dug his hands into his pockets so he wouldn't reach out and hug Carrie. She had to be strong on her own. But he could make it easier for her. "She won't be coming here again."

"Don't be silly, Will. She's your client."

"I know. I'm going out for a while. I don't

have any appointments. Just lock up when you go to lunch, okay?''

He didn't wait for a reply. He had business to take care of.

THE MORNING ROOM WAS Vivian's favorite room in the house. There the furniture was casual, more inviting than the traditional, staid décor of the rest of the Shaw mansion. The room looked out on the colorful blooms in her flower garden, and the sun cast a golden glow through the many windows, bathing the room in light. Vivian felt the brightness clear to her insides.

As she sat on a comfortable sofa and talked to her daughter, she heard the faint sound of the ringing door bell, but she didn't get up to answer it. She knew Betty would complain if she did.

Before she had a chance to wonder who it was, the door to the morning room burst open and in strode Will Greenfield. A very angry Will Greenfield, judging from the look on his face and his purposeful strides as he made his way to her.

A flustered Betty followed behind him. ''I'm sorry, but he—''

''It's fine, Betty,'' she said to soothe the housekeeper, who turned and left the room.

Standing and stepping toward the man, Vivian assumed a no-nonsense stance. "What is it, Mr. Greenfield?"

"I don't want your daughter coming to my office again, Mrs. Shaw," he blurted. Then he apparently noticed the young woman sitting there and turned to her. "Do you understand, Vanessa?"

Vivian put a hand out toward her daughter, halting any reply. "I don't know about Vanessa," she said in a strong tone to Will, "but I don't. What's wrong with my daughter coming to your office? We are your clients. We have a right to speak with you."

"Use the telephone."

"Sometimes it's more effective to speak to a person face-to-face." She could see the frustration clearly on the private investigator's face, and knew her countenance could not conceal the same emotion. Anger, too, was boiling to the surface. Where did the man get off? He had no right to make such a demand of a client, no matter how imposing he was, how broad he looked…

Before she could finish the errant thought, Vanessa came forward and placed a calming hand on her shoulder.

"It's because of Carrie, isn't it?" she asked Will. "Did she say why I upset her? It wasn't my intention."

"She blamed it on herself, but I won't have her upset. She's like my own child, and I'd do anything to protect her."

Vivian was touched by the feeling she heard in his voice. In fact, it was the first time she saw Will Greenfield display any emotion—besides disinterest and annoyance, she realized. His tender side seemed…appealing. The hard lines of his face appeared to visibly fade and in the new softness she could see how truly handsome he was. She was nearly bowled over by the realization. Every other time she'd been in Will's presence he seemed to have a chip on his shoulder, but when he dropped the attitude, he was a strikingly good-looking man. His ocean-blue eyes pulled her in so deep, it took her a minute to regain her composure.

She had to draw in a cleansing breath before she spoke.

"I think we have something in common, then, Mr. Greenfield. I know you think I trapped you into taking our case. But I'd do anything to protect my daughter."

He nodded. "Yes, ma'am, I know. If you

need to speak to me face-to-face, call me and I'll come here. Will that satisfy you?''

"It's a generous offer under the circumstances. But I'm afraid my daughter is concerned about Carrie. They were close at one time.''

"Obviously. But it's also clear Carrie doesn't want to visit with Vanessa.''

Vanessa stepped closer. "But why? What did I do?''

"I think she feels you don't have much in common now. And it reminds her of what she's been through.''

"What has she been through?''

"If she doesn't want to tell you," Will said, "that's her business.''

"But you know?''

"Yes, I do.''

"I'm going to call her and see if she'll go to lunch with me. If she says no, I'll leave her alone. Okay?''

"I suppose so," Will said, but it seemed to Vivian he agreed with a heavy heart.

Vanessa left the room, leaving her and Will staring at each other. Finally Vivian said, "Won't you sit down, Mr. Greenfield? You can give me a report since you're here.''

"Hell!'' Just like that his stern demeanor was

back, like a shutter closing out the personable, feeling man she'd glimpsed earlier. "I've only had a couple of hours to work, Mrs. Shaw. Am I going to have to give you a report every time I sharpen a pencil?" he demanded.

Vivian's lips twitched with humor, but she calmly said, "No, I don't think so. You see, I don't have a lot of interest in pencil sharpening." She crossed to the flowered sofa and sat down, crossing her legs demurely. "But what you can tell me is how you plan to find the children."

CHAPTER THREE

ATTITUDE. IT WAS ALL over Will Greenfield's expression as he faced her. Vivian could read his annoyance at being challenged by a woman. A rich woman at that. She wondered if he'd answer her or flee, wounded but ready to do battle another day. The moments stretched until finally he sat down in the wing chair.

Trying not to smile at the man, she took the seat opposite him. "Well, how do you plan to find them?"

He raked a hand through his hair and let out a breath. "Each of the states has a list that adopted children can use to find their birth parents. It's a long shot since they probably don't know their family name, but I'll read those lists, first of all."

Then he must have remembered something else he wanted to tell her, because she could almost see a thought strike him. "Vanessa asked for James Barlow's address. She wants to write him." His blue eyes met hers for the first time as he spoke, and they seemed to reach out and touch her. She could read emotion in them—concern, compassion. The same feelings that had made Will so appealing before.

"Of course it's not my call, but I think it would be better for her to wait until he's shipped back stateside. Then I could check him out before she contacts him."

An alarm went off in Vivian's head. "Why are you so sure her siblings will turn out to be rotten people? Did you find out something about her parents?"

Will averted his eyes, and Vivian felt bereft of their attention. Strange, she thought, how much she enjoyed him looking at her, warming her with his glance. She'd never actually been aware of this before with any other man. When she realized he was speaking, she fought to keep her mind on the topic at hand.

"No, ma'am," Will said. "But I know how the wealthy are, wanting to keep their distance from the lower social strata."

Vivian frowned at him. She'd thought him appealing? Well, not now. She sat up straighter in the chair. "I beg your pardon."

"Your idea of doing charity is to dress up in

an expensive gown, drape yourself in jewels and pay a fortune for tickets. You feel good about that because some of the money goes to the underprivileged.''

Vivian had sat on the boards of several charitable foundations and chaired more than her share of formal fund-raisers, but she'd also gotten down and dirty for her causes. More times than Will Greenfield could ever know. ''You know, Mr. Greenfield, I think you're showing your prejudice toward people who have money.''

''If that offends you, I can recommend another private investigator to take your case, ma'am.''

Vivian noted his rigid back, his emotionless expression. ''I don't think that will be necessary. Have you had lunch?'' Now where had that come from? One minute she was ticked off at him, and the next she was inviting him to lunch.

He was just as surprised, she could tell. ''No. I'll excuse myself so you can do so.''

''I'd like to ask you to stay and dine with me, Mr. Greenfield, but I'm afraid you might assume I'm trying to socialize with you.''

His face reddened, recognizing her use of his words.

"Of course, we could call it business if I asked you questions about our case. So will you join me?"

"No, I—" he began, but Vivian kept her gaze on him, challenging him with her eyes to accept.

He drew a deep breath. "Very well. I'll dine with you, Mrs. Shaw, and tell you about the case, to keep either of you from coming to my office. I don't want Carrie upset."

"I understand. Let me tell Betty to set a place for you. I'll be right back."

In the hallway, she saw Vanessa, heading for the door. "Vanessa? Where are you going?"

"Carrie agreed to have lunch with me. I'm going to pick her up."

"Good. Tell her she's welcome here anytime."

"Thanks, Mom. I'll see you later."

Vivian continued to the kitchen. "Betty, Mr. Greenfield is staying for lunch. Can you serve us in half an hour?"

"I can serve you in ten minutes. I thought Vanessa would be here, so I have enough for both of you. I'll be right in with fruit juice and some snacks."

"Thank you, Betty. You're a treasure."

When Vivian returned to the morning room,

she found Will staring out the French doors at her flowers. "Do you like the view, Mr. Greenfield?"

He shrugged. "The flowers are beautiful, but I'm sure they require a lot of work."

There was a sneer in his voice that irritated her. "Once Vanessa went to school, I had a lot of time. I find gardening has a calming effect on me."

"*You* do the gardening?" he asked in surprise.

"Most of it. I get Betty's husband, Peter, to help with the major projects."

"I'm impressed, Mrs. Shaw. I didn't think your hands did any work at all."

"Mr. Greenfield, you really are prejudiced against people of wealth, aren't you? Which is strange since I'm assuming most of your clients are wealthy."

"I don't limit myself to wealthy clients, Mrs. Shaw. But they do seem to have the greatest need for a private investigator."

Vivian changed the subject. "How long has Carrie been working for you?"

"Why do you want to know?"

"If you don't tell me, Vanessa will later. Carrie agreed to have lunch with her."

"She'd better not upset her!"

She put up a hand in a calming gesture. "I don't think she will. She worried for a long time about Carrie when she couldn't locate her. Her number was disconnected and the new number was unlisted."

Will gave her a skeptical look. "When you first came to see me, how come you didn't approach Carrie or tell me you knew her?"

"I heard a lot about her from Vanessa, but I didn't spend much time with the girl. Besides, when I came to your office, I was so anxious about what we needed to discuss, worried about whether or not I was making the right decision, that I scarcely noticed her."

"She can't afford to dress up much."

Vivian looked curious. "I don't remember what she was wearing. Should I have?"

"You were dressed in a designer suit and wearing expensive jewelry. I should think you'd notice that Carrie was wearing jeans."

"Vanessa wears jeans. I see nothing wrong with them."

"Fine," he said sharply. Then he looked toward the door. "Maybe I should—"

The door opened and Betty came in carrying

a tray with two glasses and a plate of hors d'oeuvres.

"Thank you, Betty," Vivian said with a smile. After Betty had left the room, she said, "Come sit on the sofa so you can reach the hors d'oeuvres, Mr. Greenfield."

With reluctance, he moved closer to his hostess. "What's in the glass?"

"I beg your pardon?"

"I don't take alcohol this early."

"Neither do I. This is a special concoction Betty makes. It's a blend of juices. She won't reveal her recipe, but it tastes like a drink I had once in Hawaii. No alcohol."

He relaxed a little and took a sip. His approving nod would have won Betty over.

"Are wealthy people all lushes, too?" she asked.

"Some of them." He took another sip, refusing to meet her gaze.

"Try Betty's pinwheels. No alcohol there, either," she added with a smile.

He glared at her, but he reached for one of the hors d'oeuvres. "Very good," he pronounced.

"I'm glad you like Betty's cooking. She's very proud of her work."

"So you don't cook?"

She sighed. The man was exasperating. "Mr. Greenfield, I can cook. My husband insisted we should have a housekeeper when we married because it befit our status. While I don't find one necessary any longer, Betty and Peter are part of our family. I couldn't fire either of them."

The man kept his head down. Finally he looked up. "I'm sorry. I'll try to be less critical of your way of life."

"Thank you."

Before Vivian could enjoy their new truce, Betty came in to announce lunch was served.

Mr. Greenfield stood and said, "Betty, the drink and pinwheels were delicious. I'm looking forward to lunch."

Her cheeks rosy, Betty beamed at him. "Thank you, sir. I'm glad you enjoyed them."

They both followed Betty into the formal dining room. The banquet-size table fit the room, but it suddenly felt way too large for the two of them.

"It's a beautiful day," Vivian said. "Why don't we dine on the patio?"

"I'd like that," he said.

"You two go on out and sit down," Betty

said at once, not at all bothered by the change of plans. "I'll bring everything out there."

Vivian led the way to a glass-topped table and some chairs set on the patio. Betty followed immediately behind them, carrying a tray with their meals. She set them down on the table.

Will smiled at the housekeeper. "Thank you. It looks great."

Betty beamed at him once more and headed back inside.

"Keep that up and you'll become Betty's favorite person," Vivian said with a smile.

He bit the thick roast beef sandwich. "Judging by this lunch, I think that might be a good thing." He swallowed and shot Vivian a look. "I thought ladies lunched on watercress sandwiches cut into bite-size pieces."

"Betty isn't fond of watercress," Vivian assured him.

"I'm liking her more and more."

"So the old saying is true?" At his puzzled look, she added, "The way to a man's heart is through his stomach." Vivian wanted to reach out and grab the words back. What made her allude to Will Greenfield's heart? She could almost feel her cheeks reddening and fought hard to keep her composure. With any luck he'd ignore her remark.

Her luck didn't hold.

"It has its merits." He took another bite of sandwich, savoring the tender roast beef.

"Y-yes, I can tell." She deflected the comment. "Too bad Betty's already married."

"I'm not in the market for a wife!" he snapped. She noticed alarm on his face, as if she were threatening his bachelor existence.

"Relax, Mr. Greenfield. I'm not interested in a husband, either."

"Because your life was so hard married to a wealthy man?"

"No. But as much as I loved Herbert, he wanted to control my every thought and action. I'm enjoying my freedom."

He showed no interest in more conversation, concentrating on his lunch.

Vivian was grateful for the silence. It was a beautiful spring day, and the sun was shining brightly, though they were enjoying the shade from the umbrella over the table. Vivian found herself oddly content, even with the difficult Mr. Greenfield.

After a few minutes, he finally spoke. "I'm sorry, I'm not much of a conversationalist."

"It's all right. I'm enjoying the peace. Have you started looking at the lists you were telling me about?"

"I went through Texas's. Since I have to read through twenty or so years, it takes awhile."

"I can imagine. And are you sure they'll still be living in the state where they were adopted?"

He shrugged his shoulders. "No. But it's the most logical place to begin. If I don't find anything there, I have some other ideas about where to find them."

"I know I get overanxious about this, but I can tell Vanessa is very excited about finding her family." There was a sadness in her voice she hadn't heard before. It alarmed her. She hoped it wasn't obvious to him.

"Are you okay with this? You haven't changed your mind, have you?"

"No! No, of course not," she said quickly. And it was true, she acknowledged. No matter these strange feelings, she knew she'd done the right thing. "I'm—I'm glad that I've made Vanessa so happy."

"You'll always be her mother," Will said softly, leaning in.

There is was again. Emotion. This time he was sympathetic. "I know. I—I just hadn't realized— She's always turned to me, and now…well, she'll have others to talk to.''

"I don't know your daughter well, Mrs. Shaw, but she seems genuinely devoted to you. I don't think that will change.'' He reached out and took her hand in his.

Vivian felt comforted by the gesture and, she admitted to herself, she liked the feel of his touch. But before she could explore that thought, he jerked his hand back and leaped to his feet.

"I beg your pardon, Mrs. Shaw. I didn't intend—''

Vivian stood also. "Of course not, Mr. Greenfield. I'll let Betty know we're ready for dessert.''

Before he could refuse her offer, she walked into the house.

Betty fussed at her for not ringing the bell she'd left on the table, rather than coming to the kitchen.

In truth, Vivian was looking for an excuse to get away from the man. Flustered, embarrassed, afraid she'd been caught with naughty thoughts, she couldn't stay next to him another second. It was almost as if— She nearly gasped as the realization hit her. She was attracted to Will Greenfield.

"What can I do for you?" Betty broke into her meanderings.

"I—I—" Vivian ceased the stammering and took a deep breath as she faced the housekeeper. "I came to ask you to bring dessert. Mr. Greenfield was a bit embarrassed because he felt sorry for me," she said softly, her gaze unfocussed as she stared across the kitchen. "I think your dessert will pick up his spirits. By the way, he loved your roast beef."

"He's a fine gentleman."

"Yes, he is, Betty, but he doesn't like people with money."

"Why?" she asked with a frown.

Vivian shrugged her shoulders. "Are you ready? He won't refuse as long as you're there." And she wouldn't have to be alone with the man, either, she admitted.

Betty scooped up a tray with two pieces of coconut cream pie. "Here we go!" she sang out and walked ahead of Vivian.

When they reached the patio, the P.I. was still standing, his arms crossed over his chest. As soon as he saw them, he stepped forward and said, "I need to go. I've got a lot of work to do."

Betty didn't wait for Vivian to speak. She put

the tray on the table, then put her hands on her ample hips. "Now you sit yourself down, Mr. Greenfield. No one turns down my pie. I make the best crust in the world. You just see if I don't!"

She took the pie off the tray and loaded the lunch dishes on it. "You come to the kitchen and tell me what you think of my crust." Then she returned to the house.

Vivian grinned at him. "So, are you staying for dessert?"

He looked frustrated and shrugged his shoulders. "I don't want to hurt Betty's feelings."

"Good." She sat down and waited for him to join her. "She's right, you know. Everyone loves Betty's pies."

He picked up his fork and took a bite. It seemed to melt in his mouth. "Man, she wasn't kidding, was she?"

Vivian shook her head, smiling. "No, she takes her reputation very seriously. And she loves to cook for a man. I—"

Just then the door from the kitchen burst open and Vanessa came out.

Much to her guest's surprise, when he stood, she threw herself into his arms. "Thank you, Will! Thank you so much!"

CHAPTER FOUR

WILL TOOK THE YOUNG lady by the shoulders and moved her away. "What are you doing?"

Vanessa beamed at him. "I'm thanking you for bringing Carrie back into my life. She's my best friend!"

Vivian stepped forward. "Darling, I don't think Mr. Greenfield is used to demonstrative people like us. I believe you scared him."

Will glared at the elegant lady. "Of course I wasn't scared. I just didn't understand what was going on." He turned to Vanessa. "And I didn't intend to lead you to Carrie. Are you sure she's okay with this?"

Vanessa was still smiling at him. "Of course she is. She was embarrassed at first, of course, but I told her she had no reason to be. I admire her courage and hard work."

"Yeah. It was hard for her."

Vivian put an arm around her daughter's

shoulder. "Will she come have dinner with us soon?"

"She worries about her mom being alone."

"Of course we'd invite her mother, too. I'd like to meet her." Vivian kissed her daughter's cheek. "Just let me know when."

"Thanks, Mom. I'll go give her a call." She started back to the house and then spun around. "Oh, and thanks again, Will."

After she disappeared, Vivian said, "I apologize for Vanessa using your first name. I realize you prefer the more formal address."

Quite the contrary, he preferred to be called just plain Will. But not by this woman. Somehow with her he felt as if he had to be on alert, on guard. He didn't stop to question why; he simply knew he didn't want to get too friendly with her. But he wasn't about to do what she expected, so he said, "No, I don't mind if you and your daughter call me Will. Most people do."

"Then you must call me Vivian." She stared him straight in the eye, daring him to refuse.

He drew a deep breath. "Sure, Vivian. I'll be glad to. Now, if you don't mind, I'd better get back to the office."

''Be sure and let us know as soon as you find out something.''

''Yes, ma'am.'' Then he got away before he was forced to call her Vivian again. He felt as if he should bow down every time he addressed her. And he didn't want to feel that way.

The thought of Mrs. Shaw being demonstrative, the way her daughter was, kept running through his mind.

He remembered the bolt of electricity that zapped through his body at the mere touch of his hand on hers. What would happen to him if she hugged him the way Vanessa did?

He'd like it.

He'd feel her body pressed close to his, from her thighs to her breasts, and he'd wrap his arms around her and pull her tighter to his chest, locking her in a possessive hold. Then he'd—

Stop! He commanded himself. Time to be reasonable and practical. There was nothing between him and Viv—Mrs. Shaw.

He shook his head to clear the mental picture and focused on the road. He'd driven past his office.

WILL WAS TIRING OF reading list after list. The last state he was checking was Arkansas. As he'd done for two days he'd look under the Bs first. If that didn't yield anything, then he would skim the entire list. His eyes studied the names.

Suddenly he jerked upright. "Carrie?" he called out to his assistant in the outer office.

"Yes, Will?" She was much happier since she and Vanessa had gotten together. Which pleased Will. He'd been prepared to fight the Shaws if Carrie really didn't want to know them again.

"How old is Vanessa?" He was just double-checking.

"Twenty-two, like me. Why?"

"I think I've found one of her sisters," Will said, studying the information given. "One of the twins. They were two years old when the Barlows died, which would make them twenty-four now. Just like her." He pointed to the computer screen.

Carrie came to stand beside him. "The one with Barlow in parentheses?"

"Yeah. She's the right age. But I'll have to see her before I can be sure. I think I'll call her." The list gave a number where the person could be contacted.

"You won't cancel tonight, will you? Mom's

counting on you being there. She's very nervous about meeting Mrs. Shaw.''

"She shouldn't be. I'm prejudiced against wealthy women, I'll admit, but Mrs. Shaw is a gracious woman." And a beautiful one, too, he added silently.

Carrie nodded. "I know. But Mom doesn't. Anyway, you'll come, won't you?"

"Yeah, I'll come. I'm going to make the call around six. That will give me plenty of time."

"Thanks," Carrie said with a big smile and a kiss on his cheek.

"Hey! You've been hanging out with the Shaws, I can tell."

Still smiling, she said, "Maybe I have. What of it?"

"Just be careful. I don't want you getting in trouble," he growled.

"I won't. And I'll see you this evening. I'm leaving half an hour early so I can get home to pick up Mother, remember?"

"Sure."

After Carrie left, Will stared across his office, thinking about the evening ahead of him. And the past few days. It seemed to him that Vivian and Vanessa Shaw were changing his world. He was resisting as much as possible, but it was as if genteel, elegant Vivian was as tough as a marine for all the effect he was having on her.

She had him thinking about her constantly during the day. Little things. Anything seemed to remind him of Vivian. Mrs. Shaw, he corrected himself. But he knew the reminder was useless. She'd gone past being Mrs. Shaw to him two days ago.

Now he saw her as a beauty, a refined but sexy woman who, somehow, had him thinking about relationships once again. Smiling once again. Feeling. Something he hadn't done in a long time—ever since his marriage broke up.

Still, he wasn't quite sure that was a good thing. In his line of work it was wise to keep his distance. And it suited his private life, too, he thought. At least he'd never be hurt again. But Vivian had broken through those thick walls of defense and he couldn't stop thinking about her.

Right now, he told himself, he had a case to work on—and his best lead in days.

He looked again at the listing. Rebecca Starrett (Barlow). How did she know her name? Did her adoptive parents tell her, too?

He was anxious to make the call, but he forced himself to wait until six. Most people were home by then. Slowly he dialed the long-distance number when his watch showed six o'clock exactly. The phone was answered on the fourth ring.

"Hello?" The woman sounded a lot older than twenty-four.

"May I speak to Rebecca Starrett?"

"She's not here. Tonight's her school night."

"She's a teacher?"

"Oh, gracious no. She goes to class one night a week."

"I see." Will cleared his throat. "I'm a private investigator looking for Ms. Starrett. I'm calling about her family."

The woman's voice rose to a higher pitch. "Oh, my! She'll be so thrilled! I think she'd given up hope."

"And who am I speaking to?" Will asked.

"I'm her baby-sitter."

"She has children?"

"Why, yes. The cutest little boy. Joey is four. He's so sweet, I just love to take care of him."

Will gave her his name and number. "Please have her call me in the morning."

"Yes. Yes, I will."

He hung up the phone, frowning. He didn't think the Shaws would be pleased with what he had to tell them. A single mother taking night classes wouldn't exactly fit their lifestyle. Maybe they'd change their minds and stop the search.

He stood. Better he get there early so he could tell them before Carrie and her mother arrived.

Besides, he didn't want to wait.

VIVIAN WAS ARRANGING fresh flowers she'd cut earlier for the entryway when the door bell rang. She checked her watch.

It was only six-fifteen. "Betty, I'll get it," she called, knowing her housekeeper would be busy in the kitchen.

She swung open the door to find Will Greenfield standing there.

"Will! You're early. No matter. Come in. How are you?"

"I came early because I think I may have found one of Vanessa's siblings. I wanted to tell both of you before Carrie and her mother arrived."

Vivian stared at him, surprised. "Really? Oh, my goodness. I'll get Vanessa. Oh, the flowers. Can you give me just a minute?"

He nodded and watched as she put the flowers in water, arranging them quickly.

"Come to the library," she said. "I'll go up and get Vanessa."

She nearly ran up the stairs to her daughter's room, knocking but opening the door at the same time. Vanessa was in front of the vanity in a half slip and bra, putting on light makeup.

"Mom? Is something wrong?"

"Will is here. He thinks he may have found one of them!"

Vanessa didn't need any explanation. She leaped to her feet. "Where is he?"

"Downstairs in the library. Put on your dress and come right down." Vivian couldn't wait one more minute to hear what Will had found out. Neither, apparently, could Vanessa, who put on her dress as she moved to the door.

"Shoes," Vivian called. "Don't you want shoes?"

"Later. Let's go hear what Will has to say!"

They rushed down the stairs to the library. Will turned as they entered and stared at them.

"I didn't mean to interrupt anything," he said, raising his eyebrows as he noticed Vanessa's bare feet.

She grinned. "At least I put on my dress! I'll finish later."

"Yes, please, Will, tell us what you found out." Vivian ushered them to seats.

"I think I may have found your sister," he

began. He gave them a brief summary. "I really don't know much. I'll have to visit her. The age is right. But I know a single mother isn't what you expected."

Vanessa ignored his remark. "When will you go?"

"You're still interested?"

Now it was Vanessa's turn to look puzzled.

Vivian spoke up. "Of course she is, Will. Even more so since her sister is alone with a child to raise."

"She might change her mind once she meets her."

"That's it!" Vanessa said, misinterpreting his remark. "I should go with you. Can you wait until day after tomorrow? I can't miss class tomorrow, but—"

Will held up a hand to stop her. "No! Absolutely not. It's my job to protect you and investigate the situation. She may not be your relative."

"But I don't want you to upset her!" Vanessa said. "You can be kind of stern, Will."

"What if I go with him in the morning?" Vivian suggested, catching her daughter's hand. "We might even be home by tomorrow evening."

Will turned and stared at her.

"I think that would be a good idea, Mom. I really can't miss that class. We have an exam. Are you sure you don't mind?"

"Of course not, dear. We'll check the airlines schedule after dinner."

Both women turned toward the door, until Will's bellowing voice stopped them.

"Wait! You can't just— You can't go with me."

They both gave him a curious look. "Why not?" Vivian asked.

"It wouldn't be proper! You wouldn't want it to get around that you went out of state with me." He glared at her, daring her to disagree.

"Really, Will, you're too old-fashioned. Of course I can. We'll probably be back tomorrow evening anyway."

"Vivian, I don't work that way. I go alone, or I don't go."

"That's up to you. I'll be glad to go by myself. If you'll just leave me her telephone number, I'll—"

"I do my job. I'll go to Arkansas and report back. That's how we're going to do it."

Vivian turned to her daughter. "Go finish dressing, dear. I'll work this out with Will."

After the door closed behind Vanessa, Vivian smiled at Will. "I will not tolerate this ridiculous argument, Will. I want to go meet this child. There's no reason for me not to go, so I don't want any more argument about it."

She turned and walked out of the room, leaving a stunned Will to catch his breath.

CHAPTER FIVE

WILL CHARGED after Vivian.

"Lady, you do not give me orders! You don't own me!"

"Will, I'm only thinking of that poor child. She's a single mother. It sounds as if she has no one to turn to. I think you might scare her. You can be a little…off-putting, you know."

Will clenched his fists, trying to control his anger. "If you're referring to my behavior toward you, you're not like this girl. She's a single parent, not some wealthy woman who thinks she can rule the world. I wouldn't be off-putting with her."

"I know you won't. Because I'm going to be with you." She smiled at him in a curiously gentle way. Then her features stiffened. "I am going, Will. With or without you."

"Damn it, Vivian. You're making a mistake!"

"Perhaps. But it's my mistake to make." She

put her hands on her slender hips, arms akimbo. "You're right, Will. I can't order you around. But we had an agreement. I paid for the information and you agreed to the terms. So I'm going to see this girl. How I go is your choice."

She was right and he knew it. He should just hand over the information and walk away. But he couldn't. And she knew that, too. Damn her!

"Fine. I'll let you know what time we leave."

"No. Peter will make the reservations for us while we dine. Then he'll let you know what time we'll pick you up. He'll drive us to the airport."

"No. I'll meet you there." He glared at her.

"Very well, Will." She actually had the nerve to smile at him before she turned away. As if they'd had a pleasant conversation.

Will remained in the library. He needed to seriously think about abandoning this case. He'd never done that, no matter what had happened. But this time retreat might be the better part of valor.

That thought rocked him. He'd never quit! Never! Why was he even thinking of such a thing? Vivian Shaw. It wasn't the work that bothered him. It was the client. He was worried about becoming involved in her life. He wanted to give her the happy ending she sought, to protect her. And Vanessa, too.

He'd crossed the line. Gotten emotionally involved. Well, he had to draw back. If they got hurt, that was on them. He'd given them both warnings. Vivian was insisting on going with him. It was a mistake, but it was her mistake. Not his.

He straightened his shoulders. Then he wandered down the hall. He didn't see Vivian. When he heard movement, he pushed open a swinging door. "Pardon me," he said.

A man turned around. "May I help you, sir?"

"Are you Peter?"

"Yes, sir."

"Mrs. Shaw was going to ask you to make reservations for us for the morning. I'd prefer that we catch a flight out of Love Field," he said, naming the small regional airport close to Highland Park.

"Yes, sir." He cleared his throat. "What is your destination?"

"Little Rock, Arkansas. Don't make a reservation for our return because I'm not sure how long our business will take." He paused and gave the man a considered stare. "It would be a lot better if Mrs. Shaw would let me go by myself. I'm not sure what we'll run into up there.''

Peter smiled at him. ''I can't help you, sir. Mrs. Shaw makes up her mind, and there's no changing it.''

Will shrugged. ''I thought I'd give it a shot.''

''Well, it didn't work,'' a cool voice said from behind him.

He turned to face Vivian. ''Can't blame a guy for trying.''

WILL LEANED AGAINST a wall, cradling a cup of coffee in his hand. The plane they were scheduled to leave on was at the gate and would start boarding any minute. Still no sign of Vivian Shaw.

Had she decided not to come? She could've let him know so he didn't stand around waiting. Shrugging, he reached in his back pocket to get his wallet and ID just as Vivian caught his eye. She waved and hurried over, Peter following.

''Sorry. I ran late,'' she said. ''Let's go get our boarding passes.''

Will stopped and gave her a critical look. ''First you need to take off that tennis bracelet and the diamond studs and give them to Peter to take back home. We don't want to intimidate

Rebecca or put ideas in her head before we know what kind of person she is.''

He waited to see if she did as he ordered. Much to his relief she removed the jewelry. Then he escorted her to the ticket counter, where they showed their photo IDs to the ticket agent and she gave them two boarding passes.

''We've started boarding, Mr. Greenfield,'' the young woman said. ''It'll be a few moments till we get to you.''

Quickly they returned to Peter, who was patiently waiting, to get Vivian's bag.

''You take good care of Miz Shaw,'' Peter ordered. Then, with a nod, he handed Will her totebag to carry, in addition to his own, and walked away.

Vivian didn't move for a minute. Then she reached for her bag. When Will didn't release it, she said, ''It's okay. Peter can't see us now.''

''What difference does that make?''

''Peter thinks I can't carry anything. But I assure you I can.'' She tugged again on her bag.

Will released his hold on it. He'd help her store it in an overhead bin, but she could carry it until then. ''We may not be seated together, since we'll be boarding in the last group.'' These quick junkets had a first-come, first-served policy. Will had never seemed to mind. Till now. It irritated him that she'd been late and now they'd probably be separated.

Vivian nodded. "I know. I'll be okay."

He said nothing else as he discarded his almost-finished coffee. "Did you eat breakfast?"

"Yes, I did. With Vanessa, Betty and Peter standing over me, watching every bite."

He smiled at that mental picture. "And you managed to get something down with everyone staring?"

She sighed. "I'm used to it. Herbert kept an eye on me until his death. Now those three watch over me. Sometimes I feel like a child."

"Maybe that's why you wouldn't agree to let me come alone. It was your chance to be the boss," he suggested.

"No, Will. I feel I have to do anything I can for these children. I could've taken them all in, keeping the family together, if I'd only fought my husband. Now one is already dead. I want to do what I can for those who remain."

He stared at her, frowning. "I thought you were doing this for Vanessa."

"I am. But for me, too." He could read the emotion on her face. This had to be difficult for her, and scary. For the first time he admired her resolve. She seemed to gather herself and continued, "if I can make the transition easier for any of them, I'll do it. If we're going to fight every time, you may want to give up the case."

So the bossy Mrs. Shaw returned, he thought to himself.

He nodded. "I don't think that will be a problem, now that I understand. I thought you doubted my ability."

She ducked her head. Then she looked up at him. "I owe you an apology for what I said. I know you would manage just fine. I was only trying to justify my going with you."

"Sir, ma'am, we're boarding," the gate agent reminded them, standing beside an open door.

They hurried over. When they reached the plane, Will found his prediction was accurate: They couldn't find two seats together. He found one for Vivian and stored her bag in the overhead bin. Then he continued on until he found another free seat about six rows back. After storing his own bag, he sat down and put on his seat belt.

Vivian Shaw was an unusual woman. There was no reason she should feel guilty. But she did, and she was willing to go out of her way to make things better for the Barlow family. He mentally apologized for his antagonism.

He wouldn't fight her anymore. But she was going to be even more dangerous to him than she'd been before. A beautiful, wealthy woman with a big heart.

VIVIAN GOT HER CARRY-ON and filed out of the plane ahead of Will. It was just as well they hadn't sat together. She was embarrassed about her behavior last night. But she wasn't going to be left behind today.

When Will came toward her, she smiled, hoping he wasn't going to hold her behavior against her. Instead of saying anything, he reached down and took her bag from her.

"This way," he said, nodding to the left. "I rented us a car."

"Oh. I didn't think of that." She followed him through the airport. "Does Rebecca live here in Little Rock?"

"Yes. I left a note for Carrie to tell her when she called that we'd be coming to see her. I guessed we'd arrive around ten."

She checked her watch. "Good guess. It's nine now. I'm going to get some coffee while you handle the car rental. Do you want a cup?"

"Yeah, thanks."

When he finished the paperwork, Will found Vivian waiting with two cups of coffee in her hands. With a smile, he took one. She picked up her bag and waited for him to lead the way.

Once they got their bags in the trunk and settled in the car, seat belts on, Will pulled out a map. "Rebecca lives on McHale Street. It's on the north side. I think our best bet will be to take this freeway," he pointed to a major road. "Is that okay with you?"

"Of course."

He gave her a stern look. "Don't be too nice. You'll spoil me."

Her grin widened. "Don't worry. I won't."

"I'm going to check in with Carrie." He dialed a number on his cell phone. "Carrie? Did Rebecca call?" While his assistant spoke, he nodded to Vivian. She felt a tiny bit relieved that the woman apparently was eager to pursue a reunion with her birth family. But was she Vanessa's sister? Her stomach tightened at the mere thought of disappointing her daughter.

Will flipped his cell phone closed. "Well, she's expecting us."

Vivian forced a nervous smile. "I'm so anxious."

"So are Rebecca and Vanessa. I hope this turns out right."

They found the address at nine thirty. Will parked in front and stared at the genteel, but run-down two-story house. "Shall we go on up, or wait until ten?"

"Let's go up. I can't wait a minute longer."

"Vivian, I'm going to introduce you as my assistant until we figure out if Rebecca could be one of the Barlows. That's why I didn't want you to wear any jewelry. So don't say you're Vanessa's mother. Not yet."

"I don't think we need to be that careful," Vivian began. When Will opened his mouth to argue with her, she acquiesced, "But I'll do as you say as long as there's any doubt."

"Thank you."

They got out and locked the car. When they reached the front door, they realized the house was divided into apartments. The name Starrett was listed in 2A. They climbed the stairs.

Will knocked on the door of the apartment, and they both heard hurrying footsteps. When the door swung open, Vivian gasped.

CHAPTER SIX

THE BEAUTIFUL YOUNG woman stared at them.
"Yes?"

Will cleared his throat. He knew why Vivian
had gasped. Standing before him was a woman
looking almost exactly like Vanessa, a tall, slender brunette. "Are you Rebecca Starrett?"

She nodded.

"I'm Will Greenfield. I called here last night
and talked to your baby-sitter."

"Yes. Your office told me you would be
here."

"We're a little early, but my assistant, Vivian,
and I didn't want to wait. May we come in?"

"Yes, please. I'm anxious to hear what you
have to say." She stepped aside so they could
enter.

The living room was sparsely furnished with
old pieces, but it was clean. Vivian sat beside
Will on the couch, while Rebecca chose an opposite chair.

Will leaned forward. "How did you learn that your family name is Barlow?"

"My mother—the woman who adopted me— told me when I...when they asked me to leave."

Before Will could respond, Vivian asked, "Why would they do that?"

The young lady straightened her shoulders. "I got pregnant and they were disappointed in me."

Will and Vivian looked at each other before Will spoke. "Did you marry the father of your baby?"

"No. As soon as he heard I was pregnant, he left. I don't know where he is."

"And your parents knew you were alone?" Vivian asked, horror in her voice.

Rebecca relaxed a little. "We made it all right."

"It couldn't have been easy," Will said.

"No, but at least she told me I had family somewhere. She said she thought I had several siblings, in fact. I signed up on that search list at once. I was hoping to find some family for my little boy."

"Do you have any pictures of you when you were younger?" Will asked.

"You mean when I was in school?"

"How about when you were first adopted?"

With a frown, Rebecca got up and walked over to a shelf unit across the room. "I should have. My adoptive father wanted nothing to remind him of me. They sent me packing with everything." She turned and explained, "he wanted a perfect child, and I didn't qualify."

"He sounds like a horrible man!" Vivian said firmly.

Rebecca smiled. "Thank you, Vivian. I appreciate your sympathy." Then she reached up to the top shelf and pulled down a photo album. "There's a picture in here taken just after the Starretts adopted me."

"That would be great," Will said, reaching in his coat pocket for the picture he had of the Barlow family.

Rebecca brought the photo over to Will. In turn, he handed her the one he had. She looked at it, then at Will and Vivian. "This is me...or that's me," she said, pointing at the two-year-old girls in the print. "Why are there two of me?"

"Rebecca, I don't think there's any doubt. You are one of the twins."

Rebecca stared at Will. "I'm a twin? We were separated? I don't— That explains— How weird."

"Mommy?"

At the child's voice all the adults turned to the door leading into a hallway. A little boy, looking just like his mother, leaned against the doorjamb, appearing a little apprehensive.

"Good morning, Joey. Come here and let me introduce you to our guests," Rebecca said, going to her little boy.

He held up his arms to her and she swung him up onto her hip. "This is my son, Joey. He just woke up. He stayed up late on my school night, so I let him sleep in this morning. Are you hungry?" she asked Joey.

He nodded, his gaze still on the visitors.

"I'll fix him his cereal. It won't take long."

Vivian leaned over to whisper to Will. "She's a very good mother."

He nodded as his eyes scanned the room, observing, looking for what, he wasn't sure.

"Can we take her home with us? Both of them, I mean?"

At that he turned to her. "Slow down, Vivian. She may not be willing to go."

Vivian didn't look happy.

Rebecca, having left her son to eat his breakfast, rejoined them. "May I see your picture again?"

Will returned it to her.

"There are six kids? I didn't expect that many."

"One of them is dead," Vivian said softly. She pointed out the second oldest boy. "His name was Walter."

"How did he die?" Rebecca asked, tears forming instantly in her eyes.

"He was in the army. He was killed in the war in Iraq a couple of years ago."

"Which child— I mean, who do you represent?" Rebecca asked.

Vivian said, "The baby. Her name is Vanessa."

"How old is she?"

"She's twenty-two, two years younger than you. You're the first one of her siblings we've found," Will explained.

"Oh. Will you give me her address so I can write her? I'd like to come see her, but I can't right now."

"Why?" Vivian asked.

"I can't miss work. I'll start saving, though, and try to drive down on a weekend this summer."

"You like your job?" Vivian questioned.

"Not particularly, but it pays pretty well. I've got some seniority."

"What do you do for a living?" Will asked, keeping Vivian in his gaze. He could feel her growing agitated.

"I'm a secretary at an insurance company."

"Do you have anyone you're close to?" Vivian asked.

"No. Mrs. Williams baby-sits for me, but she has grandchildren of her own."

"Then I think you should pack up and come with us."

Rebecca stared at her, clearly shocked. "I'm sorry, Vivian. I'd love to meet my sister, but I can't afford to do that. I'd have to find another job, a place to live, and I've heard Dallas is very expensive."

Vivian stood up. She'd heard enough. All she needed to hear. She knew what she had to do now. "I've misled you," she said simply. "I'm Vanessa's mother. It's important to her to find her family. We have room for you and Joey. We have a big house. You can go back to school full-time and we'll find a good preschool for your son. It will be great!" Vivian couldn't keep the excitement from her voice. Vanessa would be ecstatic.

But from the look on Rebecca's face she realized at once that she'd frightened her. She probably thought she was a nut case. She turned to Will. "Help me."

Will grinned. "Rebecca, she isn't crazy. Vivian is Vanessa's mother. She wants her daughter to have more family, too. Her husband died last year and she's all Vanessa has left."

Rebecca looked at Vivian. "I can understand that, but I have to think about my little boy. He might not like it there."

Vivian took the tiny opening, exploited the potential she heard in Rebecca's voice. "I should tell you about our life. We have a large house in a nice part of town. There's me and Vanessa, who is going to school to get her master's in psychology."

She paused to draw a deep breath. Then she said, "We have a housekeeper named Betty. Her husband, Peter, takes care of the cars and helps me with the garden. They both love children. They've been with me for more than twenty years. I've hired Will to find the other children, so you can all be together again."

Rebecca stared at her, openmouthed. "You— you have a...different lifestyle than me."

"How much do you make a week?" Vivian asked.

"I make four hundred a week," she said, sitting up straight.

"All right. Take a week's vacation and I'll pay your salary. Bring Joey and come with us. If you don't want to stay after a week, I'll get you back here without it costing you anything. By then, you'll know Vanessa and the two of you can keep in touch if you want to."

Rebecca got up and paced her floor. Finally she stopped and looked at Vivian. "I'll take a week's vacation and drive down. But I won't take your money. That is, if you'll put us up for a few days."

Vivian couldn't stop the smile that lit her face. "I'll be delighted to. When can we leave?"

Will spoke up. "You can see she's eager. We'll do what we can to help you get ready."

"I—I usually do my housework and laundry on weekends. I have to wash some things and—"

"So let's get started," Vivian interjected. "We'll clean the kitchen while you start the laundry."

Still Rebecca hesitated, clearly not yet convinced. "Why don't you two fly back and Joey and I will come when we can?"

"No," Vivian said. "I'm not going back without you. But we could all take the rental car. Then you and Joey could fly back if you want to come home."

"No, I can't afford that."

Vivian started to assure her that she could pay for the flight, but Rebecca finally posed a plan she felt comfortable with. "Fine," she said, "we'll all go in my car."

Vivian turned to Will. "Can you take her car and fill it up, see if it needs any repairs?"

Will smiled sympathetically at Rebecca. "You'll get used to her. She wants her own way."

"Will!" Vivian protested. But she could see from his expression that he meant no insult.

"I know, I know. May I have the keys to your car, Rebecca? And where is it parked?"

"It's in the lot behind the house. It's a beige Volkswagen. An old one."

"I'll be back in a little while." Will looked at Vivian. "Restrain yourself, please."

"Yes, Will," she assured him with a demure smile.

WHEN WILL RETURNED three hours later, he'd had the oil changed and four new tires put on Rebecca's car. The belts had been checked and the VW was running well.

Will dreaded the long drive ahead of them with the three adults and one little boy. He wondered how things would be in the apartment. Vivian tended to sweep everything the way she wanted to, but Rebecca was hesitant.

He knocked on the door of the apartment and Vivian opened it. "I'm glad you're back. I was getting worried."

"I'm sorry. I got new tires," he whispered.

"Oh, good. We're ready to go as soon as you buy us lunch." She looked over her shoulder to see Rebecca entering the room. "Rebecca offered to fix us lunch, but then we'd need to clean the kitchen again." She smiled at Joey, coloring at the coffee table on his knees. "We're ready to go, aren't we, Joey?"

"Yes," he said shyly, ducking his head.

"Here are their bags." Vivian nodded to a stack by the door. "Do you think we can get our bags in the car, too?"

"We'll manage. I'll go load these in." He hurried out. Once he got them all loaded, including his and Vivian's bags, he took a deep breath. When they'd left Dallas that morning he hadn't expected their day to end this way, that was for sure.

He pulled out his cell phone and called the office. There was no answer. Carrie was probably at lunch. Then he dialed Vivian's house and Betty answered.

"Betty, it's Will. Vivian and I are driving back to Dallas with Rebecca and her son. We won't get there until eight or nine tonight. I just wanted to let you know."

"Yes, sir. Miz Shaw called earlier."

"Okay, I tried to call Carrie, but she wasn't in the office."

"She's here. I'll tell her."

"Thanks, Betty."

He climbed the stairs to the apartment once again. "We're all packed. Everyone ready to go?" The women nodded and made for the door.

"Me, too!" Joey called, rushing to his mother's side.

"Of course, you, too." She picked up her son and gave him a big smile. Rebecca seemed to have resolved her doubts.

Vivian reached out and squeezed Will's hand. As he ushered everyone out of the apartment, he realized his hand in hers felt so good. In fact, nothing had ever felt so right.

CHAPTER SEVEN

"DO YOU KNOW VIVIAN WELL?" Rebecca asked quietly, trying not to disturb Vivian and Joey in the back seat, asleep in each other's arms.

Driving the car since they were coming into Dallas, unfamiliar territory for Rebecca, Will chuckled. "Not really. I've only known her for a few weeks."

Rebecca's eyes widened. "Really? I thought you'd known each other for a long time. You seem so comfortable together."

Will sighed. "She's a good woman. I haven't been easy to work with, but I believe she's a caring person."

And he did, he realized. No longer did he think of her as a bossy snob used to getting her own way. Vivian had revealed herself to be a gentle soul with a heart of gold. And a woman he'd like to get to know even better.

Rebecca pushed back her hair in a nervous gesture.

"I hope I haven't made a mistake. I tried to resist but I want a family so badly. Having Joey has been wonderful, but it seems like I've always been alone."

Will took a quick glance at her beautiful face. "Even before the Starretts kicked you out?"

"Yes. When you told me I had a twin, it explained feelings I could never figure out. I think I was missing my twin, even when I didn't know I had one."

"Could be. Hopefully, I can find her." He shifted lanes on the busy freeway, then continued. "I've found your oldest brother, James. He's peacekeeping in the Middle East. Vanessa took his address so she could write him."

"Is Vanessa… Is she like her mother?"

"You mean warm and overpowering?" he asked with a grin.

She grinned back. "Yes, that's what I mean."

"I think so."

He exited the freeway and turned into the Highland Park neighborhood. The houses changed, becoming larger and more luxurious.

Rebecca's eyes widened again. "Is this the neighborhood they live in?"

"Yeah, I'm afraid so."

"I won't fit in," she muttered, almost under her breath.

"You'll be fine, Rebecca. Vivian will make sure of that. Trust her. She's got a good heart."

He pulled the little çar into the graceful driveway, taking the route that would lead him to the big garage. There were lights on in the house, so he gave a brief beep of the horn as he parked the Volkswagen.

A door to the house opened and Vanessa stood there, outlined by the light behind her. Then the outside lights came on. Rebecca opened the car door and stepped out of the car, staring at Vanessa. Vanessa froze in the doorway as she caught sight of the dark-haired young woman who looked so much like herself.

Will leaned over into the back seat and gently shook Vivian's shoulder. But not before he drank in the sight of the sleeping beauty, her pink-dusted cheeks, her full lips. "Viv," he whispered. "I don't think you'll want to miss this."

She slowly opened her eyes. Then, as if just taking in his words, she struggled to get out, disturbing the sleeping boy as little as possible. "What?"

"Vanessa is coming out to meet Rebecca,"

he whispered, his gaze on the two young ladies, too.

Vanessa began slowly walking toward Rebecca, her eyes never leaving the woman. Betty and Peter stood in the doorway behind her, not moving.

Will risked a quick glance at Vivian next to him. Anxiety etched itself deeply in her face, and in the tightness of her body. With a will of its own, his arm wrapped around her in a gesture of comfort and support.

It seemed as if Vanessa was moving in slow motion, then suddenly she was hurrying, her arms open wide. Rebecca fell into her embrace, tears on her cheeks.

"Oh, my," Vivian said with relief, tears making tracks on her cheeks, too.

"Come on, Viv," Will said, ushering her forward with a hand on her back. Then he reached in for Joey. The boy stirred a little, but Will held him close and shushed him, and he fell back to sleep.

"Is he all right?" Vivian asked softly over her shoulder.

"He's fine. You go on. I'll get Betty to show me his bed."

"Peter can carry him up."

"I'll carry him, Viv. He's used to me. And I think his mother is going to be busy."

He stepped past the girls embracing and continued on to Betty. "This little guy needs a bed, Betty."

Wiping away tears, she said, "Right this way."

VIVIAN STEPPED FORWARD and embraced both girls. "Let's go inside and get something to drink," she said through her tears. "It's been a long day."

"Joey!" Rebecca said with a gasp and whirled around.

"Will carried him up to bed. He'll be fine," Vivian assured her. "Come in and let me introduce you to Betty and Peter."

Peter took Rebecca's key and went to get the luggage out of her car. "I'll be right back," he told Vivian. "Betty has a snack waiting for you in the morning room."

Vivian led the two girls there. She poured them both some tea and offered the plate of cookies and brownies. "Betty's brownies are very good," she recommended.

"I shouldn't, but maybe I'll try one," Rebecca said. She shot a quick glance at Vanessa.

"Would you like one?" she asked, passing the plate to her new sister.

Seeing the two of them together was everything Vivian hoped it would be when she started this quest. Gratitude to Will overwhelmed her. Had she even thanked him for finding this sibling? She'd make it a point later. Right now she sat back to enjoy the girls.

Vanessa took a brownie from the proffered plate. "I could use a little sugar. You know, I hope I didn't startle you, Rebecca. I hadn't realized we'd look so much alike."

"Me, neither. I—I've felt so alone for a long time. Today has been quite a shock."

"Mom and Will didn't upset you, did they?" Vanessa asked with a frown.

"No, no, of course not. But it was a shock to discover I had five siblings, one of them a twin. It explained some things. I'd thought I was half crazy." She gave an emotional chuckle that bordered on tears. But they were held at bay by Will's entrance.

"Everything all right in here?"

Vivian rose and smiled warmly. "Come in, Will. Betty made us a snack. I think she even made some of those pinwheels because you liked them so much."

"Yeah, I liked those ham and cheese things. Did you try them, Rebecca?"

"No, I'm a sucker for chocolate. I went for the brownie, and it's delicious."

Betty walked in in time to hear the praise. "You are definitely kin to Vanessa," she said with a satisfied nod. "Your little boy is cute as can be. He's all tucked in and sleeping like a baby, which he almost is."

"Oh, thank you so much. Where—"

"I'll show you when you're ready. Your room is next to his and has a connecting door you can leave open at night."

"That's perfect. Thank you, Betty."

"Miz Shaw thought that would be good. You relax now and get to know Vanessa," she said as she left the morning room.

Vivian grinned at Rebecca. "She tries so hard to make us happy. I know she works for me, but actually, she's a mother hen to all of us."

"Even me," Will admitted.

Rebecca nodded her agreement. "She's wonderful. This place is wonderful, too." Her eyes scanned the morning room. "I didn't realize—I mean, I don't really fit in here. I think maybe I shouldn't stay longer than a day or two."

"Why?" Vanessa asked. "That wouldn't give us much time to get to know each other."

"Vanessa, we won't lose each other again. I'll write and we can call each other, but my life is different. I don't belong here."

Seeing the disappointment on her daughter's face, Vivian spoke up. "You promised me a week, Rebecca. Remember? I have Will as my witness."

"Vivian," Will began, a warning in his voice.

"No, Will, I won't back off. This is Vanessa's chance to have family. And I think it's important for Rebecca and Joey, too. He'll be so much happier having family around him. You know that, Rebecca, or you wouldn't have been searching so hard. And what will the others think when Will finds them? They'll want to know why you're not here."

Rebecca ducked her head. "You're right. I promised a week. But that's all, Vivian. I won't become a burden to you and Vanessa. I can make it on my own."

"A burden? What are you talking about?" Vanessa demanded. "How could you be a burden?"

"Vanessa, I can't expect you and your mother

to support me and Joey. He's my responsibility."

Vivian stepped forward and patted her hand. "If things go well this week, we'll help you find a job for the summer. Then, you can go to school full-time in the fall and use that money to take care of Joey. We have rooms that we'll be paying for whether you live in them or not. And Betty throws out more food than you probably ever buy. She always wants to have plenty." Vivian fell silent, aware that she'd once again come on strong. "We're not trying to pressure you. Just stay for the week and we'll talk at the end of it."

Rebecca drew a deep breath. "I just want you to know I'm not looking for a free ride."

Vanessa hugged her again. "We just want to get to know you."

"I want that, too," Rebecca said with a sigh.

"Mom, I'll take Rebecca up to her room. I think she's ready for bed." Both girls stood, then Vanessa added, "Grab another brownie, Rebecca, because I have a few more questions."

"Take the plate." Vivian smiled at the two girls. Then she hugged first Vanessa and then Rebecca without any hesitation. "Good night, girls. I'll see you in the morning."

The two young women walked out with their arms linked.

Vivian stared after them, knowing they'd be up most of the night, talking and getting acquainted.

She was so happy for her daughter, tears glistened in her eyes. She moved to wipe them away and her elbow hit Will.

"I'm sorry, I—" She stopped short when she realized how close he was to her. Without saying anything, he wrapped an arm around her shoulder. It was meant, she was sure, to comfort, but Vivian couldn't deny how good it felt to be held by him. This close she could smell his woodsy aftershave and feel his heart beating next to her.

"Vivian, I'm happy for you. I know how much you wanted this reunion for Vanessa." He looked down at her and his face was mere inches from hers. His eyes looked directly into hers, and she read the sincerity there.

"I don't think I ever said thank you, Will." Suddenly shy and awkward, she lowered her eyes. "So...thank you." Why she did it, she couldn't say, but she went up on tiptoe and kissed him. His cheek was her target, but at the last minute he turned and her lips met his.

A fleeting millisecond. That was all the time

it took, but the kiss rocked her. From out of no-where came the desire to melt into Will and lan-guish in a real kiss. To let herself go and touch his lips again, to taste him, to—

No! She shrugged off his arm and scooted away from him, putting at least ten feet between them. Was that a safe enough distance? asked an inner voice. Right now, she wasn't sure being on the other side of Texas was safe enough.

Will said nothing, and she frantically searched for dialogue to break the awkward silence. "I—" In their frantic survey of the room, her eyes lit on the snacks Betty had prepared. "Why don't you sit and have some more hors d'oeuvres? You don't want to disappoint Betty, do you?" Ever the gracious hostess, she laughed to herself. Even in times of stress.

She could feel Will's eyes on her, though she didn't dare meet his gaze. Why didn't he say something? she thought. Anything.

After what seemed an eternity, he finally spoke. "Thanks, but no. I'm sorry to disappoint Betty, but it's been a long day. I need to head home. I'll just call a taxi and—"

"No, you won't. Peter will drive you."

Will hesitated, then he nodded. "Thanks. I'll go find him."

He was in the doorway when she stopped him. "Wait, Will."

He turned and once again she noticed how handsome he was. His tie and shirt collar lay open at his neck, and he'd long ago lost the suit jacket in deference to the heat and the hour. He leaned an arm against the doorframe in a classically masculine pose, unaware, no doubt, how good he looked there in her home.

"What is it, Vivian?" he asked.

"I have a favor to ask of you."

"What?" His voice sounded cautious.

"I'd like you to come to dinner on Sunday. I think Joey will be glad to see you. And Rebecca, too. I'm afraid the adjustment will be difficult for them."

"But they don't know me, either. I don't think my presence will help them, Vivian."

"It will help me. I found that out in Arkansas. That I could depend on you. I'm asking for your help again on Sunday."

He seemed to ponder the invitation. Then he nodded. "What time?"

"One o'clock." She smiled. "And thank you."

Long after Will had left, the smile still held its place. Two days and she'd see Will again.

She didn't really need him at the Sunday dinner, neither did Rebecca. But she wanted him there.

What are you doing, Vivian? asked that nagging inner voice.

She didn't know. But it felt good.

CHAPTER EIGHT

WILL TOOK SATURDAY OFF, trying to clear his head. He didn't even want to think about business. That only led back to thoughts of Vivian.

Over the last few days his view of Vivian Shaw as a wealthy woman had changed. Now he saw her as a warm, caring woman who felt guilty for not adopting six children instead of only the baby. A kind, loving woman who wanted the best for her daughter. A beautiful, sexy woman who got under his skin.

And that wasn't good.

That kiss Friday night still lingered in his mind. She'd meant only to say thank you, to give him a peck on the cheek. But he'd turned. Purposely? If he was honest with himself, he'd admit that he wanted to kiss her on the mouth. Wanted it ever since she'd walked into his office weeks ago.

But that line of thinking was dangerous.

In fact, concentrating on Vivian Shaw as a

woman at all was dangerous to his future. For a long time he'd fought any attraction to wealthy women. His ex-wife was part of Dallas society. Though they no longer had contact, he read about her every week in the society pages. He'd do his best to remember the hurt she'd caused him.

Trying to yank his mind off the subject, he read the paper from beginning to end. He watched all the sports shows on television. He went to the gym and worked out.

And through all of those activities, he thought of Vivian. He thought of how she and the two girls would be getting to know each other. How she'd be hovering over them, trying not to pressure them. How she so badly wanted a family for Vanessa.

And when Sunday arrived, she was still in his thoughts. He spent an inordinate amount of time preparing for lunch with Vivian. He wore his best suit and tie, and even debated whether he should've had his hair cut.

That thought forced him to work hard on his attitude. He was working for Vivian Shaw. Nothing else. She didn't care how he looked. All she cared about was providing her daughter with a family. He should remember that.

Hadn't she pulled back from his kiss Friday night? Enjoying the light contact he'd been ready to deepen the kiss, but she clearly didn't share the opinion. No, despite his growing feelings for Vivian, she was and would have to be just his client.

He rang the door bell, opting for the formal entry, not parking in back. He was a guest, but it was still a business relationship.

"Mr. Will!" Betty said as she swung open the door. "Come in. Miz Shaw was wondering where you were."

"Am I late?" he asked. He'd tried to time his arrival exactly.

"No. She was just wondering. Come on in. I made some new hors d'oeuvres I want you to try."

"I'm looking forward to it, Betty. How's Peter?"

"He's doing fine. He has a real challenge with Rebecca's car. He's lovin' it!"

Will grinned. Having driven the old Volkswagen, he knew what Betty meant. He followed her to the living room, a grand salon he'd never been in before.

"Will!" Vivian said with more enthusiasm than he'd expected. She hurried forward and took both his hands in hers. The squeeze she gave them, plus her desperate look, warned him something was awry.

"Good afternoon, Vivian. Hello, ladies," he added, smiling at Rebecca and Vanessa. Then his gaze encountered the reason for Vivian's distress.

An important man had stood and was waiting for an introduction. Will knew he was important by his stiff demeanor.

"Will, this Harry Browne, my late husband's business partner and Vanessa's godfather. Harry, this is Will Greenfield, the private investigator who helped us find Rebecca."

Will summoned a smile and extended his hand.

Harry Browne did not reciprocate. He stood there stiffly, staring at Will. "I don't believe in using P.I.s," he said.

Vivian reacted as if he'd slapped her in the face. "How dare you treat one of my guests so rudely, Harry! If you intend to dine in this house, you'll behave yourself!"

Will had figured she had a temper, but he'd never seen it. It tickled him that she would defend him. "It's all right, Viv. I'm not offended."

"You should address her as Mrs. Shaw," Harry informed him.

Before he could say anything, Vivian's temper boiled over again. "Will and I are friends as well as business acquaintances. Perhaps it would be better if you left, Harry."

Will protested before Harry could. "Viv, I can go. There's no need—"

"No." Her voice was cool and clipped. "I invited you to come. You are my guest. If Harry wants to join us at the table, he can mind his manners." She stared at the man, her chin up.

Will looked at Vanessa. She moved to Harry's side and slipped her hand through his arm. "Mom's right, Uncle Harry, and you know it. Will has done a great thing for me, and we all enjoy his company." Then she turned to Will. "Joey is outside with Peter, but he's been waiting for you. I'll call him in."

The change of subject eased the tension.

Will looked at Rebecca. "How's Joey adjusting?"

Rebecca looked rueful. "He's loving it. Betty and Peter spoil him rotten and Vivian is acting like a grandmother hen with one chick to hover over."

"Good for her," Will said, smiling in Vivian's direction.

"I think it's ridiculous!" Harry said, intruding on their conversation. "Vanessa doesn't need any other family. You know nothing about these people!"

Vanessa stepped forward between Harry and her sister. "Uncle Harry, Rebecca is my sister. She is my family, in addition to Mom, of course. Either you treat her nicely, or you're not welcome here. It's that simple."

Vivian put her arm around her daughter's waist. "Well said, dear." She turned to Harry. "I'm sorry this has been such a shock. I was going to call you tomorrow, to let you know what had happened. I appreciate your opinion, of course, Harry, but I am free to make my own decisions. And I have."

As if the matter had been decided, she turned to Will. "Did you try Betty's new appetizers, Will? She was eager for your opinion."

Will selected one of the hors d'oeuvres just as the French doors opened and Joey came running in. "Will, they have ducks! Peter and I have been chasing them!" The boy's face wore a delighted grin.

Will squatted down to Joey's level. "Is that right? I haven't seen them yet."

Joey grabbed his hand. "Come on. I'll show you."

Before they could take a step, Vivian knelt down beside them. "I think you'd better wait until after lunch, Joey. You need to go wash your hands because we're almost ready to eat."

The little boy hugged her neck, gave her a kiss on her cheek and said, "Okay, Grandma." Then he ran out of the room.

Will stood, giving Vivian a hand up. "Nice work, Grandma," he whispered.

"Isn't he adorable?" Vivian whispered.

"Vivian, are you sure you don't want him to eat in the kitchen with Betty and Peter?" Rebecca asked, a worried look on her face.

"Of course not, Rebecca. He's part of our family," Vivian assured her.

Will noticed Harry moved closer to Vivian's side. Obviously disapproving of the whole familial scene, he seemed eager to direct the conversation. "Did you get your invitation to the dinner party, Vivian?"

"What dinner party?" She asked, distracted by her family.

"Elaine Jankowski's dinner party. I'll escort you, of course."

Will noted that his remark wasn't a question. But even more interesting was the hostess. Her name had once been Elaine Greenfield.

"I haven't gone through my mail since Thursday. When is the party?"

Harry looked a bit peeved by Vivian's lack of interest. "Next Wednesday. It should be quite grand. She always has the best."

"I don't think I'll go."

"What? But it's an important evening. She's asking for a donation for the women's shelter." Harry turned to Will. "Sorry to talk of people you wouldn't know. But Vivian and I frequently attend parties together." There was a triumphant look on his face.

"It's not a problem, though I actually know Elaine quite well."

Now he'd gotten Vivian's attention. "How do you know Elaine?"

"She's my ex-wife." He stood there, carefully concealing his emotions, waiting for her reaction.

Suddenly she burst into laughter. "That's why—" She threw a sharp look at Harry and didn't finish her thought. Instead, she said firmly, "I won't be attending that party, Harry. Thank you for offering to escort me, though."

"But, Vivian, everyone will be there!" Harry insisted.

"*I* won't."

"Neither will I," Vanessa agreed with her mother.

"When Herbert was alive, you went to all the parties," Harry said.

"Yes, because he told me it was necessary for business reasons. I'm not involved in the business any longer, Harry."

"But I am!" Harry protested again.

"Yes, you are. But I'm not your wife, Harry. So I don't have to go, and I'm not. Elaine isn't a woman I enjoy spending an evening with." She looked directly at Will, a smile on her lips.

The shared look did not go unnoticed. Harry glanced from one to the other, and grew more upset. "I believe I'll be leaving, Vivian. I'm not feeling well."

"I'm so sorry, Harry. I hope you'll feel better soon," Vivian said charmingly.

"I'll call you this evening." There was almost a warning tone in his voice.

"How nice," Vivian returned, but she showed no remorse for his departure.

The man glared at Will and stalked out of the room. Vivian rang for Betty. "Please be sure Harry found his way out," she said when Betty appeared. "Oh, and there'll be one less for lunch."

With a broad grin, Betty said, "Yes, ma'am." Then she left.

"I'm sorry I upset your guest," Will said, watching Vivian closely.

"I'm not. You were invited. He wasn't. Sometimes, he drops in for Sunday lunch, but he was my husband's friend, not mine."

"But he wants to be your friend, Mom," Vanessa said with a laugh. "He's been in love with Mom for a long time," she added, looking at Will.

Vivian spoke before Will could think of anything to say.

"No, dear, he's been in love with Herbert's wife. He liked my obedience to Herbert's will. But Harry doesn't know me at all. He would hate being married to me."

"Then he's not that bright," Will murmured. He regretted his words when Vanessa gave him a sharp look. He wished to follow Harry's footsteps out the door. As he debated the wisdom of that move, Vivian's question distracted him.

"You were married to Elaine?"

"Yes."

"Now I understand your attitude toward wealthy women. You had me puzzled for a while."

Betty stepped into the room. "Lunch is served, Miz Shaw."

When they entered the dining room, Will noted that all five of them were seated at one end of the long table, so they could converse more easily.

Vivian took the end seat as hostess, Joey on her left and Will on her right.

The dinner was delicious, of course, and Will was enjoying the company until Vivian caused him to lose his appetite.

"Will, when did you divorce Elaine?"

CHAPTER NINE

"I DIDN'T," HE SAID, putting down his fork. "She divorced me when she realized I'd never provide her with enough money."

"Well, I think you got lucky," Vanessa said. "I can't stand that woman. She's such a snob."

Rebecca laughed. "I was afraid you were, too."

Vanessa joined her. "I should take you to the party so you'll know what a real snob is like." She looked at Will. "And how she could marry that man just because he has money? He's at least thirty years older than her."

"Vanessa," Vivian said firmly, "this might be a difficult subject for Will. Why don't we talk about something more pleasant?"

Vanessa told him about yesterday's shopping and sightseeing excursion with Rebecca.

"Did Joey enjoy it?" Will asked.

"He didn't want to go," Rebecca confessed, her cheeks turning red. "I wasn't going to leave him behind, but Vivian and he begged me to let him stay.''

"Vivian can be very persuasive," Will agreed.

Vivian chose to change the subject. "What will you work on tomorrow, Will?"

"I'm going back to Longview. I think I might be able to get some more information if I dig a little deeper."

"I could go with you," Vivian offered.

Will's heartbeat raced. "No, it won't require your time, Vivian. I won't actually come into contact with any of the siblings. We got lucky with Rebecca. I'm afraid it might take awhile to find the other two."

"I guess we thought it would be easy," Vanessa confessed, "since you found Rebecca so easily."

"I'm afraid not. As I said, lady luck was on our side with Rebecca." He addressed her. "I was surprised that your adoptive parents used the name you had from your birth parents. I'm thinking I'll go back over the lists again, after I get back from Longview, and track down all the young men with the first name of David. He was the third boy. Your twin was named Rachel. She might still go by that name, too."

"You could bring us the lists. With three of us, we could go through them much faster," Vivian suggested.

"I think you should enjoy your time with Rebecca, Vivian. She's said she's going home after this week."

Will's reminder that Rebecca hadn't cooperated with her plans didn't make Vivian happy. She toyed with the food on her plate.

"Mom, we talked about taking one day at a time, remember?" Vanessa said. With a smile sent Rebecca's way, she added, "I feel very fortunate to get to know my sister."

That subject was dropped and dinner progressed with some degree of normalcy. Except that Vivian didn't eat any more, and neither did Will. He moved the food around on his plate, but he couldn't force any down.

When they departed the table, Vivian asked Will to stay and visit.

"I really can't, Vivian." He wasn't lying. Now that he'd acknowledged his feelings for her—to himself, anyway—he simply couldn't sit with her in her home and act like nothing more than a P.I. hired to do a job. He had to go. "But thank you for lunch. It was delightful."

He excused himself to the ladies. Joey

grabbed his hand. "But you haven't seen the ducks."

"Oh, right. Let's get Peter to go with us, because after I see the ducks, I need to go. Okay?"

Joey nodded in agreement, but he didn't look happy about it. "I'll go get him."

"Thanks again, Vivian," Will said with a stiff smile. Then he hurried outside with the other two males to go find the ducks.

Betty had gone to the dining room to clear the table. But she left that task undone to question the diners.

"Was my roast beef too dry? Tough? At least two of you didn't eat much."

Vivian sighed. "Your cooking was great as always. But I'm afraid our conversation wasn't conducive to good digestion, Betty."

"Humph! I should've fixed Mr. Will a doggy bag. He could've had some roast beef for his supper."

"I don't think he'd be interested," Vivian said.

Vanessa came over to sit down by her mother. "What's wrong?"

"Will didn't want me to go with him to Longview," Vivian said, unable to keep the sadness from her face.

"But, Vivian, sometimes there's not a lot to be done. I'm sure that's why he said no," Rebecca said. "You both worked together well in Arkansas."

"I know, but something's happened since then." Their shared kiss. The quick touches. Vivian had loved them all. And she'd hoped Will had, too. "Of course, it didn't help that Harry was so rude. And that Will's ex-wife's name came up."

"That was pretty funny," Vanessa said. "I can't picture Will with that woman. I thought he'd have better taste than that."

"When you're young, it's hard to be wise," Vivian said.

Rebecca nodded. "How true."

"Maybe we can get Will to come to lunch after he gets back," Vanessa suggested. "I'll talk to Carrie. I was thinking of taking Rebecca to meet her tomorrow. I'll ask her what she thinks about Will. Okay, Mom? Assuming you're interested...?"

"Of course I'm interested in Will. As a friend, I mean."

"Well, that's not what I mean," Vanessa told her mother. "I think you're falling for him, and I'm all in favor!"

I THINK YOU'RE FALLING for him....

Vanessa's words echoed in her mind all through the night, like a nagging itch she just couldn't scratch. *Falling for him...* The words teased her, taunted her, till morning painted a blue swatch across the sky. But the sleepless night forced Vivian into an admission.

She wasn't falling for Will Greenfield.

She'd already fallen. Hard.

Like water from a broken dam, the images flooded her imagination. She and Will locked in an embrace. Her in Will's shirt and him in his pj bottoms in her bedroom suite. The two of them standing before a judge, looking into each other's eyes.

Marriage to Will would be so different from her first marriage.

She'd loved Herbert, no doubt. Only twenty years old when they'd married, she'd needed some guidance. But she'd grown restless by the time she reached her thirties. She'd challenged him several times, to no avail. Eventually, she'd come to terms with his behavior and learned to gently manipulate events.

Since Herbert's death, she'd gradually spread her wings. She wouldn't be able to return to that kind of marriage. The kind Harry Browne dreamed of.

But Will… He was a good man, a kind man. He was also a strong man. Strong but gentle.

She wanted family for Vanessa—but she also wanted family for herself. As Vanessa had said, she was still young. Her own life was far from over. And she wanted Will. In every way. So she, too, wouldn't be alone. So she could share her life with him and he could share his with her.

They'd argued in the beginning, but after their trip to Arkansas, things had changed. There was a gentleness to Will she hadn't seen before. And a warmth that left her tingling all the way to her toes.

"Enough!" she muttered. Enough daydreaming about him all morning as if she was a schoolgirl. Especially when Will Greenfield didn't even want her.

"Grandma?"

Joey had walked into the morning room and stood beside her chair, looking adorable. Instead of yearning for something she'd never have, Vivian reminded herself to be grateful for what she had. "Hello, Joey. What are you doing?"

"Mommy and Aunt Nessa went to have lunch with someone. But Miss Betty's making a good lunch. We're gonna have banana pudding! I told Mommy, but she left anyway.''

"Hard to understand, isn't it?'' Vivian said gently, smiling.

"Grandma, how come Mommy got a sister who's a big girl?'' He leaned against her legs, frowning. "I thought brothers and sisters were babies.''

"Vanessa was a baby when she came to live with us. But she didn't find your mommy until she was a big girl.''

"Oh. I told Mommy I want a little sister. She said she didn't think I would have one. But maybe I'll find her when I'm a big boy.''

"Maybe so. Or maybe you'll have cousins. They're almost as good as sisters and brothers.''

"Really? What's a cousin?''

Vivian lifted Joey and placed him on her lap. His questions kept her busy all the way through lunch.

VANESSA AND REBECCA MET Carrie at a small restaurant in Snider Plaza, an elite shopping center in Highland Park. "Are you taking the day off since your boss is out of town?'' Vanessa asked.

"No. He left me a lot of work,'' Carrie said, dipping a French fry in ketchup.

"Is he nice to work for?" Rebecca asked.

"He's the best. He's always tried to accommodate me and help me with any problems I've had. And I've had a few."

They discussed Carrie's problems for a few minutes, but Vanessa brought the subject back to Will. "Do you think he'll ever remarry?"

Carrie looked at her friend, startled. "Remarry? Why would you ask that?"

Rebecca ducked her head, leaving it to Vanessa to answer that question.

Vanessa shrugged her shoulders. "Mom seems, well, a little interested in him."

"Mrs. Shaw? She's attracted to Will?" Carrie stared into space, considering the subject matter. "Yes," she said softly. "I can see that."

"You can?" Vanessa asked.

"Sure. You know, in the beginning, he didn't want to take the case. But I can tell he's gotten involved in it. Personally, I mean. But do you know about his ex-wife?"

"Yes," Vanessa said, though she didn't add anything.

Rebecca came to Vivian's defense. "I should think he'd be taken with Vivian. She's so pretty and generous. Just the opposite of his ex-wife, from what Vanessa has said."

Carrie's eyes widened as she looked at her friend. "Do you know her?"

Vanessa nodded. "I do. She's disgusting, marrying a man thirty years older than her for his money. I heard she had to sign a prenup, but she's sure spending the money while he's alive."

"I didn't ever know her name."

"It's Elaine Jankowski." Vanessa paused but then added, "She's giving a big party this week. My uncle Harry thought he'd take Mom to it, but she refused."

"Wouldn't it be funny if she went with Will?" Carrie suggested, a big grin on her face.

"I don't think so." Vanessa leaned forward. "I want Mom to be happy. She's still young. Why, some women even have children at her age. I want you to help us get them together. Will you do that, Carrie?"

"Sure. As long as it doesn't hurt Will."

"Good. Let's make some plans."

CHAPTER TEN

WILL PULLED OUT HIS cell phone. "Carrie? I'm on my way back. I'll probably be in the office by four-thirty."

"Oh, good. Vanessa is so anxious to hear what you've found, she insists we both come to dinner. I hope you don't mind."

Will blew out a long breath. So much for the resolution he'd made while driving, to keep his distance from Vivian. He'd finally decided there was no point in making himself miserable. "Carrie, I'm pretty tired. Why don't you call and tell them I didn't find much? I'll report tomorrow."

"But, Will, you have to eat anyway. And Betty has already started dinner. She loves to cook special things for you. I told them you wouldn't be able to stay late. Please?"

It was bad enough trying to resist Vivian. A combination of Betty, Carrie and Vanessa was too much. "Don't you want to tell me Rebecca will be upset with me, too?"

"Well, I *know* Joey wants you to come."

"Fine, Carrie," he said with a sigh. "Tell them I'll be there. But I won't stay late." He hit the end button.

"So much for resolutions."

AS SOON AS SHE HUNG UP the phone, Carrie immediately dialed Vanessa's phone number.

"I talked him into dinner, Vanessa, but I don't think he'll stay long. He sounds pretty tired."

"Good job, Carrie. We've got everything arranged. Someone will call and offer us theater tickets, we'll go and he and Mom will have dinner on their own. I hope this works out. I don't want Mom upset."

"I don't want Will upset, either. He might stop speaking to me."

"You know, I have a good feeling about this. It will work out," Vanessa said emphatically. "But just in case, keep your fingers crossed."

TOO STAID. TOO BUSINESSLIKE. Too formal.

All these clothes and nothing was right.

Standing in front of her closet, Vivian fretted. What should she wear to see Will?

Maybe he wasn't even coming, she thought.

"Mom, it's all set up." Vanessa burst through her door, as if on cue. "Will will be here at six."

"I hope he didn't mind."

"Of course not. Now, what are you going to wear?"

That was the question of the day, Vivian thought. "I'm not sure. What about this dress?"

"No, too...ladylike. Wait a minute." She went to the door and called out for Rebecca. "Help me choose what Mom should wear."

"What do you mean this dress is too lady-like?" Vivian demanded.

"It looks like a dress Dad picked out for you," Vanessa explained as Rebecca came into the room. "We've got to find something sexy for Mom to wear."

Sexy? Vivian drew a deep breath and fought her fears. When Rebecca found a dress in a soft green that clung to her figure and matched her hazel eyes, both girls declared it to be perfect.

"I'm not sure," Vivian muttered, staring at herself in the mirror after she had put on the dress.

"Will will fall on his knees and beg you to marry him!" Vanessa assured her.

"Marry him!" Vivian echoed. She could feel her pulse begin to pound. "Now you're being silly. Besides, I don't want to trick him into w-wanting me."

Rebecca hugged Vivian. "He won't object. You deserve him, Vivian."

"Thank you, dear." She embraced the young woman. "But I don't even know how to flirt!"

Vanessa put an arm around her mother. "That's what makes you irresistible."

"I don't know about that, but I'm so nervous, I'm not sure I can wait until six o'clock." Vivian looked at herself in the mirror again, trying to get used to her new image. "Are you sure he'll like this dress?"

"We're sure," Vanessa and Rebecca chorused together and burst out laughing.

An hour later, they were all gathered in the living room, waiting for the guest of honor. Carrie kept checking her watch.

"Are you sure he said he'd come?" Vivian asked again.

"Yes, ma'am. He got into the office about four-thirty."

Vanessa looked up. "Did he find out anything?"

"He didn't really say. He just said he got a few clues to look for."

The door bell got everyone's attention.

"Okay. Does everyone know what they're supposed to do?" Vanessa asked.

Everyone nodded in agreement just as Peter escorted Will into the living room.

"Good evening. I hope I haven't kept you waiting," Will said stiffly, looking everywhere but at Vivian.

Vivian stood and walked toward him. "Not at all, Will. Would you like some fruit juice?"

"Sure," Will said, still not looking at her.

Vivian thought she'd be too afraid to encourage Will. But she discovered she was irritated with his attitude. She picked up one of the glasses of juice on the tray and carried it back to him. "Here you go," she said, but she didn't turn loose of the glass even when he tugged on it.

Her plan worked like a charm. Will looked up and forgot all about juice. "You look very… charming, Vivian."

Vivian beamed at him. "Thank you, Will."

Will almost chugged the glass of juice. Then he opened his mouth to give his report so he could leave as soon as dinner was over.

Before he got his throat cleared, the phone rang. Vanessa hurried over and answered it. Will frowned. For some reason, everyone was watching her. He risked another look at Vivian. He was a little disturbed by her sexiness tonight.

"Oh, really? Oh, yes, I'd love them. You'll

leave them at the box office? Oh, thanks so much.'' Vanessa hung up the phone and spun around. ''That was Patty, one of my friends. She has three tickets for the theater tonight for that play I wanted to see. She can't use them.''

Before Will knew it, the three young ladies made their goodbyes and disappeared, leaving him alone in the room with Vivian.

''What happened?'' he asked.

''Didn't you hear? They got tickets for a play Vanessa wanted to see. They said they'd eat when they got back,'' Vivian assured him.

''But—''

''Shall we go in to dinner?''

''I shouldn't stay, Vivian. I'm sure you've got things to do and—''

''Why, no, Will. Nothing except have dinner with you. Shall we go?'' She crossed and took his arm without waiting for an answer. ''Let's eat outside, since it's just the two of us. I think Peter has some lights up out there.''

When they stepped out onto the patio to find plenty of lights, a table set for two, and food already on the table, Will stopped short.

''Vivian, when did you tell Betty we'd be eating on the patio?''

''Why?'' she asked, looking at him from under her lashes.

"Because it seems to me this table was arranged before I got here. How did Betty know the girls were going to leave?"

Vivian felt like a thief caught in the act. She was probably blushing. "Er, I think maybe she heard Vanessa talking on the phone."

He put his hands on his hips and stared at her. She never could lie. Best to try the honest approach, she thought. "Will, you're being difficult. Don't you want to have dinner with me?"

"Of course I— No, I can't— This won't do!"

Vivian gasped. "Why not?"

"Because we've got to keep things on a business level, Vivian. This is too…too intimate."

"I see," Vivian whispered, dropping her head down. "I was afraid it wouldn't work."

"What wouldn't work?" Will asked sharply.

"My dress, getting you alone, trying to make you pay attention to me." She turned her back on him. "It's okay if you leave."

"Look, Vivian, I can give you the name of a good man to take over your case. He'll find the other kids."

"But you won't?" She kept her back to him.

"Honey, I— I mean, Vivian, I can't stick to business. I know all you want is for me to find the kids, but—but I can't keep my mind on business."

She spun around, staring at him. "Why not?"

Will drove his hand through his hair, frustration on his face. "Look at you, Vivian! You're beautiful, generous, kind. I was okay as long as I thought you were a selfish, wealthy woman, like Elaine. But I know better now."

She smiled, thrilled by his remarks. "Thank you. That's what I wanted."

"What?"

"I wanted you to notice me, to l-like me."

Will took a step closer. "Honey, that's not a problem. I can't help but notice you. But I need to remember that I'm not someone you'd be interested in."

"Why not?"

He actually glared at her. "Because I'm not in your league. You probably spend more in a month than I make in a year."

"Why does that matter? I'm not interested in you for your money." She stepped closer.

"Good thing," Will muttered.

"But money doesn't matter."

"Yes, it does. You wouldn't like living in my apartment," he told her, his lips tightly pressed together.

"I wouldn't have to live in your apartment. This house is paid for. You could live here with me."

"And have everyone say I married you for your money?" he roared.

"Will, do people talking about us bother you that much? Enough to keep us apart?" She looked at him, her heart in her eyes.

"Damn it, Viv, how do you expect me to resist when you look at me that way?"

She put her hands on his chest. "I'm hoping you don't," she whispered.

He wrapped his arms around her. "Are you sure this is what you want?"

"Oh, yes," she said. He took her breath away before she could say anything else, as his lips captured hers in a kiss.

This was the kiss she'd been waiting for. Nothing accidental, but deliberate. All the feelings he'd kept pent up were spoken on his lips now, and she replied in kind.

She wrapped her arms around him and leaned into his chest. Finally! her mind rejoiced. That was her last coherent thought as he deepened the kiss and she prayed it would never end.

It probably wouldn't have, were it not for the clapping and cheering that distracted them.

They looked up and saw Vanessa, Rebecca and Carrie standing by the door, clapping and cheering. Betty was standing outside, her arms crossed over her chest, a grin on her lips.

"What are you all doing here?" Will demanded, still holding Vivian against him.

Vanessa winked at him. "I've been looking for a new dad, and it looks like you're the perfect candidate."

"I don't want your mom pressured into anything," Will growled. Then he looked down at Vivian's smiling face. "Are you okay with this?"

"Depends on what 'this' means," Vivian said, finding that she did know how to flirt. "Are we talking marriage? Or do you just want to have your way with me?"

"Vivian Shaw!" Will said with reproof. "I would never— Well, I would, but I want you to be my wife. And I've got witnesses, too."

"Yes, you do, and I accept," she told him, standing on her toes to kiss him again. Will participated with enthusiasm. When he finally lifted his head, there were more cheers, clapping and laughter.

"You're my witnesses," he called out. "Right?"

"Right," Vanessa agreed. "Mom, I think our plan worked. Will seems pretty ready to move in."

Vivian wrapped her arms around his neck.

"Yes, he does, doesn't he?" Delight filled her voice.

"When?" Will whispered.

"As soon as possible. I wanted Vanessa to have family. Now I'll have family, too."

"Always, Viv, always." He kissed her again.

When he raised his head this time, Vivian sent the ladies away. "Will and I are going to have dinner and make plans."

"We could help you plan," Vanessa suggested.

"Not this time, dear," Vivian told her. "This kind of planning is best with just the two of us."

Having family was great, but there was something to be said for privacy at a time like this.

* * * * *

Be sure to look for Judy Christenberry's next book,
THE LAST CRAWFORD BACHELOR,
an April 2004 release
from Silhouette Romance.

Dear Reader

Private Scandals. Are there any two words in the English language capable of capturing a writer's attention more? Especially when those writers delight in mapping out the shadowy labyrinth that is the human heart with sizzling sensuality as their guide? You can bet we happily accepted the opportunity our editor Brenda Chin extended to us to not only contribute a story to the *Private Scandals* anthology, but to spin off a three-book Blaze miniseries, stories specially designed to set your heart to pounding.

In "Sleeping with Secrets," driven businessman Gabe Wellington seduces sexy attorney Rachel Dubois…mind, body and soul. He is everything a woman could want in a man. But what happens when the secrets of his past threaten Rachel's dreams of tomorrow? Are some sins too dark to be forgiven?

We hope you enjoy Gabe and Rachel's sensual journey to find the answers to these questions. We'd love to hear from you! Write us at P.O. Box 12271, Toledo, Ohio 43612, or visit us on the Web at www.toricarrington.com.

Here's wishing you many sexy journeys of your own,

Lori and *Tony Karayianni*
aka *Tori Carrington*

P.S. Make sure you check out the three connected Blaze titles in February, April and June!

SLEEPING WITH SECRETS

Tori Carrington

We humbly dedicate this story to our editor
Brenda Chin and everyone at Harlequin Books
for continuing to challenge us as writers
and nurture us as people. Thank you.

CHAPTER ONE

A DARK SECRET lurked in Gabriel Wellington's past. A secret that could never be shared. In fact, if the wealthy denizens of the northwestern Ohio city of Toledo knew what lay in his past, they'd issue a collective gasp.

Gabe's fingers tightened around the delicate crystal champagne flute. Scratch that. Only some of them would be appalled by his secret. Others would be both covertly and openly amused by how Gabriel Wellington IV, the only male descendent of one of the city's founding families, had gone about regaining the family fortune.

Gabe stood in a ballroom surrounded by the citizens in question, hating every moment.

Lord, he had forgotten how torturous these infernal events could be. Then again, there were probably few people with an ounce of common sense that enjoyed these balls. Especially excessive black-and-white ones in the dead of winter when even the cold wind blowing in off Lake

Erie worked against him, preventing him from stepping outside to catch a breath of fresh air.

And Gabe was seriously in need of some fresh air.

A waiter passed and Gabe nodded at him, indicating that his flute was still full enough. He slowly sipped the expensive fizzy liquid then took in the ornately decorated room at Stranahan Theater's Great Hall. Women's perfumes and men's colognes clashed even as their simple black-and-white attire harmonized, creating a deceptively pleasant atmosphere that quite accurately reflected the people in attendance. Greed and philanthropy weren't words that fit easily together no matter how hard one tried. Most would argue that if you did more good than bad at the end of the day, then it was one of your better days. That wasn't enough for Gabe.

Of course, that hadn't always been the case.

He absently wondered where he would be now if things hadn't gone down the way they had when he was twenty-two. If his parents hadn't died in an automobile accident on a wet winter night. Would he have gone on to law school and become an attorney? Would he be married with three children and walk a dog named Spot every morning?

Would he be like these people who really didn't have a clue what existed beyond the marble and crystal they used to buffer themselves from the life everyone else lived?

Gabe pushed his cynical musings aside. What was…well, was. And he couldn't change that. Wouldn't even if he could.

At any rate, it wasn't who was wearing which designer that nabbed his attention. Rather, he familiarized himself with the people he had grown up with and was seeing again for the first time in ten years. Funny how the more things changed, the more they stayed the same. College sweethearts continued on down the road and married. Men his own age were beginning to look more and more like their fathers while their fathers looked more and more like their fathers before them. Too much time devoted to inactivity and not enough to physical pursuits. And those who did sport tans were either golfers or their color had come out of a cosmetician's bottle or a tanning booth.

He hadn't known what to expect when he'd returned to polite Toledo society. But it certainly wasn't the detachment he felt watching people he used to think were family. Then again, it didn't help when that same family had shunned him and nearly run him out of town on a rail a decade ago.

Gabe glanced at his watch, mentally beginning the countdown to when he'd be able to leave the event. The ball was serving to jumpstart the local and statewide political season and was being thrown for Municipal Court Judge Jonathon Dubois who had just tossed his hat into the ring for Ohio Supreme Court Justice. Gabe wasn't acquainted with the man, but he was familiar with the name. While Toledo's population was only four hundred thousand, the wealthiest one percent numbered at four hundred and they made it their business to know each other very well. Still, every now and again you stumbled across someone you hadn't met. Of course, having lived in L.A. for the past decade, Gabe was a bit out of the loop.

But that didn't stop others from wanting him to contribute to their campaigns. He'd already shaken more hands than he could count and his jaw ached from all the smiling he had done.

But the simple fact was that just as the candidates needed his money in their bids for election, *he* needed *them* to help him in his next step to regain everything his father had lost.

The sweet reverberation of a woman's deep-throated laughter captured his attention, simply because it was out of place among the orchestrated chuckles and affected female laughter. The sound caught him off guard and sent heat sluicing down his frozen back. He turned slightly to appreciate a splash of scarlet red in the sea of black and white and the woman who unabashedly had dared wear the color. His lips curved up in a real smile for the first time that night and the black and white that had been his mood mere minutes before vanished, leaving only vivid color in its wake.

The provocative woman in question stood with her back to him, so he couldn't try to place her, but he could take in the smooth slope of her creamy bare shoulders and the way her short, rich brown hair curled against her elegant neck. His gaze slid lazily down her back to her narrow waist, then down even farther to a decadent slit in the side of the long skirt that showed off a pair of killer legs in sheer black stockings. White gems flashed at her wrist and her ears. She turned her head slightly, offering up an attractive profile and showing that her hair was slicked back. He'd bet that at any other time the soft coffee-brown strands would be a riot of sexy curls.

Sexy...

The word definitely fit the woman. She represented that breath of fresh air that he'd been seeking only a moment ago. And just as the frigid January air would have robbed him of breath, so did this woman, this siren, this one person who dared to defy the dress code for the night and seemed to relish doing so. In the midst of the soft jazz music and the formal atmosphere, her beauty was timeless. She could have easily been plucked straight from the nineteen forties.

And more than likely she was there with someone even if her left ring finger was gloriously bare.

He gave a shrug. Not that it mattered. Gabe was known to take what he wanted when he wanted it. And, with fierce intention, he decided he wanted this woman.

And by night's end he would have her.

In his bed.

Writhing under his body.

Shuddering in response to his touch.

Her throaty laughter melted to a soft purr then into deep, soulful moans.

Gabe caught movement out of the corner of his eye as someone came to stand next to him. Male, he knew, because Gabe smelled him before he saw him, the man's overpowering scent of expensive designer cologne polluting the air at least three feet ahead of him.

"You aren't going to give up, are you, Wellington?"

Gabe narrowed his eyes though his gaze continued to drink in the lovely sight in red across the ballroom floor.

Lance Harkin.

"Depends on what you're referring to," Gabe said, betraying none of the resentment that seethed in his veins toward the other man.

Lance waved his free hand. "Coming back here to Toledo. Buying your parents' old place. Trying to relocate the headquarters of G.B. Wellington here." Lance chuckled without humor, the sound grating further against Gabe's taut nerves. "I'd have thought the first humiliation would have been enough. But no. Here you are, back for more."

Even the muscles in Gabe's ankles tensed at the gibe. Who would have believed that he had not only grown up with the man next to him, but that they had roomed together at Princeton and had been best friends for most of their early lives?

Now Gabe could barely tolerate the sight of Lance Harkin. And not just because of the guy's rude behavior and chilly welcome upon Gabe's return. No. There was the little matter that Harkin's family was directly responsible for the loss of the Wellington fortune. And Lance made no secret that he'd like to repeat history.

Gabe forced himself to look at his old friend, now the man he planned to destroy. "Excuse me, won't you?" he asked with a calculated grin. "I think I just spotted the woman I'm going to marry...."

ABSOLUTELY DELICIOUS...

That's how Rachel Dubois felt in the decadently cut red dress.

She quelled a shiver as the satiny material shimmied against her skin.

Okay, so maybe being rebellious and wearing her older sister Leah's latest designer dress hadn't been the brightest idea, but Rachel couldn't deny the little thrill of wearing the rich, vibrant material. Then there was the matter of having everyone notice her. After all, she was usually the one too easily forgotten. "You were at the ball, dear? I'm sorry, I don't recall seeing you," she might hear from a person she'd spent a half hour talking to.

Of course, she didn't know if "Oh, yes, I remember. You were the one who wore that loud, horrifying red dress" was any better. Particularly since this was an event to encourage contributions to her father's election campaign. She fought to keep from rearranging the slit at the side to cover her left leg. Ah, well. It was a little too late to reconsider now. She was wearing the dress. She was here. And she had every intention of having a good time.

Because, as her sister was so fond of pointing out, somewhere over the past year she seemed to have forgotten how to have a good time.

Of course what went unsaid was that it was almost one year to the day since they'd lost their mother to breast cancer. And Rachel had moved back home, a quiet part of her afraid that her father might harbor thoughts of following his wife of the past thirty-five years.

She briefly closed her eyes, not wanting to think about that now. Not wanting to pine for her life before Patricia Dubois had called the family dinner meeting to share her numbing news. Not wanting to recall how her father, Municipal Court Judge Jonathon Dubois, had seemed like a shell of his former self after the funeral. Not wanting to remember how it had taken a mammoth effort to drag her father back to life after she'd moved back home.

No. Right now, other more positive things vied for her attention. She'd just bought a small house in the Harmony area—of which she was District 7 city councilwoman—and after two more weeks of renovations she'd be all set to move in. And her father was not only living again, he was running for Justice of the Ohio Supreme Court.

Rachel caught herself pressing her palm against the back of her neck then dragging it down over her shoulder, slowly, almost sensually. The move wasn't anxiety-induced. Or even self-conscious. Instead, it was that her skin felt sensitized, aware, as though alert to something…or rather someone in the vicinity. She slowly turned her head and scanned the crowd, her gaze settling on a dark-haired man sauntering toward her like a dangerously graceful black panther. She languidly dropped her hand to her side, her gaze locking with his deep brown eyes as he looked at her. Her breath hitched in her chest, the lace of her bra chafed against her suddenly overly sensitive nipples and the heat between her thighs shot up ten degrees.

She shifted, causing the material of the dress to rustle. Oh, yes. Things were very definitely looking up.

She swallowed hard. Okay, this was not a reaction she should be having to Gabriel Wellington IV. Considering that he had a rezoning proposal up for consideration with the city council's planning committee, on which she sat. While it wasn't illegal for her to be lusting after him, any public connection between a councilwoman and a man who had something to gain from her would be enough to raise a few brows. Not to mention that the mere appearance of impropriety could be enough to sink her own political career and smear her father's campaign.

She licked her parched lips. But who knew Gabriel Wellington IV would look so hot in a fitted tux?

And who knew she would find him looking at her as though he wanted to swallow her whole?

"Ms. Dubois. So nice to see you again." His voice skimmed over her, making her shiver.

"Mr. Wellington," she said with a simple nod. "I wasn't aware you knew my father."

His eyes narrowed the slightest bit. "Your father being the Honorable Judge Dubois?"

He hadn't known. She smiled. "One and the same."

"Then I don't. Know your father, that is." He slid his right hand into his slacks' pocket, pulling her gaze to the way the rich, black material pulled against certain strategic areas. She forced her attention back to his face. A purely wicked twinkle danced in his eyes as if he knew where she'd been looking.

"You don't know him?" she repeated.

"No. I'm just a concerned citizen who likes to put good people in office."

"I see."

He swept a hand toward the ballroom floor. The Toledo Orchestra had been contracted for the event and was set up at the far end of the hall. Here and there, couples showed the results of finishing school dance classes. "May I have the honor?" he asked.

Rachel had never taken dance classes. She hadn't had to. Every step she'd ever needed to know her parents had taught her during Saturday night family get-togethers at their estate in the Old West End. Back then her father had dusted off his 78s and played them on the old Victrola in the library where he would dance with her or her sister or her mother out onto the marble-tiled foyer.

She remembered thinking that she'd never meet a man as charming as her father.

But as she sank deeper into Gabriel's breathtaking eyes she wondered if perhaps she'd been mistaken.

Of course, it wouldn't be proper protocol at all to be seen dancing with Gabriel, especially in public. But the pianist began playing the opening chords of the familiar Ella Fitzgerald classic "More Than You Know." The timing couldn't have been more perfect.

"The honor would be mine," she murmured, putting her gloved hand into his.

After all, what could one little dance hurt? And with Judge Dubois so busy working the room, the odds weren't in favor of her getting a dance with her father.

All thoughts drifted from Rachel's mind as Gabriel gently pulled her into his arms, his left hand supporting her right, his left foot skillfully working between her feet. The heat of his right hand at the small of her back made her gasp quietly as she stood still, staring up into his eyes.

"You know, it's probably not a great idea to be doing this," she whispered, unsure if she'd said the words or if they were stuck between her brain and her mouth.

"I know," he murmured, then pulled her closer.

In front of the orchestra the soulful Black female singer lightly touched the microphone singing about a man with a questionable past....

Gabriel gently guided her in one direction in a smooth two-step, then back again. Rachel tried to tear her gaze from his but found it impossible. And the more she looked, the heavier her heart seemed to thud and the more her palms seemed to sweat beneath the material of her gloves.

The singer told of her desire to take her man, give him what he needed....

By mere millimeters Rachel felt Gabriel moving her closer to him. And she was helpless to stop him. The couples dancing around them disappeared. A sort of white mist seemed to buffer them from reality. Her throat tightened to an uncomfortable degree. And a desire so complete, so overwhelming, swept over her so that her knees nearly buckled under her.

Gabriel seemed to sense her need for support and tugged her closer still. His fingers tightened perceptibly around hers. His tux jacket skimmed against the front of her dress, teasing the hard tips of her breasts. His left thigh briefly met the swollen flesh between her legs, making her wetter than she'd been in a long, long time. Her breathing grew shallower. Her steps slower.

Rachel couldn't remember a time when she'd been more turned on merely by dancing with a man. Perhaps the answer was never. Especially when he leaned forward.

"God, you're beautiful," he whispered.

His lips skimmed lightly against the shell of her ear as he pulled away, making her breath snag.

The singer shared her helpless plea to give her man all she could, which was her love....

Rachel's eyelids fluttered closed as she gave herself over to the words of the song...the feel of the man against her...the molten sensations flowing through her system. Her womanhood throbbed and hungered. Her skin tingled and sang. And she wanted this man more than anything else she could name in that one moment.

She swallowed hard, feeling inexplicably vulnerable by her spiraling emotions. "You know, this isn't going to help in your zoning bid."

Gabriel's lips turned up just the slightest bit, pulling her gaze there, making her mouth water with the desire to kiss him. "I know."

The pianist played the final chords of the song but Rachel only distantly realized it. Even the spattering of applause wasn't enough to break the sensual spell Gabriel Wellington had put her under. She didn't want the dance to end. Didn't want this man to release her hand. She wanted him to press his thigh more tightly against the tender flesh between her legs. Wanted a more intimate feel of his hard, powerful body. Wanted to escape into the Ella Fitzgerald song and be someone else. Somebody, anybody other than herself. A woman who could make a naughty suggestion to this wildly handsome man and tempt him home with her.

Rachel felt him step away from her and she languidly opened her eyes, meeting his dark and brooding gaze. She watched as his eyes moved from her mouth to her neck then to her breasts.

He slowly removed his fingers from her waist, released her right hand and applauded the orchestra.

Rachel forced herself to do the same even as her cheeks grew hotter.

"Thank you," she murmured, gathering fistfuls of her skirt in her hands and hurrying from the dance floor.

GABE STOOD ROOTED to the middle of the dance floor watching as Rachel Dubois fled. And fled was the word for it. He'd no sooner released her than she'd practically run away, her red skirt swishing behind her.

He suppressed the urge to groan, remembering the way her red, red mouth had bowed open as if she was out of breath. The way her breasts had heaved under the rich silk. The hot feel of her gloved hand against his and the even hotter feel of her body brushing all too briefly against his.

I want her…and I'll have her.

The thought set him in motion. He strode purposely from the dance floor, then fished his cell phone from his jacket pocket. At the same moment the handheld receiver vibrated in his grip, signaling an incoming call. Not recognizing the number in the Caller ID box, he allowed the call to transfer to voice mail. He didn't want any distractions from his intention to track down one unforgettably sexy Rachel Dubois.

"How can I be of service, Mr. Wellington?" Gloria, his secretary, picked up his call on the second ring.

No matter how many times he asked, his executive assistant refused to call him by his first name. And no matter where he was, or what time it was, she always picked up by the second ring, ready to please.

He told her what he was after then waited as she

looked up the information. It was ten o'clock on a Saturday night. He suspected that Gloria was never more than thirty seconds away from a computer and the Internet and her vast number of resources.

"You know, it's probably not a good idea to be contacting a city councilwoman outside office hours," she said quietly.

Gabe knew she'd gotten the number. "It probably wasn't a good idea to dance with that city councilwoman, either, but I just did."

"Pardon me?"

Gabe smiled. "Never mind. Give me the number."

She did. "It's to her cell."

She hadn't had to tell him that because he recognized the number as the one that had flashed on his display screen mere moments before. "Thanks, Gloria."

"I assume you'll be late returning home tonight, sir?"

"You assume correctly."

"Good night, then."

"Good night."

Gabe disconnected then pushed the button to retrieve his voice mail messages. Three were from business associates, two in town and one in L.A. But it was the fourth that interested him.

Rachel Dubois's breathless voice read off an address he recognized as being on the outskirts of town. "Meet me there. Half an hour."

He grinned then looked up to see her standing near the coat-check counter. Her lush lips curved up into a smile as she accepted her stole. She winked then was no more than a wistful memory as she disappeared through the front doors.

Gabe slid his phone back into his pocket, then headed for the same door Rachel had used. A half an hour was much too long for him to wait....

CHAPTER TWO

SHE WAS CRAZY...

    Mad...

    Certifiably insane...

And Rachel Dubois wanted to feel Gabriel Wellington's mouth crushing against hers more than she'd wanted anything else in a long, long time.

The old house she'd recently bought was cold. While still unoccupied, the gas furnace had to be kept running to prevent the pipes from freezing in the January cold and the electricity kept on for the subcontractor's power tools. The antique furniture that had come with the place was covered for the most part, lamps unplugged and moved out of the way for the painters. She didn't have any clothes here yet, so she couldn't change out of the red dress. She bent to light a fire in the large fireplace in the living area thinking that she might not have the courage to follow through with her plans if she could change her clothes. The dress seemed to make her more impulsive somehow. Provided her with a bolder, more daring persona. An escape from the staid, empty life she'd been living as of late. A state she hadn't even recognized until tonight. Until she'd taken Gabriel's hand and gotten lost in his eyes.

She stood up and rubbed her hands against her bare arms. Maybe that wasn't entirely true. The seed for her current actions had been planted a while ago. When her sister had stopped by for Sunday brunch a few months ago, Leah had forced her to stand in the front door of her father's house and held her chin so she had to look outside. Only it hadn't been the autumn foliage she'd wanted Rachel to look at. Rather she'd wanted her to look beyond the perfectly manicured lawn expected of a judge, outside the stately home…beyond the person she'd become.

"We talk about a part of Dad having died along with Mom," Leah had said to her quietly. "But what about you, Rachel? Has a part of you gone with her, too?"

Rachel had taken a good long look at the rut she'd made for herself over the past year and decided right then and there to climb out of it and start working on a new one.

Only she'd had no idea in which direction to take it.

Until a growing something inside had compelled her to invite a virtual stranger to her new house, to a place where no one would know where she was, in the middle of the night.

She shivered straight down to her toes, the illicit nature of the midnight rendezvous with Gabriel making her feel real, alive and so completely hot she really didn't need the fire to warm her.

"Are you cold?"

Gabriel's voice reached out from the darkness behind her. Rachel swallowed a gasp, keeping her back turned to him, her heartbeat immediately kicking up at the thought of him watching her without her knowing. How long had he been here? What were his thoughts? Did he think her slightly off her rocker to be standing in a dark, mostly empty house under renovation in the middle of the night waiting for him? Or did he feel the same forbidden thrill at their meeting that she did?

But right that minute she didn't feel much like a city councilwoman. And Gabe wasn't a wealthy business owner with a proposal in front of one of her committees. He was simply a sexy man to her needy woman.

"No," she whispered, still not having looked at him.

She felt his hands on her bare arms before she

knew he had even moved. No easy feat given the old floorboards beneath them. She remembered comparing his movements to a black panther earlier and thought that's exactly what he was.

His fingers skimmed over her skin, leaving a flash fire in their wake. "You left before I could properly say goodbye."

Rachel caught her breath at the feel of his fingers against her hip. "Goodbye wasn't exactly what I had in mind."

She couldn't seem to budge from where she stood. Not to face him. Not to touch him. All she was capable of was standing still, anticipating his next move.

"And your date?" he asked, his fingers fluttering over her hip and toward her front.

Rachel's knees nearly gave out from under her. "Who said I had a date?"

"A woman as beautiful as you always has a date."

She fought weakly against the sensual silk that had begun clouding her mind. Of course, he was right. She had been accompanied by someone tonight. Someone who had been displeased with her provocative attire. Someone who was more an occasional escort than a real date. And someone who seemed preoccupied and hadn't blinked when she told him she was calling a cab to go home.

"You're right."

His lips skimmed over her bare shoulder. "I'm always right."

She laughed low in her throat, heat, sure and swift, filling her belly.

"And the identity of this date?"

Rachel could hear her own breathing grow shallower. She forced herself to concentrate. "I'm surprised you don't know already. You were talking to him before you asked me to dance."

Was it her or did his fingers tighten against her flesh the slightest bit?

"Is something wrong?" she whispered, longing to feel his hand touch more intimate places.

"To the contrary. Everything is very right."

She felt his other hand curve over her left hip, then he was gently pressing her bottom against his hard body. Every molecule of air rushed from her lungs in a soft sigh.

"I wouldn't have left a woman like you alone for a second," he murmured just above her ear, sending shivers scooting everywhere.

"Why?"

"Because I'd be afraid someone might steal you away."

Like you? Rachel wanted to ask.

Instead she said, "And your date?"

She felt him smile against her neck. "I'm all yours for the stealing, Rachel."

His face was parallel to hers, putting his decadent mouth within kissing distance. She smoothed her hands tightly over his where they rested against her hips, then turned her head so that her senses were filled with the feel and smell of him. He didn't wear any sort of overpowering cologne. In its place was the subtle scent of sandalwood. His soap, perhaps. And when combined with his heat the smell made her mouth water with the desire to run her tongue along the surface of his tanned, smooth skin.

He pressed his lips softly against the corner of hers. She moaned and tried to turn in his arms. He stayed her with his hands, trapping her there, his front pressed enticingly against her back. Her movements limited when she wanted to explore every inch of him.

His tongue dipped out and into her mouth. She allowed him entrance, feeling her breasts heave against her bra as her breath quickened. Then his hands moved, hers still on top of his. They dipped briefly downward, toward her throbbing sex, then slowly up until all four hands cupped her breasts.

Rachel felt as if she were on fire. As if the flames from the fireplace had leaped out and licked along her exposed skin. Gabriel gently squeezed her breasts, easily finding her erect nipples and pinching them through the material of her dress and bra. She resisted the knee-jerk reaction to shy away from his touch. She'd always been self-conscious about the size of her chest. Leah had once told her that she had the breasts of a tease. Full and round and irresistible to men. She'd spent her teenage years hiding them behind oversize blouses and her books. In college she had finally tried some close-fitting turtlenecks and cotton shirts. But never anything that revealed her cleavage the way this dress did.

Gabriel kissed her deeply, then dipped a finger inside the right cup of her bra. The rasp of male skin against her overly sensitive female flesh made her gasp. He moved the attentions of his mouth to her left shoulder and used his hand to coax her nipple out and over the top of her bra and dress, openly watching his progress. Rachel found her state of dress incredibly naughty and freeing all at once.

But the sensation was nothing compared to the feel of Gabriel cupping her bare breast and pushing it up until he could lick the distended nipple with the very tip of his tongue.

A strangled sound escaped her throat, answered by a low growl from Gabriel. He grasped her hips again and pressed her more insistently against his arousal. During their earlier dance she had guessed at his strength and size, but now she knew exactly how large he was, the stiff ridge of his erection extending from the top of her bottom to the middle of her back.

Dear God…

Rachel had been intimate with two other men in her life. And neither of them had prepared her for the man skillfully stoking her passions to life now. In fact, she suspected that Gabriel Wellington would put most men to shame. Not just with his size. But his charm. She got the feeling that few woman could resist this tall, dark man who had a grin only the devil could have made.

And his touch…

Finally he seemed to grow impatient with their position and he released her so he could pull her toward him, face-to-face. She willingly let him, so overwhelmed by finally feeling him pressed to her front that she cried out. She tunneled her fingers through his thick dark hair. Rubbed her bare breast against the front of his tux. Ground her hips hungrily against his rigid hardness, leaving no mistake as to what she was after.

He backed her against the edge of a sofa that had been slid out of the way so the contractor could move unhindered. Gabriel knelt down, his gaze imprisoning hers, and then he slowly lifted the satiny fabric of her dress up her stocking-clad legs. Rachel tightly grasped the sofa back and caught her bottom lip between her teeth as he hesitated, apparently having discovered that she wore thigh-high stockings. She cried out when she felt his mouth against the flesh between the lace top and her scrap of underwear.

Oral sex was so far outside of her realm of experience that she didn't know whether to encourage him or to stop him. The act seemed so selfish. So intoxicatingly greedy.

Made her feel so exceedingly vulnerable.

For while he would coax her to the heights of desire, she would go there alone.

He licked her inner thigh and she gasped, curling her fingers into his soft hair. Maybe he wouldn't go there. Maybe he would stay where he was then come back up to meet her mouth. Maybe she wouldn't have to worry about making the decision of letting him continue or…

She gasped as he moved the crotch of her panties aside, baring her tender flesh to the cool night air.

Maybe he was going to do it.

And maybe she wanted him to.

Before she had a chance to decide, he fastened his mouth over the most sensitive part of her, shooting her up into the stratosphere of sensation. It was no longer pitch black with only the golden light of the fire to break the darkness. Behind her eyelids the world emerged red and hot and explosive.

She caught herself spreading her legs even farther and wantonly pressing her womanhood even more tightly against his mind-blowing mouth. He swirled his tongue around and around her aching bud then covered it completely with his lips and sucked it deep inside. Rachel was forced to grip the side of the couch to keep from either collapsing or falling to the floor at his feet. Her breath came in ragged gasps. Soft mewling sounds filled her ears. Then she was catapulting to the other side of sensation and into a world she had not seen before. Her womb contracted, her body shuddered and every inch of her burned and twitched, alive with glorious sensual awareness.

She slowly regained control of her breathing to find Gabriel hadn't stopped. Rather he was still crouched between her legs, leisurely lapping the generous proof of her climax that ran from her as a result of his expert attentions.

Rachel restlessly pulled at the lapels of his tux, not giving in until he was standing, wedged between the trembling cradle of her legs…

RACHEL DUBOIS TASTED like a fine tangerine at the peak of ripeness, her hot juices flowing when you bit into her. Gabe kissed her deeply, savoring the taste of her sex melding with the sweetness of her mouth. He didn't think he'd enjoyed going down on anyone more than he had just now. Watching the conflicting emotions play out over Rachel's beautiful face had taken his breath away. It was obvious she hadn't been given the pleasure before, and knowing he was the first caused a primal side of him to react. To want to claim her unlike anyone had before. And to perform in a way that no one else would ever be equal to.

"Please, please, please," she said over and over, slanting her mouth first one way then the other, apparently unable to get enough.

But coming from a lifetime of restraint, Gabriel was still in complete control. He always held a part of himself back, watching, dissecting, considering what to do next.

He took in her red, red mouth, the deep color more from his kisses now than her lipstick, then lowered his gaze to where her breast still rested above the top edge of her dress. He bent to take the engorged nipple into his mouth but she held him still with her hands on either side of his face, her dripping sex pressed against the front of his slacks. She released one of her hands then moved it between them, restlessly trying to open his zipper. Gabe took a deep breath and held it, the feel of her unpracticed maneuvers threatening his control. He ground his back teeth together as she finally tugged the metal zipper halfway down then tunneled her hand into the front of his silk boxers, her fingers seeking for and finding his hard arousal.

He shuddered, the reaction catching him so far off guard that he was surprisingly close to coming.

Control, he reminded himself. He was the one who needed to be in control.

And for the briefest of moments he knew a desire to hand that control over to Rachel. That was something he couldn't let happen again.

He took a condom out of his back pocket, edged her hand away, then easily sheathed himself. He held her chin still in his other hand and gazed deep into her glistening hazel eyes as he nudged her thighs farther apart, rubbed the knob of his penis through her dripping channel, then slowly entered her.

The depth of passion that burned in her eyes made his stomach clench. Her eyelids drifted closed and she moaned in a genuine, unabashed way that made him feel like an imposter.

He pulled out then filled her to the hilt as if to reassert his control. Instead he lost the last of whatever threads of control he possessed.

For the first time in over a decade Gabriel Wellington was overwhelmed by sex.

He clenched his every muscle, fighting off climax, willing himself to return to the point of control. But Rachel's restlessness wasn't helping. He opened his eyes, refusing to look into her face this time. Instead he stared at their exposed sexes. Her thighs spread, opening her swollen pink folds to his gaze. Her curls only lightly trimmed and unwaxed. Girlish.

His own sex. Long, hard and throbbing.

He slowly reentered her, watching her moist, tight flesh accept him, and then he exited again. He repeated the movement several times until he felt himself slip into that control zone again.

"Please, Gabriel. Oh, please love me."

The plaintive sound of her voice, Rachel's voice, again robbed him of all thought as she gripped the side of the sofa and thrust her hips fully against his, grinding mindlessly, insatiably against him.

Gabe's control gave a final snap. Gone were his measured thrusts. His calculated caresses. His carefully placed licks. Instead he roughly gripped her soft hips, bit the exposed flesh of her shoulder, and thrust in and out of her until blind need filled him, wound through him, demanded his complete surrender.

Then he felt Rachel's slick muscles contract around him and knew she was climaxing. And he was helpless to do anything but follow right after her.

CHAPTER THREE

SUNDAY BRUNCH at the Dubois house was a tradition that went back as far as Rachel could remember. With few exceptions, the family gathered every Sunday at 10:00 a.m. for the meal. Such a short time ago that "everyone" had always included Rachel's mother, and Leah's husband, Dan, and their ten-year-old daughter, Sami.

Since her mother's death and her sister Leah's divorce a year ago, however, more often than not it was just Rachel, Leah and their father.

Rachel used a kitchen towel to pick up the lid of the double boiler on the stove and roll the béarnaise around. Her face burned hot and she was pretty sure she'd already ruined the front of the white blouse she had on over black Lycra pants. For some reason she couldn't quite seem to concentrate this morning.

She caught her finger toying with the top button of her blouse. She knew exactly what was behind her distractedness. Or, rather, who.

At the mere thought of him her breasts swelled and heat rushed to her sex.

Gabriel...

"I'm sorry I'm late."

Rachel jumped, dropping the lid she was holding as her sister swept into the kitchen, grabbed an apron from the pantry, then tied it around her slender waist. She looked at Rachel and stopped dead.

"What's wrong?"

Rachel swallowed hard and bent to pick up the pan lid. "Wrong? Why should anything be wrong?"

Leah crossed her arms over her chic chocolate-brown turtleneck that went perfectly with her tweed riding pants. "Rachel, nothing, I mean nothing usually startles you."

Rachel stepped back to the stove and took in the contents of the double boiler, two skillets and one saucepan in various stages of cooking.

"And you're never late," she flung back at her sister.

Leah came to stand next to her, repeating Rachel's move with the béarnaise then considering the rest of the pots. "Touché." She sighed.

"Dan was late picking up Sami this morning—again." She grabbed a nearby spatula and used it to check the browning red potatoes. "And your reason?"

Rachel shrugged, unable to conquer her distracted lethargy. Every since she'd returned home very early that morning everything seemed to move in slow motion. The second hand on the clock ticked by torturously. It had taken her a half an hour to wash and cut the potatoes when it usually took her ten minutes. And she seemed acutely aware of every beat of her heart. "Late night."

Leah glanced at her. "How was the event? Oh, my God, I almost forgot! How did the dress go over?"

Rachel felt her cheeks heat anew.

"You did wear the dress, didn't you?"

Rachel laughed and nodded. "Oh, I wore the dress, all right. I'm sure I'm going to be the talk of the town for at least five minutes."

Leah smiled and leaned into her as she turned the potatoes. "Good. It's about time you set some tongues to wagging."

Rachel nearly choked. She would do a lot more than that if anyone found out about her and Gabriel.

She rested her hand against the side of her neck. If sleeping with a man who was in the midst of petitioning city council for rezoning wasn't enough, then going to a ball held in her father's honor with one man then leaving with another was enough to tarnish her name for the next decade. In fact, she could probably forget about substantial backing during the next city council election.

Then there was her father's election campaign and what he would make of the whole situation.

She hadn't been aware she'd groaned until she found Leah staring at her.

"What?" Rachel asked.

Leah continued staring. Then she finally blinked and shook her head. "Nothing."

Nothing.

When Leah said "nothing" there was very definitely something going on behind her deep brown eyes. Unfortunately, over the past year Leah had been focusing that sharp mind of hers more on Rachel's personal affairs than her own.

Had it really only been a year ago that Leah had been seduced into having an affair, left her husband and daughter, only to have her lover walk out on her?

Rachel turned away to get the fresh-squeezed

orange juice out of the refrigerator where she'd put it to chill. Oh, God, what was she getting herself into?

"Rachel?" Leah's soft voice reached out for her. "If there's anything, you know, that you want to talk about, I'm here."

Rachel put her arm around her older sister's shoulders and squeezed. "I know."

They stood side by side for a while, both of them tending to the food. Rachel was so lost in thought that she nearly didn't hear her cell phone until the third or fourth ring and a curious glance from Leah.

She wiped her hands on a towel and excused herself to pick up the phone from the kitchen table. She didn't recognize the number on the display so she punched the button to answer.

"Good morning, Rachel." Gabriel's deep voice filled her ear.

Shivers scooted down Rachel's arms and up her back. She immediately stepped farther away from her sister, trying to hide her smile. "Good morning, yourself," she murmured, purposely not saying his name in case her sister could hear.

"I won't keep you. I was just thinking…I'm up for the same time, same place tonight if you are."

She hadn't been sure she'd hear from Gabriel again. That she not only had, but he was asking to see her again, made her feel all weak-kneed again.

"Um, sure."

A pause, then, "Very good, then. I'll see you tonight."

His pleased tone made her stomach pitch to somewhere close to her feet.

She absently pressed the disconnect then stood for a long moment with the phone pressed to her chest. The sound of Leah taking something from the stove finally snapped her out of her reverie. She quickly put the phone down, straightened her hair—although she wasn't entirely sure why she thought it needed straightening—then rejoined her sister, afraid of what she had given away and what Leah might ask.

"Dan and I are talking about reconciling," Leah blurted more than said.

Rachel nearly dropped the wooden spoon she'd picked up. "What?" Rachel stared at her sister, wondering if she'd lost her mind.

Leah nodded, her head suspiciously held straight as she pretended to concentrate on breaking eggs into a second hot skillet. "Actually, we've been talking about it for a month now. That's the real reason I was late. He wanted—'' she briefly twisted her lips ''—he wanted to discuss family counseling options.'' She flipped her blond hair over her shoulder. ''I guess there's this great guy in Sylvania who's known for working miracles on dead marriages.'' She fell briefly silent. ''And you already know that Sami wants more than anything for us to reconcile.''

''And you?''

Rachel barely dared whisper the question.

Out of everyone, she was probably the only one who hadn't blamed Leah for what had happened. Most likely because she'd known all too well how cold her sister's marriage had been. Dan Burger had always cared more about his career as a top attorney than he had about her sister. And he'd seemed to take a perverse pleasure in letting Leah know that.

Leah smiled at her, but it wasn't a true smile. ''I'm going to tell Dad during brunch.''

Which basically meant that she was as good as going through with it. Jonathon Dubois had looked upon Dan as the son he'd never had and had made no secret of his disappointment when the two had divorced.

Rachel cleared her throat. ''Remember what

you just said to me? You know, about your being there if I need to talk?'' She caught and held
her sister's gaze. ''Ditto.''

Leah hugged her, appearing as distracted as
she felt. ''I know.''

TWO DAYS LATER Rachel sat in council chambers downtown, barely able to concentrate on the
zoning and planning committee proceedings.
She'd spent most of the morning in her law office downtown where she conducted her personal practice, then had hurried here.

She didn't know if she could survive another
midnight rendezvous with Gabriel. While he
made her body hum while they were together,
when they were apart she had to feed her body
complex carbs constantly to keep her system
from collapsing altogether. Little more than five
hours of sleep in three days could do that to a
person.

Hours and hours of wanton sex could do that
to a woman like her.

''Councilwoman Dubois, where do you
stand?'' the committee chair asked her.

Stand? Right now she was lucky to be sitting
upright. ''In favor.''

The vote to recommend the council rezone a

business parcel to residential moved to the next committee member and Rachel fought not to collapse back in her seat. Since she sat on the zoning and planning committee, she already knew that they were no closer to agreeing on Gabriel's request than they had been last week. So the item would be brought up, then shelved until the next planning meeting. Namely because she and two other committee members stood opposed to the stretch of land in the far southwest corner of the city being rezoned for commercial purposes. Which meant no shopping mall there for Gabriel's company, G.B. Wellington. It wasn't only because long, unbroken stretches of land were a growing rarity in Toledo proper, but because this particular parcel was the unpreserved site of a minor revolutionary war battle and preservationists were fighting against Gabriel's commercial plans.

Rachel plopped her head in her hand and doodled on her notepad, knowing she should be doing some serious thinking. But, honestly, she couldn't seem to budge her brain from Gabriel. And her thoughts had nothing to do with business.

Of course, the quicker she removed the zoning

question from the equation, the easier it would be for her.

"Rachel?"

She blinked at the councilwoman to her right. "Hmm?"

"In favor or opposed?"

"To what?" She sat up straighter and looked around council chambers. The others were in various stages of leaving.

Janet smiled. "To lunch."

Rachel laughed then gestured with her hand. "Never mind me. I just bought a house and I'm having trouble with the contractor."

"Ah. Yes, that will do it." Janet slung her purse over her shoulder. "I've got some errands to run. Can I pick you up anything?"

Rachel shook her head. "No, thanks. I need some fresh air, anyway."

Janet left her alone and Rachel watched everyone else move away, as well. She fished her cell out of her bag and checked her messages. One was from her secretary saying a case had been rescheduled because of a heat outage at the courthouse. The second was from Leah saying she needed to borrow a plain suit to visit the post-marriage counselor. Rachel stared down at her nice, gray suit and made a face she was sure wasn't very attractive. Need a plain suit? She was definitely the person to see.

"Hello, Rachel." Gabriel's voice was her third message. "I've had my secretary reserve a table for you at Georgio's for lunch at noon. Hope you can make it."

Rachel's eyes widened as she looked around the empty chambers. Surely Gabriel wasn't suggesting that they go out in public together, was he? At least not while he still had a proposal up before the planning committee. His appearing to woo her might call her vote into question, no matter which way it went. While neither of them had broached the subject of their taboo relationship, he had to know that she couldn't afford to be seen with him in a public setting.

Right?

Of course, he hadn't said that his secretary had reserved a table for them. Rather he said she'd reserved one for her. Which meant what, exactly?

Not that it mattered. A thrill shot through Rachel's veins at the mere thought of seeing him again, taboo or not.

She began to slide her cell back into her purse when it began vibrating in her hand. She looked down at the unfamiliar number then answered, hoping it was Gabriel so she could tell him she couldn't make it.

Instead, she found her father on the other end of the line.

"Hi, Rach. Are you doing anything for lunch?"

Five minutes ago she'd been facing a brisk walk to the Spaghetti Warehouse by herself for a quick bowl of pasta. Now she had offers for two lunch dates by the two men in her life.

But considering the odd comment her father had made when she got home this morning, she wasn't sure she was up to facing him across a lunch table just right now.

I hope you're not doing anything I wouldn't do, he had said when she'd let herself into the house after five that morning still wearing yesterday's clothes, her hair a mess, and no question as to what she'd been up to.

Unfortunately, she had been doing what the Honorable Judge Jonathon Dubois would never do.

A widower of nearly thirteen months, her dad hadn't even hinted at being interested in dating again. Which wasn't surprising since he'd been married to her mom for thirty-five years.

And his reaction to Leah's goings-on a year

ago left no doubt in her mind about how he would react to her sneaking around with Gabriel Wellington.

"Sorry, Dad, I'm already booked. Zoning stuff," she said vaguely.

"Ah. A rain check, then." A heartbeat of a silence, then, "How about dinner?"

Rachel swallowed hard. "Dinner?"

Her father chuckled. "Yes. You know. That meal that one generally eats at around 6:00 p.m.? It's been a while since we've had dinner together."

"We just had dinner on Sunday."

"We had brunch."

"It was a meal."

He fell silent again. "Why am I getting the impression you're avoiding me, Rachel?"

Oh, that judge's voice had always been enough to strike the fear of God into her. She remembered classmates talking about cajoling their fathers into this, sweet-talking them into that. Her father? While no doubt a charmer, when it came to discipline, neither she nor Leah had ever questioned his authority.

Rachel's throat choked off air. "Because you have an overactive imagination," she said, hoping to fend him off.

Why was it her father always made her feel as if she was a criminal? Of course, in this case, what she was doing was borderline. While her affair with Gabriel could be looked upon as scandalous, it wasn't illegal as long as no money exchanged hands.

Was it?

"Unfortunately the rain check will have to wait until a later date, Dad. I'm taking a suit to Leah's tonight and will probably catch a bite there."

"I see."

Rachel bit hard on her bottom lip to keep from filling the void he left, likely purposely. She'd gotten herself into more trouble in the past babbling when she would have been better off keeping her mouth shut.

"Is she seriously considering this reconciliation with Dan?"

Rachel raised her brows. Did she detect the slightest bit of disapproval in her father's voice? No. That couldn't be. Jonathon Dubois had been very disappointed at Leah's breakup.

Still, he wasn't celebrating in the way she would have expected him to.

"I suppose so, yes," she finally answered.

"Very well, then. Give her and Sami my love."

"I will."

"So, will I see you tonight? Or will we be running into each other again tomorrow morning?"

Rachel wanted to die right then and there.

"Never mind," he said when she didn't respond immediately. "Have a nice lunch."

"Um, I will. You, too."

Rachel slowly sat staring at the cell phone before finally disconnecting from the call.

Her eye caught on the time in the display.

Ten till twelve.

Oh!

She shot from the chair. She had just enough time to primp a bit before she made that noon reservation at Georgio's, a short five-minute walk away.

She shivered again, wondering just what Gabriel had in mind....

CHAPTER FOUR

SHE'D COME...

Gabriel Bradford Wellington IV always took advantage of every opportunity thrown his way.

Then why was it that he was sitting across from two prominent New York bankers who could make or break his business plans, and all he could concentrate on was Rachel Dubois where she sat across the room from him at Georgio's?

She'd come.

He hadn't been sure she would. He'd purposely left the message on her voice mail rather than talking to her directly. Talking to her would have allowed her to do some verbal maneuvering to get out of the invite. The message...well, the message had been more suggestive. Forbidden. Harder to deny. More enticing.

Damn, but she looked good. Too good. While her suit might be on the conservative side, her cheeks were pink from the cold January wind and her hair had that windblown appearance that made her look sexy as hell.

And made him think about everything but balance sheets and financial statements and return investments.

He watched as Rachel looked over the menu, her right hand toying with the top button on her blouse. She didn't even seem to be aware of her actions as she unbuttoned one, then two of the buttons, smoothing the collar of the white blouse back so that he could see a stretch of her smooth, creamy skin.

Gabe reached for his water glass, found he had already drained it, then put it back down for the server to refill.

Rachel's mere presence in the restaurant per his request spoke volumes. He'd left his message vague so she'd had no idea whether they would be dining together or if she would be expected to sit alone. Her coming told him she'd been open to either possibility. Considering how much was on the line, her decision made him so hot for her he could concentrate on little else.

Reckless was not a word he would have used to describe business attorney and City Councilwoman Rachel Dubois, the woman he'd first seen last month sitting at the council table, her pretty face almost completely devoid of makeup, her features sober as she listened intently to her fellow council members.

Of course, the Rachel Dubois of the red dress at the black-and-white ball was someone else entirely.

And it seemed it was that Rachel who had come out to play today.

Still looking at her menu—something Gabe didn't need to do because he dined often at the critically acclaimed, upscale downtown restaurant—Rachel shifted in her chair until her legs were off to the side, hiking up her skirt in a casual way that was anything but. Gabe watched as she opened her legs just enough to give him a good look at her white panties before she slowly crossed her legs. Then she looked up from the menu straight into his eyes, setting his blood on fire.

Damn, how he wanted her.

Now. Here.

He'd designed the meeting to get her to reveal something about her feelings for him. Instead, Gabe seemed to be learning more about himself.

"But, of course," Phil Chandler was saying, "all this is for naught if that rezoning proposal is denied."

Gabe blinked and fought to refocus on his companions. Nothing wasn't being said now that hadn't been said a hundred times before. Everything rested on that council vote. He took a business card and a Mont Blanc pen out of his inside jacket pocket, jotted something down, then started to rise. "If you'll excuse me, gentlemen, there's someone I must say hello to."

He placed his napkin on his chair, straightened his tie, then strode across the room toward Rachel's table.

He waited for her eyes to widen in fear that he might join her. Instead she smiled and seemed to relax into her chair, as if hoping he might sit next to her.

And damn if Gabe didn't want to forget about his scheduled lunch meeting and take the seat opposite her. Instead he stopped, held her even, charged stare, then slid his business card onto the table in front of her.

She turned the card over and read his words. "Meet me at your place. Now."

Then Gabe grinned and moved on.

A HALF AN HOUR LATER Gabe let himself into the quiet empty old house that he'd seen more of in the past week than he had his own place. Rachel was closing the curtains in the front room, her jacket lying on the back of the sofa, her bottom round and lush and all too tempting under the simple gray skirt.

Gabe caught her from behind, reveling in her surprised gasp as he slid his palms down and over her slender hips then pressed his arousal firmly against her.

"Mmm," she intoned, instantly relaxing into him. "We have a half hour before I need to get back to a committee meeting and before the contractor returns from lunch."

He ran his tongue the length of her neck that she unwittingly exposed to him. "I was hoping for more time."

Her laugh was low and sexy. "And here five minutes would probably be enough for most men."

He almost roughly pulled her around so that she faced him, staring down darkly into her eyes. "Haven't you learned yet that I'm not like most men?"

He watched her elegant throat work around a swallow. She opened her mouth once or twice as if to speak, then merely nodded.

Gabe didn't think he'd ever seen a woman so openly, unabashedly consumed with desire. And he'd certainly seen his share. More than his share, really. And knowing that he was the one responsible for Rachel's tumultuous state sent his own need for her soaring off the charts.

It wasn't so much that he enjoyed turning the good girl bad. Instead, there seemed to be something…more about her. Something that drew him in. Made him forget who he was. Where he'd come from. What he'd done over the past decade. And just made him feel…alive somehow. Not so obsessed with his need to reclaim his family's stake in Toledo society.

She snaked her hands around to the back of his neck then lifted on her toes to kiss him. Not a tender, slow kiss. Rather a hungry, devouring one. At the same time, she rubbed against his erection in a way that made him groan.

Gabe tightened his fingers on her hips and abruptly moved her until her back was flush against the freshly painted wall. He possessively positioned his leg between hers, nudging her thighs apart, demanding that she open to him. She not only did so without hesitation, she slid her right leg up the outside of his left one, hooking her calf behind his knee. He dragged his hand up her thigh, only then realizing that she hadn't only taken off her shoes but her stockings, as well. His fingers branded her smooth flesh as he drove up her raised leg, moving the hem of her skirt ever upward until he touched her hot, swollen flesh, also blessedly bare.

He'd once believed that good girls were boring. That one time was enough to grow tired of them. And experience had shown his belief to be all too accurate. But Rachel...Rachel might be a good girl on the outside, but a very naughty girl resided inside.

He burrowed his fingers into her soft, damp curls, then with the tip of his finger, parted her burning flesh. She shuddered, her body briefly sagging against his, her mouth freezing as her eyes fluttered closed.

Sweet Jesus, had he ever had sex with a woman so wonderfully responsive? So completely into what they were doing? So sensitive to his touch?

''Please, please, please,'' she whispered, staying perfectly still, waiting for him to make the next move.

He waited a torturously long moment before simultaneously plucking her petal-soft core and sliding a finger into her dripping wet channel.

Rachel's soft moan wound around and around him, cocooning him from their surroundings, from the time of day, from everything except the need to bury himself deep inside her.

She made clear her thoughts on the matter as her

hands dove restlessly for the waist of his slacks. She'd gotten better over the past couple of nights and made quick work of his belt, button and zipper, not stopping until she cupped his throbbing, engorged length in her cool hand.

Gabe stretched his neck and gritted his teeth as she gave an experimental squeeze, then ran her fingers down the length of him and back up again.

"Condom," he rasped against her ear, nipping the flesh below it. "Back right pocket."

Her hand slid around to his backside and into his pocket. He took the condom from her and within moments he was sheathed and ready.

Gabe gazed down into her flushed face. At the way her full lips were slightly parted. At the sleepy, sexy state of her eyes as she returned his stare. At the way her breasts heaved against the white of her blouse.

Sexy.

Hot.

Utterly intoxicating.

Pushing her skirt up the rest of the way, he bared her to his gaze, taking in the wedge of tight, dark curls, the swollen flesh just beneath, the way her pink folds puckered open, inviting him in.

When Gabe was with Rachel, this moment was all he could think about. When he was away from her, it was also all he could think about. This pause of anticipation. The instant right before he thrust deep into her tight flesh, knowing that the moment after that would be even better, even sweeter than his imagination was capable of conjuring.

He slid his fingers up the backs of her thighs, then lifted her so she had no choice but to join her ankles behind his back. She made a soft sound, her back flattening against the wall as she sought purchase against the unyielding surface with her hands.

Gabe held her still then fitted the knob of his arousal against her portal. Her muscles contracted, her body readying itself to accept him. Eager, anxious, hungry for his entrance. He tilted his hips, watching as his erection breached the slick opening. It took every ounce of strength he had to slide back out rather than thrust in to the hilt. Rachel made a soft sound of objection, then gasped when he slid in again, this time a little deeper, coaxing her to open to him.

Her hands left the wall and grabbed for his shoulders. The new stability allowed her some freedom of movement. Gabe braced himself as she slid herself slowly down his length until her pubis was flush with his. Her shudder was so powerful, so complete that he could almost swear it had come from him.

He'd be damned if he didn't want to come right then. Feeling her completely encircling him, squeezing him, every inch of her trembling with desire for him, sent heat surging through his every cell. For a long moment he was completely incapable of movement. He could merely stand, supporting both of their weight, scrambling to find the self-control that seemed in such sort supply whenever he was deep inside Rachel Dubois.

She clung to him, her breathing ragged, forcing him to take on even more of her weight. He stumbled slightly, then regained his balance. Then with the shear strength of her legs she lifted herself from his throbbing shaft, then sank down again.

A growl ripped from Gabe's throat as he grasped her hips, trying to hold her still. But she wouldn't have any of it. Her teeth dragged along the edge of his ear. "Take me, Gabriel. Take me, hard."

He nearly slammed her back against the wall and drove into her like a man gone mad. And he was. Mad with lust. Mad with his inability to control himself with her. Mad at her for making him feel this way.

And oh so damn happy that she did.

He worked his hand up under her blouse, grasping her right breast almost roughly through the fabric of her bra. She gasped and he thrust deep again…then again…and again.

"Yes!" she cried, throwing her head back against the wall. "Oh, Lord, yes!"

In…and in again…deep…deeper. Gabe thrust and squeezed and grabbed until he felt his gut clench with pent-up passion. Then he grasped her hips, pulling them forward so he could drive deeper still. Somewhere in the back of his mind he was afraid he was hurting her, afraid he might bruise her, but he couldn't help himself. He slammed into her sweet, hot flesh as if there was no tomorrow. And he didn't stop until he heard the deep moans that foretold her climax. Only then did he allow himself the release his body sought like food for a starving man.

And somewhere in the shadows of his mind he knew a fear that he *was* a starving man. And that Rachel was the only food his body would accept.

MUCH LATER that same day, after they had parted then come back together again at the empty house, Rachel wrapped herself in a sheet, more to protect herself against the draughty old house than out of modesty, and collected the basket of foods she'd brought with her from the foyer.

She rejoined Gabriel where he lay stretched across the rug that lay in front of the blazing fireplace. Rachel knelt down next to Gabriel on the thick white wool, taking in the way he had his hands crossed behind the back of his neck, his eyes closed, completely comfortable with his nakedness.

And, oh, what glorious nakedness it was, too. Her chest tightened in awe as she allowed her gaze to flutter over his fine physical form down to where he was still semi-aroused, the thick flesh resting against his upper thigh.

"Open," she whispered. He began to open his eyes and she put her other hand over them. "Not your eyes. Your mouth."

"Mmm. I don't know if that's a good idea," he said, keeping his teeth together.

She laughed. "Why? Are there any allergies I should know about?"

He caught her wrist tightly in his hand, making her gasp at the sudden roughness of the move. "No. But I do think you should know that I'm not very good at surprises."

If her heart-pounding reaction to his quick move was any indication, she wasn't very good at surprises herself.

He opened his mouth. Her hand shaking, she carefully lay a square of sharp cheddar cheese against his tongue. "Okay, you, um, can close now."

He did. And slowly began chewing. "Mmm. Cheddar."

She shifted on the soft, white wool rug, trying to shake the shadow of uneasiness caused by his forceful move. If she were honest with herself, the shadow seemed to be a constant presence between them. Gabriel could by turns be breathtakingly seductive and gently coaxing. He could also be dark and demanding in a way that she admitted sometimes intrigued her, other times almost frightened her.

She'd never known a man to be as fierce as he was. So passionate.

"That was an easy one." She forced herself to lighten up as she caught him peeking at her through cracked eyelids. "Am I going to have to blindfold you, Mr. Wellington?"

He finished eating the cheddar then grinned at her wickedly. "You'd do so at your own peril."

She shivered straight down to her bones. "Close your eyes again."

He did so and she slipped a slice of kiwi between his teeth.

He correctly guessed the fruit and the next five things she fed him. Then she gasped when he grasped both her wrists and flipped her over until she was lying flat on her back.

"My turn."

Every inch of her skin quivered at the prospect. "You forget, I packed the food so I already know what's there."

"Yeah, but you don't know how I intend to feed it to you."

Rachel's womb contracted in anticipation while he reached over to pick up something from the nearby sofa. She realized it was his tie and he was moving it toward her eyes.

The breath rushed from her lungs. "I don't..."

"Shh. I let you have your way with me."

Rachel lifted her head so he could tie the material in the back. "For a whole two seconds."

She felt his tongue move over her right nipple, causing her to shiver in anticipation. "You wanted more?"

"Yes," she whispered, admitting that there was an even darker side of herself that wanted him to be fierce. Wanted him to possess her. Take her. Claim her as his own.

She waited for something from the basket she'd prepared to be placed against her lips. Instead she felt something cold and wet touch her right nipple. Her back arched up off the rug and a soft sound exited her mouth. Gabriel swirled his tongue around and around the ultra-sensitive tip then took it deep into his mouth. Rachel could have sworn her moan had come from somewhere else. Somewhere deep inside her. A place she wasn't familiar with. A place she wanted to explore and examine and visit for a long, sweet while.

Gabriel's fingers cupped her breast from underneath then lifted it high on her chest. Then he was kissing her mouth. Slowly, hotly, coaxing her head forward in order to keep contact with his mouth. He pulled slightly away, alternating between her mouth and her nipple. He hesitated slightly and she felt him drizzle something over her breast. Then he was kissing her again. He switched his attention to her breast then came back to her mouth. She tasted the thick, sweet essence of honey there. He cupped her breast again and lifted it until Rachel discovered she was licking her own nipple with the very tip of her tongue.

Gabriel's fierce groan indicated that he liked watching her. Liked watching her very much.

Rachel strained her hips against his, trying to force a more intimate contact. Her anticipation grew when he slid his hand between them and parted her thighs. Then he sank into her in one, long stroke, filling her to overflowing and taking her straight to the brink and beyond. Chasing away all her concerns and shattering her reservations.

For now…

CHAPTER FIVE

THE FOLLOWING DAY at his office on the top floor of the towering glass Owens-Illinois building, Gabe signed off on five letters of correspondence he'd had Gloria type up, read through a sixty-page contract, then put it all off to the side of his desk and leaned back in his chair. But he didn't see the expensive, carefully selected antiques the decorator he'd hired had filled the large office with. He didn't see the two burgundy leather couches, the mammoth desk he sat behind, or even the view of the Maumee River thirty floors below his floor-to-ceiling windows. All he seemed capable of concentrating on was the memory of Rachel's exquisite face flushed with passion. The way her back arched when he touched her. The soft sounds she made when he first entered her.

He absently rubbed his closed eyelids. He'd been working nonstop since seven that morning. He'd been so consumed by his need to regain his family's standing in Toledo for so long, the mere suggestion that someone was capable of distracting him seemed impossible. But there she was, Rachel, forever on the fringes of his thoughts, waiting for the opportunity to rob him of his concentration and strip him of the ironclad control he'd always had over himself and his life.

A simple one-night stand. That's all he'd been looking for when he'd asked her to dance...was that really only four days ago? A few hours of escapist sex to help take the edge off his negotiations with his New York business partners.

Now his business partners and Toledo zoning laws were the furthest things from his mind.

Instead, he kept looking at his watch, wishing the minutes to tick by faster until the time he could lose himself in Rachel's sweet flesh again.

To him, sex had always been just sex. A physical need that could be satisfied with anyone who caught his eye. In fact, the words "making love" seemed so incongruous to him that he'd never used them. He was the only child of parents that had died together ten years ago. Since their death, he'd been so driven by his ambitions, he supposed he hadn't given himself time to see if there was something behind the words.

Then again, he hadn't exactly given himself

time now, either. Not when everything he had worked so hard for was within his grasp. Rather, Rachel had *stolen* the time.

A knock on the door, then his executive assistant stepped in, her hands full of files and correspondence and message slips. "Shall I order in lunch?" she asked.

Gabe glanced at his watch, surprised to find it was half past two. But rather than remember the last thing he ate, he wondered what Rachel was doing at that moment.

He dry washed his face with his hands. "No. Just bring me some coffee if you get a chance."

Silence.

Gabe dropped his hands on his desktop and looked at his fiftyish executive assistant. He'd brought her with him from L.A. He'd liked her on the spot because she didn't even blink in the face of his most brooding stares. Never flinched on those few occasions when he was in a foul mood and barked at her. And she ran his office like a well-loved car.

She'd worked for him...

"Gloria, how long have you worked for me?"

She regarded him carefully. "Long enough to know that something's bothering you."

He didn't answer.

"Eight years."

He nodded. Eight years. Yes. He remembered now. He'd had that dusty old office on Wilshire Boulevard and Gloria had been the first person not to blink when he told her there'd be no medical and she'd sometimes be required to work twelve-hour days with no overtime.

Last month he'd given her a six-figure Christmas bonus.

"Do you want to talk about it?" she asked, her gaze steady.

Gabe raised a brow. Sure, he knew Gloria had three kids, four grandkids and that her youngest son had just announced that he was gay. But most of that information he'd found out by overhearing various phone conversations over the years and by the pictures she kept and changed every now and again on her desk. Casual conversations between them were kept to a minimum. He knew about her youngest because she'd simply told him she had to take a Friday off to fly back to California to attend some sort of "Help, my child's gay and I don't know how to handle it" type of counseling. Her words, not his. And she hadn't expected a response, either. Not that he would have given her one.

He distantly wondered what kind of counseling his parents would have gone to with him had they lived to see just exactly how he'd gone about regaining the family fortune.

Gabe squinted at Gloria. Had she ever guessed at how he'd acquired his initial startup money? He didn't know. If she did, what did she think of him? Both then and now?

He absently rubbed his chin. Had they ever shared a meal together that didn't include work? Had he ever been to her house? Did he even know where she lived without having to refer to her employee file?

He got up from his chair and shrugged into his jacket. "Have lunch with me, Gloria."

She blinked at him. "Pardon me?"

He cracked a grin. "Grab your purse and coat. I'm taking you out to lunch. Oh, and leave your steno pad behind."

She blinked as if he were speaking a foreign language. "I'm not sure I'm following you."

He rounded the desk, took her arm then steered her from the office. "I'm asking you to have lunch with me like two normal people would, Gloria. What's to understand?"

She seemed dazed and more than a little confused.

"Okay," he said, stopping beside her desk. "Have lunch with me, Gloria, or you're fired."

She smiled at him. "Just let me get my coat…"

The telephone began ringing. Gloria made a move to get it.

Gabe halted her with a hand. "Let me do the honors."

He picked up the receiver, about to tell the caller to call back later when a familiar voice came over the line.

"Well, well, well. If it isn't Mr. Important picking up his own phone."

A familiar coldness took hold of Gabe as he identified the voice. He had been expecting this call, although he had hoped that it would be a face-to-face meeting.

"Lance," he said calmly. "I'd really like to talk to you, but I'm on my way out to lunch with my executive assistant. You'll have to call back."

And with that he hung up the receiver on the man he intended to make pay for destroying his life.

He turned back to face Gloria's shocked expression then held his arm out with a smile. "Shall we?"

"DRESS UP. We're going out."

Two days later, Rachel shivered when she retrieved Gabriel's message from her voice mail just as the regularly scheduled council meeting was drawing to a close. Going out. As in public. As in let the world know what was going on between them. They wouldn't be having lunch at separate tables. Rather they would be going out as a couple. Together.

She was helpless to stop her mouth from smiling, her nipples from tingling and her thighs from quivering at the thought of shouting to Toledo and the world at large how she felt about Gabriel Wellington IV.

She glanced around at her fellow city council members. Did each of them have their own Gabriel waiting at home or by the phone or out there somewhere planning a special night just for the two of them? Did all of them know what it felt like to be truly loved by another? To have a person who rocked your world down to the foundation, turned black to white, and made you forget your name with one skillful touch?

Loved…

She slid her cell phone back into her briefcase and gathered up the papers in front of her. Yes, she full-heartedly admitted, she loved Gabriel. Had fallen in love with him the instant he'd extended his hand to her and asked her to dance.

And what a dance it was turning out to be.

Rather than ending on that ballroom floor, the dance they'd indulged in kept going on and on. Each of them showing the other new steps. Alternately leading then following. She'd shared parts of herself with Gabriel that she'd shared with no one else. Bared her soul in a way that should have left her feeling naked and vulnerable but rather made her feel sexy, safe and loved.

Loved…

There was that word again.

Did Gabriel love her? Or was it far too soon for him to recognize his own emotions?

She tucked her short hair behind her ear. Of course, she'd be the first to admit that their relationship could very well be one-sided. More specifically, on her side. But while the possibility existed, that's not what her heart told her. Her heart whispered that the expression on his face when he looked at her, when he touched her, when he shared his body with her could be caused by nothing else but love.

And now he wanted to make it public.

Janet gave her a shoulder a squeeze as she got up. "Well, I guess that's that."

Rachel blinked at her. Yes, she thought with a mental smile, that definitely was it. She loved Gabriel.

And she couldn't wait to tell him….

NOT THE RED DRESS. No. But something even better. Something more Rachel. And sexier than Gabe could have put together in his fantasies.

"Is something the matter?" Rachel asked after she'd slid into his vintage Jaguar and he'd closed the door and rounded to climb into the driver's seat. Gabe hadn't realized he'd been staring until that moment.

He fought the urge to pull at his bow tie. "No," he said, reaching over to skim the back of his index finger over the side of her exposed neck. "Everything's perfect."

And it was. Oh, the close-fitting black, crystal-covered dress Rachel wore looked respectable enough. And probably would have fit in fine at the black-and-white ball last weekend. But not everyone would see what he did. Namely that when the light hit it just right—as the setting sun was hitting it now—it was completely sheer. His mouth watered with the desire to put his mouth over the faint outline of her right nipple. And his eye kept pulling to where the material bunched in her lap to cover where he suspected she wore absolutely nothing underneath.

His intention to take her to the Valentine Theater where the Toledo Opera was performing nearly flew straight out the window. Instead he wanted to pull onto a darkened street and explore all the many ways the dress didn't cover her…and uncover her even more.

"Something is wrong," Rachel said when she caught him staring again.

Gabe looked into her big, beautiful, hazel eyes rimmed with charcoal and felt something give in his chest. It was as though a dam had broken against the powerful current pressing against it. He recognized the resulting pounding waves within him for what they were: his feelings for this one woman he could no longer deny.

He skimmed his finger down her soft cashmere wrap to her hand, then lifted her palm to his mouth. He placed a soft kiss there then ran his tongue the length of it, taking in her shiver. "Everything's just right, Rachel."

He knew the exact moment when he'd decided that what was happening between him and the woman beside him was something more than just sex. It had occurred while he was sitting across from Gloria at Georgio's and she had asked him if his change in temperament had to do with a woman. And he hadn't hesitated when he'd told her yes. Not only that but he'd gone on to tell her all about Rachel. How she made him feel. How he thought about her every single minute of every day. How even at that moment he longed to be with her.

Gloria had smiled, telling him something that he hadn't realized until that very moment.

He loved Rachel.

"Let's go, shall we?" he asked.

Rachel smiled. "Are you going to tell me where we're going?"

To heaven and beyond, he wanted to say. "You'll just have to wait and see."

She softly cleared her throat. "I'm not very big on surprises."

He remembered saying the same thing to her the other day. "I think you'll like this one."

Of course there were some other things that she probably wouldn't like about him. Namely his past. But he wasn't going to think about that now. The past was the past and Rachel was his future. If his not telling her was a sin, it was the sin of omission. And he was ready to face the consequences when and if she ever found out.

Until then, he was going to make her fall as deeply in love with him as possible.

He shifted the car into gear then pulled away from the curb outside her house.

THE OPERA...

Rachel hurried to the powder room at intermission, more to recompose herself after the Toledo Opera's rendition of La Bohème than due to any real basic need. While she'd enjoyed operas since she was six and her father had taken her to see Les Misérables, she had never felt as moved as she had while sitting next to Gabriel in the restored balcony of the Valentine Theater. She supposed her own raw emotions for him might be to blame. Or that she now understood the depth of the love the heroine sang about. Whatever the reason, she felt so completely stripped of any semblance of self-control that she needed a few precious moments to herself before she rejoined Gabriel in the lobby.

The well-appointed room was already filled with other women by the time she entered. She recognized a great many of them and chatted about the performance until a spot opened up in front of the mirror. She checked her mascara and began to apply more lipstick when fellow councilwoman Janet McClellan took the spot next to her with another woman she didn't recognize.

Rachel smiled at her. "Enjoying the performance, Janet?"

"Oh, very. Have you met Catherine? She's a friend visiting from California."

Rachel regarded the other woman amiably. "No, I don't believe I have."

Something they remedied with a quick, polite shake of gloved hands.

Rachel leaned forward to separate a lash.

"Is that Gabe Wellington you're with?" the new acquaintance asked.

"Do you know him?"

The woman's eyes twinkled in a way that Rachel wasn't all too sure she liked, but couldn't say why. Old enough to be her mother, she looked as though she'd gone under a cosmetic surgeon's knife more than once. The skin on her face was a little too tight, her forehead a little too… unwrinkled. "Oh, I'd definitely say I know him." She glanced at Janet who had moved away to allow someone else access to the mirror. Catherine moved closer, making Rachel leery of her sudden friendliness.

"So, tell me, have his prices dropped now that he's in Ohio?"

Rachel blinked at her. "Pardon me?"

Catherine laughed. "I'm talking about Gabe's services, dear. Very skillful, that one. And worth every penny."

Rachel found it suddenly impossible to breathe.

This woman wasn't saying…she couldn't possibly be inferring…

"You don't know what you're talking about."

Catherine looked her up and down. "Well, maybe I'm wrong about you. But I definitely know what I'm talking about when it comes to Gabe."

She squinted at her. "Oh, dear. You didn't know, did you?"

"Know what?" Janet asked, coming to stand next to them.

Rachel held Catherine's curious gaze. "Nothing. Maybe you're right, Rachel. Maybe I'm wrong about everything."

Unfortunately Rachel had the sinking sensation that she was very, very right.

She realized then that she'd never asked Gabriel how he'd regained his family's wealth. She'd just assumed he'd gone about it in the usual way. Only that's not what had happened, was it? The way Gabriel had regained his family fortune was by doing favors for wealthy women. Favors that commanded a high price and probably had nothing to do with lawn work.

She all but ran for the door.

CHAPTER SIX

SOMETHING WAS DIFFERENT. Gabe couldn't put his finger on it, but all through the late dinner he'd arranged following the opera, Rachel had seemed somehow more distant. Inaccessible to him. And his reaction was to pull back from her.

After dinner, he'd taken her to his place for the first time. His houseman, Arthur, had had champagne and strawberries waiting for them in the atrium looking over the lighted back garden and Rachel had seemed impressed but reserved during their brief tour through the house he had grown up in, his father had lost, and that he had bought back and restored to the way he remembered it.

And now, as he lay her across his king-size antique sleigh bed, he was filled with a fierce urge to break through the barrier she'd erected between them. Destroy it, force her to give in to his will, offer herself up to him in all the ways that mattered.

She stared up at him. The passion was there in her beautiful face. But so was an inexplicable sadness, a question she couldn't seem to bring herself to ask.

As the scent of sandalwood and of her warm skin filled his nose, he lowered his mouth to hers and began his seduction with a deep kiss. No touching. No caressing. Just a soft plundering that molded his mouth to hers, his tongue sliding between her lips, tempting it to come out to play. She relaxed into the burgundy-colored luxurious bedding, threading her fingers through his hair almost roughly, curving her naked body up against his. With his eyes closed, it was almost easy to imagine that nothing had changed between them. Almost. If not for the slight hesitancy in her movements.

Gabe put his hand between them and stayed her with his fingers against her upper torso even as he stared deep into her eyes. He tried to uncover what lay there, in the depths of her dark pupils, see what she was hiding from him, what kept her from connecting to him the way he desperately needed her to do. He edged his hand down her smooth skin until he could curl his fingers into the soft wedge of hair between her thighs and watched as her eyelids fluttered closed and her neck arched so she could take in more air.

Physically, he had her. But emotionally…

Gabe clenched his jaw, sheer determination to dominate her entirely surging through his veins. He dropped his head to her neck and licked her there at the same time he lightly pinched the bit of flesh between her legs. She automatically opened to him and he slid his index finger into her channel, finding her hot but dry. Something he intended to remedy posthaste. He made his way back up to her bud and circled it as he continued licking his way up to her ear.

Come to me, Rachel, he silently commanded her. *Give yourself to me.*

He returned to her entrance, finding her wetness growing. Without preamble, he thrust two fingers up deep inside her and twisted them. Her breath hitched and her back arched up off the mattress, her juices instantly dripping around his fingers.

That's more like it, baby. Give it to me.

He withdrew his hand and rubbed his thumb against the wetness, then thrust his fingers deep inside the tight, wet aperture again, pressing the pad of his thumb against the puckered skin between her buttocks, not breaching the entry, merely causing a different kind of chaos to shudder through her body.

Rachel gasped then shied away from his bold, forbidden touch. He moved his thumb away and concentrated on the careful movements of his fingers, twisting and thrusting them up deep inside her. She moaned and he pressed against the forbidden entryway again, satisfied when she didn't move away. If anything she seemed to strain against him, as if tempting entry.

Yes...

Gabe's blood thickened, making his heart beat faster to keep it flowing through his body. He ran his other hand the length of her smooth body...down the side of her neck...between her breasts...down over her flat stomach... Then he pressed the heel against her damp curls and felt the movements of his fingers inside her.

In one swift movement he rolled her over to lie on her stomach. She gasped, then moaned, instantly, hungrily offering her sweet, rounded bottom up to him, her fingers fisting into his Egyptian cotton sheets. Gabe studied her flushed profile. The way her lids drooped over her glassy eyes. Her lips had bowed open, taking in quick breaths. Damp tendrils of her cinnamon-brown short hair lay plastered against her cheek.

He positioned his knees shoulder-width apart then grasped her hips, his fingers making indentations in her soft flesh. He lifted her up and back until her sex rested solidly against his rock-hard arousal. Her womanhood was swollen and hot and wet.

He quickly sheathed himself then penetrated her wetness, holding her still when she bore down, attempting to take more of him in. He withdrew, then ran his arousal along her engorged flesh, back and forth, before entering her again, this time a little deeper. Her deep moan made him shudder and pushed him closer to the point when he'd lose that all important control he was counting on to break through all her barriers tonight.

He withdrew again, smoothing a hand over her bottom then following the shallow crevice of her bottom with his thumb. She whimpered and tried to grind against him. He thrust again, this time to the hilt, filling her deeply. She gasped, her exquisite body quivering from head to toe.

"Oh, please, Gabriel…" she said, her voice sounding suspiciously close to tears. "Please take me."

He leaned forward until his chest rested against her back and his mouth touched the sensitive shell of her ears. "Give yourself to me, Rachel."

He heard her thick swallow. "I'm yours, Gabriel. All yours."

He closed his eyes, breathing in the scent of her perfume mixed with her own unique musk. *No, baby, you're not. But you will be…*

He pulled himself upright again and positioned himself just so before hauling her sex fully against his. As he knew she would, she ground against him, his turgid flesh deep inside her as she rubbed her sex against his scrotum. He ran his hand up her side and her arm, then gently took her hand, moving it so it was reaching between her thighs. Then he curved her fingers around his swollen sac and pressed them to where they were still connected. She moaned at the feel of the crisp hair of his sac making contact with her sensitive nub. He released his grip then allowed her the freedom to explore. She caressed and squeezed him then pressed him harder against her, her quivering growing more pronounced, her juices flowing freely around his erection and out to cover them both.

He tilted his hips forward and she moaned. Then he withdrew and drove home again, watching her arch her back even farther, take her hand away from him and clutch the sheets again.

Yes, that's it...

He thrust into her hard and deep...again and again... Her breathing grew more labored. Her body shook all over. He wanted to bring her a pleasure that she would never forget. That would claim her as his for eternity.

The force of his need to do that surprised Gabe. He'd never felt the desire to possess someone in the way he longed to possess Rachel. Always confident in his ability to seduce someone physically, now he was afraid he'd never be able to do it emotionally. Never convince someone to love him.

The thought caught him off guard. But no more than Rachel's bold and telling movement as she pressed against him, reminding him of the dereliction of his duties. Indicating her willingness to be taken in any way he wanted.

His hips jerked forward, as if on their own accord, and he slowly, very slowly, entered her again, dragging out the sensation of filling her. She gasped then held very still. He withdrew, listening to her ragged breathing, her deep swallows. Then he groaned when she pressed against him again, indicating she wanted more.

And more was what he gave her.

With the skill of a master in his element, he introduced her to a whole new world of vivid sensation. There was no feral thrusting now. No. He handled her gently, carefully, using a restraint he rarely tapped into to amplify her pleasure. He slowly expanded her muscles, inch by torturous inch. And when he finally had moved in to the hilt, she cried out, her beautiful body dissolving into an endless series of contractions and spasms and deep, soulful moans.

And Gabe followed right after her.

RACHEL HAD NEVER FELT so exposed...so vulnerable...so utterly at someone else's mercy. And coming on the tail of what she'd learned about Gabriel earlier, it made the moment all the more emotional. One minute she was soaring higher than she ever had before...the next she was so low she was half afraid she'd never find her way back to solid ground.

Raw emotion balled up in her chest, turning and twisting like razor wire until she couldn't help the ragged sob that ripped from her throat. Gabriel still lay against her back, his hands holding her gently, possessively. Everywhere she looked, he surrounded her. He'd even breached the delicate walls of her heart, slashing them to shreds.

He stirred and she sensed him looking at her profile. She closed her eyes tighter and tried to turn her head away, wipe the tears sliding out from under her eyelids onto the soft sheets beneath her cheek, but he stayed her with a hand on her hair.

"Rachel?" His gravelly voice filled her ear.

She caught her bottom lip between her teeth and bit down hard, trying to staunch the flow of her tears. She only succeeded in making them more intense and another sob filled her mouth.

Gabriel rolled from her and gathered her up in his arms. He didn't ask if he'd hurt her. Didn't presume that there was something he could say to soothe her. He merely held her. His hands smoothed over her hair and face where she rested against his bare chest, then down over her back.

She'd never felt so loved.

She'd never felt so much despair.

"Is it true?"

Rachel hadn't been sure she'd said the words aloud until Gabriel's hands stilled against her skin, his relaxed posture stiffening a bit. Not in a way that anyone else might notice, but Rachel did.

She wiped the dampness from her cheeks with her open palms then looked up at him, though the tears had yet to stop. "Is it true you used to be a…"

His eyes seemed overly dark in the wholly male room, the heaviness of rich walnut paneling and the burgundy and brown color schemes relieved only by the white candles flickering on the bedside table. "A what, Rachel?"

She sensed that he knew exactly what she was talking about but was going to make her say the words. "A…male escort."

The upturning of his lips wasn't so much kind as it was cynical. "That's one way of putting it," he said. He stroked his index finger down the side of her face then seemed to absently consider the wetness transferred there. "Gigolo would be more accurate."

Rachel searched his stern, handsome face for a sign of remorse. Of regret. She came away wanting.

She moved to roll away but he held her fast.

She snapped her head back to him abruptly. "Why didn't you tell me?"

His eyes narrowed. "When would you have

had me say it, Rachel? During our dance at the ball? Or mention it casually during one of our many rendezvous?"

She winced at his blatant sarcasm.

She lay there for a long time, desperately trying to get a handle on the situation. Trying to deal with the tumultuous emotions roiling through her.

"Why?" she whispered. "Please, make me understand."

He didn't respond for a long moment. Didn't move. Didn't make a sound. Then, finally, "Make you understand what, Rachel? Something I did in the long-ago past? Why? So you can take away my Mr. America title?"

She tried to pull away again, and he again prevented her from doing so, this time more roughly than she was comfortable with.

"I've never had to explain my actions to anyone, Rachel."

"I need you to explain them to me. I need to…"

"Understand," he said simply.

She nodded.

He released his grip on her and she rested her cheek against his chest again, freeing herself from the fierce darkness in his eyes.

"Tell me what it is that you want me to help you understand, Rachel," he whispered harshly. "Why my parents instilled in me a history of family, of success, of wealth...then left me unprepared for the sharks that would come feed on all of it when they died?" She shivered, swearing she felt his body temperature drop. "Why not one of my family's supposed friends stepped up to lend a helping hand? Why the only job I could get in my own hometown, despite an Ivy League education, was that of short-order cook? Why I didn't have enough money to start up my own venture and my own friends turned their backs on me? Why I felt the only way I could regain everything my parents lost was by leaving the only place I'd known as home?"

Rachel swallowed hard, her ears hearing the words, and her heart responding to the emotion behind them. The vehemence. The bitterness. The hurt.

"The day after every last one of my parents' belongings—this house, the business, the heirlooms—were auctioned off to satisfy their debts, I hitched my way out of town. I didn't stop until there was no more road to travel. And with no work, no money for a room, I didn't know what I was going to do...."

The image of a handsome young man still grieving for his parents, losing everything he'd ever known in his life then heading out into the big unknown made Rachel's chest ache.

"But..." she whispered. "Why did you do what you did?"

"Say it, Rachel," he said sharply. "Gigolo. I was a gigolo."

She shook her head, unable to say the word.

He laughed humorlessly. "Trust me, it's not something I planned on. No child grows up thinking, 'Gee, I think I'll prostitute myself for money.' He rested his chin on top of her head. "There I was, standing on Long Beach staring at the Pacific Ocean and half wondering if I should just throw myself in it when destiny drove up by way of a vintage Bentley." His voice dropped to a murmur. "The woman in the back was older, attractive. I was fresh out of ideas and her dinner invitation seemed like as good an offer as any I'd had for a long while." He fell briefly silent. "Even though she was a good decade older than me, she was beautiful. And kind. She took me back to her place where I showered and enjoyed her company. Then the following morning I found the money she'd left on the table—a lot of it—along with a note asking me to call her. She wanted me to escort her somewhere that weekend.''

Rachel tried to envision it. The type of man who would accept money. The type of woman who would offer it. Both images were so outside anything she'd ever known.

''I didn't take the money the first time. But I did the second. And every time after that.''

Silence. Then, ''You judge me badly for taking it? The money that got me off the streets and into an apartment? The friendship I developed with the woman and other women like her?''

Rachel squeezed her eyes tightly shut. ''I don't know what I think. But I know how I feel. Hurt. And betrayed.''

He ran his hand over her short hair, his movements light, feathery. Experienced.

She decided she no longer liked that word.

''Then you know how many of those women I became friends with felt. Betrayed. By their husbands.''

She shifted her head to squint up at him in the candlelight.

He smiled at her softly. ''You see the type all the time, Rachel. The ballroom was filled with them the other night.''

Her stomach tightened. "What?" she whispered.

"That's right. The women I dated were usually long married to philandering husbands who had probably already had mistresses set up before they married their wives."

"So that makes what you did okay?"

He shook his head, his gaze shifting over her face. "You asked me to help you understand. You're not hearing me, Rachel. My arrangement wasn't about sex. It was about companionship. But mostly it was about power. These women had felt so powerless in their relationships for so long that they needed to feel in control of something. And giving me money for my company gave them that." She watched him rest his head against the backboard of the bed. "If not, I'd have gladly dated them for free."

She swallowed hard. "You say dated..."

He nodded as he closed his eyes. "That's how I viewed it. I was never with different women at the same time. And I didn't date outside seeing them. So it was dating."

"With benefits."

He cracked his eyelids open, staring at her. "With benefits that allowed me to begin my trek back. Gave me the capital I needed to restart

G.B. Wellington out in L.A., then build it up again until I could come back here in the same position my family had been before I lost my parents. Back to where I am right now.''

Rachel considered him for a long time. While what he'd said wasn't what she'd expected, she still felt somehow betrayed. ''And where are you now, Gabriel?'' she asked, not really expecting an answer.

And he said nothing. Then the bed squeaked and the bedding rustled as he moved out of her arms. Rachel let him go.

''One more question,'' she said, pulling the top sheet up to cover her breasts.

He sat on the side of the bed, his back wonderfully muscled, his physical presence so appealing and irresistible.

And not so long ago, much in demand.

He turned his head so she could see his profile. ''What?''

''Did you sleep with me with an agenda in mind?''

Every cell in her body throbbed with fear and pain as she waited for his answer.

He shifted until he could look into her face. ''No,'' he said, simply, strongly.

Rachel couldn't look at him anymore,

couldn't be sure of her own feelings for him, wasn't convinced she could trust him with them. "Are you sure? Because if you had, you got what you wanted. Council voted to pass your bid to rezone."

He reached out for her but she moved farther away to prevent the contact, another sob crowding her throat.

"And I'll have you know that as much as I was against it, I voted for it."

She finally dared meet his gaze. "The only problem is now I'm questioning why."

Rachel dropped her chin to her bare chest and stared at where her hands clutched the sheet to her breasts, as if she was no longer comfortable being naked in front of him.

"The past has no power over you but what you let it have, Rachel," he murmured. "I learned that quickly. I learned that the hard way."

Silence.

"Now, it's my turn to ask you a question," he said.

She waited without looking at him.

His voice was soft yet held a hard edge. "Why did you come back home with me tonight if what I did ten years ago bothers you so much?''

Rachel's lungs suddenly refused to take in air. ''I don't know,'' she whispered, barely hearing the words herself over the pounding of her heart.

He gripped her chin in his fingers, forcing her to look up at him even though she tried to turn away. ''Maybe that's something you should find the answer to.''

He withdrew his hand then got up, walking toward the connecting bathroom without putting anything on. Rachel watched him go. Thinking of how much everything had changed in one heartbeat. Thinking of her father and what news like this might mean to his bid for Ohio Supreme Court Justice. Thinking of her sister and the trouble she'd gotten into and the trouble Rachel had sworn she would never get herself into.

Gabriel paused briefly at the door. ''I think you'd better go now, Rachel.''

She blinked, watching as he entered the bathroom then closed the door behind him.

CHAPTER SEVEN

THREE DAYS LATER Rachel sat listlessly at the kitchen table in her father's house, toying with the toothpicks that sat in a crystal holder in front of her, watching as the winter sun set over the back lawn. Barely five o'clock and soon it would be pitch-black outside. Surely somewhere it was still daylight. Australia, her mind provided. Yes, in Australia it was summer. And the water went down the drain counterclockwise. And they had kangaroos and koalas.

She frowned at the ridiculous direction of her thoughts, then found them unbiddingly circling back to the person who had caused her lethargic state. The large house was quiet. The bagels left over from the previous day's awkward family brunch untouched on the counter. She'd eaten little over the past two days and supposed she should try to force something down now. But she couldn't seem to scare up the energy to do more than play with the toothpicks she had just dumped out of the holder and absently begun stacking.

Betrayed. That's how she felt. Betrayed and hurt and…used. Gabriel had played her body like a finely tuned instrument toward an end that she hadn't seen coming. Sure, she'd considered what others might think of her dating him given his zoning petition. That they might see him as a man who'd sell himself for favors. But she'd never thought that their musings might be the truth.

As for his skills in the bedroom…

She squeezed her eyes shut. She'd been so busy responding to his touch, giving herself over to the myriad sensations he presented to her like a gift, she'd never stopped to think that he was so good at what he did because he'd once done it for a living.

And what had he said about the women at the ball the night they'd met? That they were like the women he had "dated"? She swallowed hard, wondering if he'd been…hired by anyone she knew.

She thought of her father and a soft sound pushed from her throat.

How many others knew about how Gabriel had gone about regaining his family's fortune?

Was she the last in Toledo to know about his shadowy past? Or was she the first? And did it really matter when all was said and done? Scandalous skeletons like that had a way of springing out when you least wanted them to. And with her father running for a seat in the Ohio State Supreme Court, closed closet doors that might spring open at any time were something no nominee wanted to deal with.

The cell phone at her elbow vibrated against the tabletop. She cracked her eyes open to stare at it, then automatically picked it up.

She answered, disappointed when Lance Harkin said hello. "Oh, hi, Lance. This really isn't a good time for me."

They may have dated on and off for the past year, but when she'd met Gabriel she'd understood what had been lacking between her and Lance. Essentially any chemistry whatsoever. She didn't see his mouth and long to kiss it. She didn't stare at his hands and wish they would touch her. She didn't find it difficult to breathe just being in the same room with him.

Her heart didn't ache when she knew she couldn't see him again.

"Definitely not the reaction I was hoping for," Lance said dryly.

"Sorry, that's the only one I can give you right now."

A heartbeat of silence, then, "Rachel, you and I have to talk."

She closed her eyes and absently rubbed her forehead. She'd always hated when people said that. Why not just cut the drama and come out with it?

"Forget that Gabriel Wellington has the power to sink not only your, but your father's political ambitions, he's only using you to get back at me and my family."

Her eyes flew open. "What?" she whispered.

"You heard me. You made a mistake by going out in public with him last weekend. A very grave mistake that could end up costing your father his judgeship. And you public humiliation."

Rachel squinted at the table in front of her but really didn't see it. She'd never known Lance to be a spiteful man. He'd always been kind and courteous. Which made the words he was uttering now all the more difficult to comprehend. "Lance, you and I only went out occasionally. It's not like I betrayed you in some manner."

A humorless laugh. "You think this is about

us, Rachel? Like you said, there never was an 'us.'"

She grew even more confused. If this wasn't about them, then what was it about?

"I'm sorry, Lance, but I really have to go."

She heard him begin to object but she'd quickly pushed the disconnect button. She sat for a long while with the receiver pressed against her chest, trying to make sense out of his words. She was so deep in thought that she didn't immediately hear the quick knock on the front door

The door opened, then Leah's voice disturbed the silence. "Anyone home?"

Despite the relief she felt at the visitor being her sister, it seemed to take every ounce of energy for Rachel to say, "Back here."

Moments later Leah swept into the room wearing a soft, formfitting cashmere dress and supple black suede boots. The subtle scent of gardenias filled the room as she put her camel hair coat, purse and the suit she'd borrowed, freshly dry-cleaned and wrapped in plastic, on the chair next to Rachel. "Where's Dad?"

"In Columbus."

"Oh, I forgot he was going down there this week. Wheeling and dealing his way into Columbus politics."

Rachel stared at her sister. Leah and their father had discussed the trip at great length at brunch yesterday, filling in the silence left by Rachel's preoccupation.

"Okay, I hadn't forgotten. I came to see you," Leah admitted with a heavy sigh. "Have you eaten anything yet?"

The toothpicks that Rachel had been making a small teepee out of collapsed to the table. "Don't you have a family you should be feeding?"

Leah blinked at her. "Yes. You." She waved her hand as she took things out of the refrigerator, tucking items under her other arm then grabbing the plate of bagels. "Dan took Sami to his parents' for dinner. The monthly Monday night get-together."

"Shouldn't you be with them?"

Leah made a face as she put lox and cream cheese and strawberries alongside the bagels on the kitchen table. "Our counselor thinks it's a good idea if we take this reconciliation thing one step at a time."

Leah stared at the suit, having forgotten why her sister had needed it in the first place in the face of her own dilemma. "How did the first session go?"

Leah sat down gracefully. She never plopped, as Rachel was known to do on occasion. She shrugged as she uncovered the bagels and began halving them. "As well as can be expected, I guess. Dan was only twenty minutes late." She smiled, her brown eyes twinkling. "That gave me time to prime the counselor to my point of view."

She skillfully creamed and loxed a bagel half then handed it to Rachel. Rachel took it automatically, dragging her finger through the cream cheese then sticking it into her mouth. "Doesn't that defeat the purpose?"

"Depends on which purpose you're talking about." She took a small bite out of her own plain bagel. "Anyway, my life is consumed with all this reconciliation stuff and I'd just as soon not talk about it right now. I came over here to find out who's to blame for your lovesick condition."

Rachel abruptly stopped chewing. "What?"

Leah eyed her. "You know, that's the problem with love. You're so caught up in it that you don't realize that other people are noticing your condition."

"Are you talking about your own situation?"

Leah visibly winced. "Ouch." She shrugged

again and put her bagel half down. "Let's just say that I know this from personal experience."

Rachel stared at her own bagel, surprised to find it almost gone when she couldn't remember eating any of it. Had it really only been a year ago when she'd noticed her sister's edginess? Her distracted state? Then guessed at her having an extramarital affair?

"So who is he?" Leah pressed. "Have you finally fallen for Lance?"

Rachel nearly choked on the last bite of bagel. She accepted the glass of iced tea her sister handed her.

"Not Lance then," Leah said when Rachel's coughing fit ceased.

"Not Lance." The mention of the man's name brought back his disturbing words.

"Anyone I know?"

"Hmm?" Rachel's shoulders sagged. "I don't know."

"Well, how are we supposed to find out if I know if you don't tell me who it is?"

"Oh, Leah. It's all such a non-issue now."

"It's not if you're sitting here building toothpick houses."

"They're teepees."

"Okay, whatever." She handed her another bagel half.

"And my mood is because it is such a non-issue. It…whatever it was…is over."

"Ah."

Rachel felt the uncharacteristic desire to see if her bagel would stick to her sister's perfect dress if she smushed it against the soft material.

"I'm not even going to ask what that evil smile is about. I'm just happy to see you smile at all."

Rachel made a face. "Have I been that bad?"

"Worse. Even Dad noticed, and he not only commented on it, he asked me to check up on you while he was gone."

Rachel groaned and dropped her head to the table, only after a few moments remembering to chew and swallow the bite of bagel still in her mouth. "That's bad. Dad never notices anything."

Leah held up a finger. "Wrong. Dad notices everything. He just doesn't normally comment on it unless he's really concerned."

"And that's better?" Rachel dragged her head off the table and picked at her bagel, her meager hunger satisfied. Or chased away. At any rate, she didn't think she could swallow another bite.

"How do you think his bid for the Supreme Court seat is going?"

Leah's eyes narrowed the slightest bit. Though she'd gotten married in college and stopped short of reaching her degree, Rachel always thought her by far the smarter of the two Dubois girls. Not necessarily in the decisions she'd made in her life, but she was always the first one to pick up on a problem, see through a lie.

And Rachel was afraid she'd given away a very important part of her problem with her simple question.

"Why? Are naked pictures of you about to pop up on the Internet?"

Worse, Rachel thought. News of her illicit involvement with a man who'd had an important proposal in front of city council and who had a dark and shady past was about to make Dad's bid a whole hell of a lot more complicated.

Leah wiped her hands on a napkin. "Wait, don't tell me. You're forging drug prescriptions and going through the drugstore drive-thru to fill them?"

That made Rachel laugh. But it was a tinny sound that did little to lighten the darkness now pressing in around them.

Leah glanced at her watch and sighed. "Sami has probably inhaled Iris's meat loaf and is demanding to be taken home. You're not going to tell me who this mystery man is or what this is about in the next five minutes, are you?"

Rachel shook her head.

"I didn't think so." She got up, collected her coat and her bag then stood looking down at her younger sister. "Just so you know, I'm going to be stopping by tomorrow night. And every night after that until you give."

Rachel turned her attention back to her tee-pees. "I wouldn't expect anything less."

She felt Leah's hand on her shoulder, surprised when her sister leaned down and kissed her temple. "You know, if Mom were here she'd know exactly what to do."

Rachel was even more startled by the comment. It seemed a long time now since any of them had openly mentioned Patricia Fitzpatrick Dubois and the important role she had played in all of their lives.

"Gotta run," Leah said. "See you tomorrow."

Rachel nodded, listening as the door closed behind her sister, leaving her completely alone in the echoing emptiness of the house. She reached toward the wall behind her and flicked off the overhead light, throwing the room into complete darkness. And she allowed the tears crowding her chest the release they sought.

NONE OF IT MATTERED...

Later that night Gabe stood in his office suite in front of the floor-to-ceiling windows at the top of the tallest building in Toledo and looked down at the dimly lit river that wound through the city. He'd regained his family's fortune. He'd bought back his childhood home. He'd restored the estate to its former glory including a great many of the heirlooms he'd had an interior designer track down and buy back. He was on the verge of making the family business even larger than it had been before. And his plan to destroy the family that had destroyed *his* family was nearing completion. Careful leveraging and shrewdly worded exclusivity agreements with the Harkins's longtime suppliers and business contacts would soon bring them to ruin. The Harkins themselves had yet to figure it all out.

Gabe took his right hand out of his slacks' pocket and ran his fingers through his hair. For the past ten years he'd been obsessed with these goals. Ironic how little all of it mattered to him now.

With slow, measured steps, he moved around his

carefully designed office. The walls held his university degrees, along with photos of him with local and national politicians and actors and actresses—a space behind his desk even boasted a shot with the former president. He paused at the picture of his parents at the groundbreaking of their first shopping center. They'd taken the money his father's father had made making auto parts and channeled it into expanding Toledo's commercial facilities.

Finally he stood in front of the scaled-back model of the three-tiered shopping center he planned to build on land that had once been swamp, then the location of a minor revolutionary war battle. He absently rubbed his chin, just then realizing he'd forgotten to shave that morning.

The intercom buzzed. "Mr. Chandler on line one," Gloria told him.

He crossed to his door rather than his desk and opened it, startling Gloria. "Tell him I'm out. In fact, tell everyone I'll be out for the remainder of the week. A family emergency. Then call it a night and go home. Bright and early tomorrow morning we have a lot of work to do. A lot of…changes to make."

Gloria blinked at him. If anyone knew how hard

he'd worked to be standing where he was now, it was Gloria.

And she, as well as everyone else, also knew that he didn't have family.

He suddenly realized that perhaps that was the hole he'd been trying to fill all these years.

To his surprise, Gloria smiled. "It will be my pleasure."

Gabe considered her for a long moment, remembering their three-hour lunch together the other afternoon. Did she know something he didn't? If she did, he wished she'd tell him. Because right now he didn't have a clue about what he was doing, or was going to do.

All he knew was that in order to do whatever it was, he had to stop what he was doing now.

He listened to Gloria tell Chandler that he was out, then he stepped back into his office and closed the door. Of course, everything would go much more smoothly if he could start making sense even to himself.

FRIDAY AND THE WEEKEND loomed before Rachel like an eternity of loneliness. Her father had returned from his trip to Columbus. And every night like clockwork Leah had stopped by as promised to hand-feed her. But with every tick of the clock,

Rachel's melancholy seemed to grow darker and deeper rather than easier to deal with.

As she stood at the kitchen sink washing the few dishes they'd used for the stroganoff Leah had brought over, she thought about her house. The renovations were due to be complete by the middle of next week. Whereas just a short time ago that information would have brought her joy, now she couldn't even conjure up the image of her packing her things and moving there, much less being happy in that place. The place where she had shared so many intimate times with Gabriel.

Gabriel...

She was no closer to sorting out her feelings on the matter than she had been nearly a week ago.

Rachel shook the water from her hands then reached for a nearby towel. She'd canceled three appointments with her interior designer. She'd wanted to consult with her about updating the look of her new house without compromising its original integrity. Maybe she should give her another call, see if they could meet for an hour or so in the morning. Something, anything, to fill the time. To make her forget the passion she'd shared with a man she could never be with. A man who presented more questions than answers. A man she loved.

But could she ever trust that he loved her?

The week had seemed to drag by no matter how she tried to hurry it along. They say that everything heals with time. But if every minute seemed like a week, how were you supposed to get through that time? And just how much time did a broken heart require? Definitely more than a week, because she was no closer to forgetting about Gabriel than she'd been yesterday. Would a month be enough? Two months?

It seemed unfair to her that such a brief affair should leave such a lasting, branding mark.

Of course it didn't help that she scoured the papers at work every morning, searching for some news snippet on him or his company. She'd fully expected to see a groundbreaking ceremony now that the rezoning had been ordered. Or see him smiling alongside area politicians and fellow fat cats celebrating the coup. Or being quoted on what was to come.

But she'd found nothing. Not one single word had been written up on Gabriel Wellington IV.

She looked down at where her hand sat next to her cell phone. All it would take was a few seconds and she could find out what the papers couldn't tell her. She could call him to see if he was thinking about her even a fraction as much as she was thinking about him.

Her palm touched the cool plastic, but she didn't make a move to pick it up. She couldn't call him because she was afraid he'd ask her to answer the final question he'd posed to her before she'd left his house last week. Namely, why had she gone back to his house with him if she'd known about his past?

Had she, as the women before her, been after just the sex? Had she suspected since the moment that she'd first taken his hand in that ballroom that whatever happened between them would be temporary? Had she ever imagined a future, never looked beyond the few hours they stole away with each other nearly every night?

But why should she have? They'd been seeing each other for far too short a time to consider anything permanent.

Then again, she'd dated Lance on and off for months without even sleeping with him, but she had considered a future with him....

It was all so confusing.

There was something about the single-mindedness that had been behind Gabriel's drive to regain his family's fortune that unnerved her. If a man was willing to sell his body to the highest bidder toward a superficial goal, then how much was his soul worth?

Or had his goal been as superficial as it appeared?

For a short time she'd practiced criminal law before switching to business. And whenever clients had come into her office, she'd always strived to give them the benefit of the doubt, no matter how damning the evidence against them. Had she given that same consideration to Gabriel? Or had she tried and convicted him without uncovering all the evidence?

"What evidence?" she whispered to herself. "He slept with women for money…"

She stood for a long time, her hand still on the cell phone, her heart beating loudly in her ears.

"This, too, shall pass," she said, mimicking the words her mother used to say. Whether it was a skinned knee or the disaster that turned out to be her senior prom date, that was her mother's answer to everything.

The problem was, Rachel wasn't convinced she wanted this to pass.

The rumble of voices drifted down the hall into the kitchen. She slowly turned to look in that direction. Her father had retired to his home office right after they'd finished dinner and she hadn't seen him since. Did he have a visitor? She hadn't heard anyone ring the door bell.

No…it wasn't voices. But rather a voice. Singing.

Her heart dipped low in her stomach. The old Victrola in the library hadn't been used since before her mother died.

As if on their own accord, she found her feet leading her toward the sound that flooded her mind with memories. Saturday afternoons spent doing swing dances or the Charleston with her father and mother and sister. A tradition that had been switched to Sunday afternoons following dinner after she and Leah had moved out of the house.

She stopped in the hall outside the open double doors. Her father stood in the middle of the room in his old deep red smoking jacket that her mother had bought him for Christmas one year, the white cravat she and Leah had given him on the same day folded neatly at his throat.

Rachel put her hand over her mouth to squelch the soft choking sound that escaped her throat. Jonathon Dubois had always been a handsome man. Tall and lean, he had a grin designed to melt any little girl's heart. Watching him now, the sound of Etta James's version of "More Than You Know" filling the air, it was all too easy to imagine that her mother would step from the shadows and into his arms at any moment.

Only her mother was gone.

But Rachel was here.

Her father held his hand out to her. "May I have this dance?"

The words reminded her all too much of Gabriel's words such a short time ago. Dropping her gaze, she nodded, then moved the steps needed to place one hand in her father's, and one on his shoulder. Then she waited for him to lead the way.

He leaned down and lightly kissed her cheek, then pulled back to smile at her as he lead her in a simple two-step.

It hit Rachel all at once that the song was the exact number that had been playing when Gabriel had asked her to dance.

"I had a visitor in chambers today," her father said quietly, slowly twirling her then bringing her back to face him.

Rachel swallowed hard to keep the tears at bay. The nostalgia for yesterday and the pain from today swirling around in her chest was almost too much to bear. "Oh?"

"Mmm. A nice young man by the name of Gabriel Wellington."

Rachel stared at her father.

He focused his gaze over her shoulder and continued dancing in a way that told her he might not continue.

"And?"

"Shh," he said. "This is my favorite part."

He caught her off guard by dipping her.

"And," he continued, "he asked me the strangest question."

Rachel couldn't read his expression. It was the same expression she'd seen him wear in court when about to render his decision or read a jury's verdict. She didn't know if he was about to let her off on her own recognizance or remainder her to state prison for the rest of her natural life.

"And, um, what might that have been?" she forced herself to ask.

Judge Jonathon Dubois met her gaze. "He asked for your hand in marriage."

Rachel's knees almost gave out from underneath her.

He led her through a turn around the room. "You can imagine my surprise, since I didn't even know the two of you had been courting."

Courting—such a traditional word. And so unfitting for what had passed between her and Gabriel.

Rachel nodded and dropped her gaze to the familiar cravat.

"I, of course, granted him my complete and full permission."

Rachel stopped dead in her tracks, staring at her father as if he'd just announced plans to take out a contract on the mayor. "What?"

"Keep up, Rachel," he said, still dancing.

She forced herself to concentrate on following his lead because she wasn't having any luck following what he was saying.

Gabriel had asked her father for her hand in marriage?

Her father had granted him permission?

But...

Her father leaned closer to her. "I know about his past, Rachel."

He pulled back and she stared at him.

"Everything."

But how? How could her father possibly know? Had Gabriel told him? And if he did know everything, how could he possibly approve of her marrying him?

"The past only has power over you if you let it."

Rachel widened her eyes. The words were so similar to the ones Gabriel had said to her.

"Remind me to tell you a story about my own past sometime, Rachel," her father whispered as the song came to an end. He twirled her one final time as the last notes faded.

Etta's next song began. Rachel caught her breath as she recognized the opening strains of "The Very Thought of You."

"May I cut in?"

Rachel's heart expanded in her chest until she was afraid her ribs would crack under the pressure as she turned to find Gabriel standing with his hand out.

CHAPTER EIGHT

GABE WAS AFRAID Rachel would refuse him the dance. He was afraid she might accept. Despite fortunes won and lost, despite all that he'd ever had on the line, the mergers, the buyouts, the leverages, the deals, this one moment loomed more important to him than any he'd ever encountered before in his life.

He stood holding his hand out for what seemed like an eternity before Rachel finally slid her fingers from her father's grip then turned to him. The feel of her silken skin against his again after so long made him want to close his eyes and savor the sensation.

Rachel stepped into his arms, but he noticed that her posture was stiff, her intention to keep as much distance between them as possible.

Out of the corner of his eye he saw Jonathon Dubois leave the room, then heard the soft sound of the front door closing shortly thereafter. Rachel didn't appear to notice. Then again, Rachel was probably trying to work through what had just transpired.

Gabe dared move his head closer to hers, needing to smell the sweet scent of her hair. Oh, how he missed even the smallest things about her. The way she caught her bottom lip between her teeth when she was uncertain about something or when she was trying to hold back her climax. The soft material of the clothes she chose to wear. The way she had of always touching him, even in a nonsexual way, as if subconsciously she desired a physical connection with him.

"Marry me, Rachel."

He hadn't meant to blurt the words out that way. He'd had a whole speech worked out. A whole laying of his cards on the table. Just as he had laid them out for her father earlier that day. But holding her like this made everything vanish but the need to have her in his life forever.

She searched his eyes, wariness in the depths of hers. He wanted to wipe it away, erase it and leave only the hope he also saw lurking in there.

"All these years I've been working toward a single-minded goal," he spoke softly, evenly. "I wanted to build back up what was taken from my family. I gave my all to that goal. I worked until I couldn't see straight, pushed forward without any regard to where I was going or the road I was taking to get there."

Rachel's gaze moved to somewhere over his shoulder.

"But all that changed when I first danced with you."

She met his gaze, hope beginning to edge out the other emotions shining in her eyes.

"I've never regretted a single thing I've done in my life...until the moment I let you walk out of my door, Rachel."

"Gabriel, I..."

"I'm not done."

She caught her bottom lip between her teeth in that telltale way. But far from thinking he had her, he knew a fear that he might never hold her in his arms again. Not in a dance. Not in love. And that possibility scared the hell out of him.

"Rachel, you made me realize that the hole I had in my chest couldn't be filled with things. No matter how much money I made, how many of my family's belongings I recovered, how many people I made pay for what happened, that hole seemed to grow bigger rather than smaller.'' He stared down at her. ''Until you filled it with love.''

He watched her skin flush.

''That shopping mall? I've donated the land to the state park system with the stipulation that none of it ever be sold.''

She stared at him as if incapable of believing what he was saying.

''I love you, Rachel. More than anything else I have ever loved in my life. The thought of going on one more day without you is unbearable to me.'' He pulled her to him, burying his nose in her hair, unable to look at her should she refuse him. ''I can't change the past, baby. But I can give you my future. Please accept it. Please say you'll be my wife.''

Somewhere along the line they had stopped dancing and merely stood clutching each other in the middle of her father's library. The old gramophone played on, but Gabe barely heard the song over the hammering of his heart.

''You told my father?''

He spoke into her hair. ''Yes.''

She pulled back to look at him. ''But that could have ruined everything. What if he'd said no?''

"I would have risked anything to make you mine, with no more secrets, no more hiding."

She didn't seem to know what to say. Then she burrowed deep into his arms, rubbing her cheek against his shoulder as she looked away from him. "Oh, God. I've been so awful to you. I was hurt...confused. But that's no excuse for the way I've treated you."

Gabe held her so tightly he was afraid she couldn't breathe. "Let me get this straight... you're apologizing to me?"

She nodded her head and his belief that he didn't deserve this woman multiplied exponentially. "I don't care what you did in your past. I don't care if you've been with a thousand women or just one. All I care about is that I love you. And I don't want to be away from you anymore."

Gabe pulled her back just far enough to claim her mouth with his, to seal the words there so she couldn't change her mind. To remind himself how damn good she tasted, and feel how much she did love him.

He pulled a ring box out of his pants' pocket and took out the marquise-cut solitaire inside. "This is the ring my father presented to my mother. I'd be honored if you'd accept it."

He saw the tears in her eyes and felt compelled to clear his own throat.

"Only promise me something, Rachel. Promise me we will be together and in love until we're old and gray."

He put the ring on her finger and looked into her eyes.

She smiled. "I promise."

As Gabe kissed her, he knew that he'd always love Rachel Dubois-soon-to-be-Wellington more than she'd ever know it was possible to be loved.

* * * * *

And the scandal doesn't stop here!
Don't miss Tori Carrington's
SLEEPING WITH SECRETS
miniseries, available April through June,
only from Harlequin Blaze.

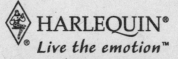